# The Toxic Bachelor

978-1-8380729-0-2 – Print
978-1-8380729-1-9 – eBook

*For my family.*

# Contents

# Chapter 1 – Katie

Her name is Katie and this is the third date. At the same time it feels like both the blinking of an eye, as well as an age in getting to this point, and my mind flicks back to the first trawl when I identified her as one among number of possibilities on some dating site. It would be a lie to say that she had stood out then, her picture (taken some years and a few pounds ago on a foreign holiday) did not leap out from the roll-call of the desperate on the website, and her profile was so generic that I have long forgotten the details. I had been feeling particularly lonely that evening and had messaged a dozen women across my dating sites. It gives you an idea of the success rate when only one of those approaches has made it to this point. It took two long months from my first contact, through online messaging and then texting, to get to where we are: the third date. The process seems to have followed a tightly written script with a huge amount of effort to arrive at this critical point, and yet all I want to do is go home and get an early night.

None of this shows in my outward appearance. I smile, take a keen interest in anything Katie has to say, no matter how banal (and believe me it is banal), and laugh at her jokes. I hold her gaze to show I'm interested and try not to feel a tinge of victory when she leans over the table and touches my hand. I have learned to be a skilled actor, attentive and fascinated, as if I have finally discovered someone special among the endless catalogue of women I have met. The truth is that I knew before the first date – much delayed due to babysitting issues and other social engagements – that I had no real interest in her. I can hear Ben in my head: "*If you don't like her, why have you been leading her on?*" My mind quickly flits away from the uncomfortable question.

Katie, on the other hand, has decided that this is the night we are going to sleep together, and I knew the moment she walked into this second-rate Italian restaurant. Our first date was at a garden centre, always a safe place for a walk, a chat and a cup of coffee, and she had dressed in comfortable baggy clothes. I had her laughing and giggling within two hours with a repertoire of self-depreciating humour, which has become honed by far too much practise. I was awarded a kiss on the cheek and a lingering stare.

The second date was a rushed drink after work, but this time she had made the effort to change out of her work clothes and to touch up her makeup. The drink became two and it was only the fact that we were both driving and she had a friend looking after her two children that called a halt to the evening.

This time she has pushed the boat out. She is wearing tight black trousers, high heels and an elegant blouse that has been cut to show off her cleavage. She has been deliberately leaning forward all night to show it off, as well as to give glimpses of her embroidered bra. Her hair has been freshly cut and her makeup has been applied with great thought. All of this was far too much effort for an indifferent restaurant on a Thursday night. However, it was her first sentence on greeting me that had broadcast her intentions: "The children are with their father tonight."

She was taller in her heels, and able to kiss me on the cheek (and dangerously close to the mouth) without going onto tiptoes. She had placed a hand on my shoulder and lent in close for the greeting, whispering the words into my ear as she bathed me in the scent of perfume and shampoo. The meaning was a clear declaration that we were going back to her house after the meal and only for one reason. The first time a woman had done this to me, I had been giddy with excitement and don't get me wrong - I'm not completely dead inside! – I still had a flicker of arousal earlier tonight. Job done. You did it. She wants you. But soon after the challenge had faded, the boredom reared its ugly head.

I study Katie closely. I do like her. She would make a great colleague. The sort of person who would remember people's birthdays and bake cakes regularly. I mean, she is nice but three dates and a barrage of electronic messages have told me that we have nothing in common. Part of it is the differences in education, and yes I do know how awful that sounds, but mostly it's the fact that we just don't like the same things. I don't have time for reality TV shows and especially not people who organise their days around their broadcast schedule. We both like to travel at least, but I like to explore off the beaten track, hiking and swimming. She likes to lounge around the pool, read trashy novels and top up the tan. I love exercise and being out, she likes to eat and stay in. And then there's the children. She has two of them, and sooner or later that will become an issue if things get serious. Normally, I steer clear of women with baggage, just as I do of any mention of a cat, but at my age that's narrowing the field quite considerably.

"So," purrs Katie, now in full seduction mode on the off-chance that I have missed the other blatant signals and was in danger of being chivalrous. "Shall we have desert?"

I am tired. I have work tomorrow. Had I known that a night of passion was on the cards, then I would have pushed the date back to the weekend. I will be fifty next birthday and sometimes all I want is an early night and a good sleep. I'm not past it or anything; I still maintain an exercise regimen that has kept the flat stomach and broad shoulder of my youth. And even though my once dark hair is white at the sides, it's a look that works for a mature guy. I dress well. My extravagance is clothes and I have long appreciated what a good tailor can do for an aging figure. But I'm just not digging this. I know how it will work out and in the morning I will be wishing I just had gone home and told Katie that I wasn't that into her.

I make a point of looking at the desert menu. It is distinctly average. Just like the wine. Just like the main course. Just like the service. I imagine that if I were to walk into the kitchen, I'd discover that the food came from the ready-meal aisle of a supermarket — just unpacking and microwaving required. I know deep down that if I had been keen at all I would not have recommended this place for dinner. We would have gone somewhere nice, not somewhere convenient with good parking.

"I'm not sure that I have enough room for desert," I reply carefully, rubbing my stomach to show how full I feel despite having sent half a lukewarm plate of pasta back.

"I know what you mean!" replies Katie with a predatory smile through lips stained by cheap, red wine. "Well, why don't we go back to mine for a coffee?"

And there it is. 'The offer'. She is staring at me, watching for my response. I feel like we're playing poker and I'm having to ensure I betray none of my thoughts. I know the best thing to do is to decline. Make some excuse but be polite. Yes, she will be disappointed but it's far better than the hurt from the alternative. I have already checked her out closely and I know that physically she's not my type. That impressive cleavage will lose its shape as soon as the bra comes off. She has no waist to speak off, and I can tell her legs will be shaped like two sausages under those trousers. I can hear Ben in my head telling me to stop being so shallow, that this is what happens with age and having two children — who apparently are her world (she has mentioned that on all three dates and I can't help but think she is warning me that my status in her life will be third-tier at best) — but it's a far cry from the pictures on her dating site profile. It wasn't me that got to enjoy her legs when they were shapely and toned, and she didn't surrender her waist and get stretch marks giving me children. The so-called 'laughter lines' around her eyes did not come from humour we had enjoyed, and the grey roots of her hair were not from worries we had shared together.

"Coffee would be nice," I reply.

I switch my expression to slightly shy and bashful. Katie grins wider, enjoying the control of the situation. I reach across the table and squeeze her hand, she squeezes back tightly. I am now committed to going home with her. My face does not betray my inner despair. I cannot keep doing this. Something needs to change. My life is a mess and yet I squander so much of my time on chasing and dating people I feel no connection with. I don't know which is worse for me: the feeling of being alone or the guilt of short term liaisons. I know that going home with Katie is a bad idea but the worst part is that my mind has already moved past this, and is cataloguing my next best options on the dating sites.

I call for the bill. It takes an age. This is a critical time in how I perceive the quality of the service and therefore decides the size of the tip. I never understand why waiting staff never get that and drag their feet. Of course, perhaps they do know best. I'm on for a promise with my date and I'm not going to damage the magic by arguing about slow service or looking tight-fisted with a miserly tip. I go through the motions and the bored waitress puts on a false smile and makes a show of thanking me with a small bow. The expression turns back to deep boredom before she has even turned away.

"Shall we?" I say.

We stand up and I help Katie with her coat. As we walk towards the door of the near empty restaurant, I place my hand on the small of her back. She looks around and up at me, and I take the chance to kiss her on the lips. It's a gentle, nuzzling, lingering kiss rather than a crude snog, but it does the trick and leaves her grinning. The waitress makes no secret of watching us, finally being provided with some distraction from the tedium of her job.

# Chapter 2 – Chimera

I work at a non-descript company called Chimera, which rents space in one of the many industrial estates clustered around Reading. The building was built sometime in the 1980s with an economy of effort, leaving a soulless brick and glass office block for companies on a budget. Everything about it is tired and insipid: the sun bleached sign on the outside, the broken double glazed windows, and the fact that there are about half the number of car parking spaces needed. The surrounding buildings are no more inspiring, chosen by companies cutting costs on their way to final bankruptcy, or smaller start-ups trying to find their way to growth. Needless to say that there is a lot of turnover in both camps, and it hardly seems worth making the effort to learn the name of the companies or exchange more than a passing nod with their employees in transit. In this way, Chimera is the exception. It has been here for nearly a decade, relocating after its buy-out by an American company that needed a European office.

I always arrive early. I don't have the patience to hunt for a space in an area where every road will be choked with parked cars by half eight. Better to get in before everyone else and take one of the spaces right outside the front door. It is a situation that drives a lot of my behaviours: why I like to get to bed early on a weekday, why I like to get up early even though I am not a morning person (and won't be until at least three cups of coffee later), and why I bring both breakfast and lunch into the office. Once I have my space outside, I will not risk losing it. It's one of the things that makes people say that I'm inflexible, but I don't care. Sometimes it's better to arrange life to avoid hassle rather than continually have to battle with crowds and traffic. Ben says I should move off to some quiet, isolated village and to be fair, he has a point. I look up at the building but make no move to leave my car. Now I have my space – my favourite one right by the door – I am in no hurry to get into the office. I pull out my phone but it is off. Part of me wants to start checking through my texts and dating website messages. There are several irons in the fire at the moment and I have an innate need to see how they are progressing, but there may also be a message (or messages!) from Katie and once I've seen them I shall feel the need to respond.

I sigh heavily (another dramatic habit I have picked up in the last couple of years) and fire it up. There are four messages from website women, all of which hold promise but are clearly progressing at different rates. One is clearly desperate, two seem ambivalent and the final one is obviously keeping me on the hook in case her first choice does not work out. That's fine. I have learned to keep my options open. I start to mentally compile replies with the right balance of flirtation and nonchalance but I don't rush to reply immediately. I switch to my texts. There is one from Katie.

**'Hey Hun, u ok? Thanx for last night. Amazing. R U free this weekend? Wanna see u again! Xx'**

My heart falls. I hate text speak. I could put up with it when phones were new and rubbish and took an age to send a text, but with a modern smartphone it just makes people look thick and inarticulate. I had hoped that a night (well, less than an hour before I called a taxi) of lacklustre passion would have put her off. It's not like I didn't try, I really did, but my heart was just not in it. The low lightning had been unable to hide her settling figure and her heavy perfume had not masked her body odour. It was not good. Despite this, she still seems keen. I have to shut this one down quickly. It is another chore for the day to resolve but first I need coffee.

I climb out of the car, lock it, and then make sure it's locked at least twice before feeling safe to walk the ten yards to the front door. The outside door is access controlled for the four companies that share the empty reception. A four-figure code is needed to unlock the door and the keypad is so worn that one can tell immediately the numbers if not their order. I tap the code in without thinking. It hasn't changed in the years I have worked here. The reception has a small desk, a phone, a sign-in book for visitors, and a plastic pot plant that is thick with dust. There are a few posters stating the fire procedures and the health and safety briefing that must be read out to visitors. There has never been a receptionist and it would be cruel to have kept someone in such a cramped office. I move through to the corridor behind and scan my card at the entrance to Chimera and push through the inner door.

The office is open plan and more spacious than one would think from the outside. There are a dozen or so desks — only half of which have occupants — an area for making tea and coffee, which is complete with a fridge and a microwave, a couple of meeting rooms, a makeshift lab and the manager's office. I move quickly to my desk before heading to the kitchen area to get the kettle on and eat the stale croissant which is my breakfast. It is quarter to eight, three quarters of an hour before the office officially opens, but my two closest work colleagues are already here. Denise is sat at her desk and poring over the schedule for the week. She is in a world of her own, caught between managing the office on behalf of the supposed manager and the countdown calendar where she is marking down the days to her operation which occupies her thoughts. She has her back to me, lent over her desk, and I steal a glance at her long legs which are on display today, noticing her heels.

Ben looks up at me and gives me a crooked smile. He is always in early so he can be gone by four pm to do the school pick-up for his children. His wife does the morning run but then has to make up her hours later. His shirt is crumpled, a non-iron shirt that really hasn't been ironed, and his nylon tie is lop-sided. I suppose we are friends. Well, work friends anyway since it's very rare for us to have a beer outside work despite the fact that Ben is the nearest thing to a life coach or at least a confessor I have. He is fifteen years younger than me but is settled and at least seems content: proper house, a stable marriage and happy children. I do occasionally wonder how he has managed it but then I've met his wife. She's nice enough, but nothing special. I know that I'm never going to drop my standards just to have somebody. And then I worry that I'm never going to have anybody. There was a time that I used to dwell on this and it would eat at me, but then I discovered dating sites and since then, if there ever is a twinge of concern, I just log on and take comfort in the catalogue of available women out there. The perfect one must be out there in all those people and nothing dispels doubt as quickly as action.

"Good morning, Johnny," says Ben.

"You alright, Ben?" I reply.

I keep moving, not waiting for an answer. I drop my bag on my desk and head for the kitchen. The kettle has recently boiled and has enough water for two, so I make Ben a coffee as well. I'm nice like that. I eat the croissant in about three bites and I know that my stomach will be rumbling by ten o'clock. I walk slower back to the desks and hand Ben his coffee.

"Thanks, mate," says Ben.

He sits back in his chair and regards me. His body is beginning to betray his sedentary existence of someone who balances childcare with a career. There is a clear paunch over his belt and his shoulders have lost the tone he had when he was a keen kayaker. Our desks are opposite each other and although there is a small divider between them, one would need to hunker down low for it to provide any cover. I start turning my computer on and organising myself when the interrogation starts.

"So last night was the third date, wasn't it?" asks Ben.

I pretend to consider the question before giving a dismissive nod.

"What was her name again?"

"Katie," I reply. I am typing my password into the computer and pretending to be distracted.

"Good night, was it?" he pushed.

Denise has noticed my arrival. She has not said anything but is sat up and making no secret of the fact that she is listening intently to the conversation. She refers to my love life as "the soap opera" and makes a point of never missing an episode. She got drunk at the Christmas party and called me a male chauvinist, the kind of man she would never have anything to do with, and claimed that I was addicted to chasing women. She apologised in work the next day, even giving me a little hug, but our friendship has never been the same since. I had thought that my stories amused her, and was a bit shocked to discover that she was as disgusted as she was fascinated by my behaviour.

"Yeah, it was okay," I mumble.

I am not in the mood today for a cross-examination. There are times when it is indeed therapeutic to share and I seem to have lost most of my male friends as the years have gone by, in no small part from the disapproval of their wives and girlfriends. My subconscious has already sorted through the four options on my phone and made an initial selection of who to pursue. I am now itching to get my phone out and start messaging and this conversation is a distraction.

"Did you sleep with her?" asked Ben innocently.

I don't reply but I don't stop my expression either. I pull a face involuntarily: a sort of half sneer when I screw up the left hand side of my mouth. It is something my colleagues have come to recognise the meaning of. Denise gives a small gasp and rolls her eyes.

"So you shagged and now you're not keen on her?" pushes Ben.

Needless to say, this is not the first time that we've had this conversation. Sooner or later, it seems to get to this point, and recently it always seems to be sooner. My mind flashes back to Katie and last night. We had barely made it through the door when we started kissing. It wasn't bad to be sure and for a moment, I had thought that we may be onto something. We never made it to the kitchen and there certainly wasn't any coffee, and after a few minutes of fumbling, we managed to kick our shoes off and went upstairs. Her bedroom was cramped and stuffy. This was the point I realised that I wasn't really into it but it was too late to go back. I should have asked her to open the window but she was on a mission at this point, and began to rip my clothes off rather aggressively, pausing only to help me undress her.

"Have you told her yet?" asks Ben.

"No, no yet," I reply too quickly.

"Has she messaged you?"

"Yes, but I have not replied yet. I will."

"But she messaged you this morning? And I haven't seen you touch your phone yet so she must have sent the message early. Like right after she woke up. And that means she's really keen," continued Ben relentlessly. He really should have been a barrister or something.

She had been rather sweaty to say the least. I had slipped my arms around her and felt a trail of moisture from her armpits, and her back was sticky. The result pretty much killed me in the trouser department and so to distract her, I had pushed her onto the bed, pulled off her underwear (which was a struggle and a half as they were two sizes too small and welded into her hips) and put my mouth to work between her thighs. I had to wipe off the cheese around her labia first — another turn off — before wishing that I could switch off my senses of smell and taste on occasions.

"She's not right for me," I reply weakly.

"And you hadn't worked that out before the clothes came off?" snapped Ben in mock exasperation. "Or was she just too fat again?"

There is some truth in this. Quite a lot. I don't want to say that outright because Ben's wife has piled on a few pounds over the years and I don't want to offend him, plus Denise may well go off on one for me being shallow. I mean, it's fine for women to say that a man is too short to date but heaven forbid that you're honest and admit that a woman is too fat.

"She wasn't my type physically and we didn't have a lot in common," I reply carefully.

Denise rolls her eyes again and makes some comment under her breath about it being typical of me. I allow her that in light of the previous evening. I have finished my coffee now. Cheap, instant coffee. I wish that there was somewhere within easy walking distance where I could get a decent cup from. My phone is burning a hole in my pocket and there are people I need to be messaging. This is the quiet time before the manager is in and perfect for organising one's social life without disapproving glares.

"You are right," I concede to Ben. "I should really say something. Let her down easily. It's unfortunate that it didn't work out but there is no point in being cruel."

I stand up to leave but Ben isn't having any of it.

"So you're going to give her a call then?"

I hate this bit. He knows that I have no intention of doing that. Once I've lost interest, then it's over. They should be grateful to even get a text. I don't need to answer because this too is nothing new.

"Dumping her by text? After you slept with her?" snaps Denise, breaking into the conversation. "What is it with men like you?"

"Men like me?" I ask, taken back by the ferocity.

"Middle age, middle class men with entitlement issues," snaps Denise.

"The Jeremy Clarkson of the office," chimes in Ben unhelpfully.

I am aghast and lost for words. Is this how they really see me? I start walking back towards the reception, where the toilets are. I do not need a lecture on treating women right especially as they are no different when they lose interest in men.

***

The toilets are a great place to hide. I miss having an office with a door but I also realise if I ever get back to that happy state, then I will spend all day on my phone and get nothing done. Probably not a good idea on reflection. I review my messages from the website and quickly choose Rebecca to move forward with. Her photos are new and one of them shows her doing yoga, and despite the fact that she's in her forties she has a perfectly toned body and a delicious bum. There is also a photo of her on the beach looking good in a bikini, and another of her out partying and holding a cocktail. Great legs. Long, golden, curly hair. Deep green eyes. The website vultures will be circling and so I better move quickly. Her interests are boringly predictable: travel, yoga, sailing, healthy cooking, loves to shops, likes to go out for nice meals but also enjoys quiet nights in. Has children. Less good. But no cats. I send her a message saying that I think we have a lot in common and am looking to take up yoga as part of a better lifestyle. I also decide to push it and ask her if she wants to meet for a drink tonight. I mean nothing ventured, nothing gained and it's not like I have other plans.

After sending the message with a certain sense of satisfaction that I've hit the right notes, I turn my attention back to Katie. I really want to just ignore it and hope that it goes away, but I know that will never happen and it's best to kill it quickly. Yes, it will upset her but she'll be back on the horse in no time: there are hundreds of other options out there.

**'Hi Katie. I enjoyed last night too. This weekend is looking quite busy for me and I'm not looking for anything too serious at the moment. Maybe we should give it a few weeks and see how we feel? Johnny x'**

I hit send with a quick prayer that she'll get the message. I really don't want this to get ugly, it's such a waste of emotional energy. I flick back onto the website and search for any new profiles. It is Friday after all and always good to catch the fresh meat before too many others get there. Best to get a connection established quickly and leave the rest of the prowlers out in the cold. I normally only look in the age range from thirty to forty five but this draws a blank for new profiles. I have several active accounts but my experience is that you just keeping bumping into the same old people on different sites. Again, it's a waste of time. I extend the range down to twenty five and am rewarded with some new faces. It's the age old problem for men my age: do we chase after younger women and put up with the fact that they are immature and have nothing to say, or do we go after older women, who, to be blunt, are a damn sight more interesting, but who are physically on the wane? While I ponder this, my phone pings and I see a new message has arrived from the website messaging service.

**'Drink sounds good tonight! I'm usually at Savannah's around eight. Pop by for a drink? Rebecca x'**

You'll notice that she does not sign off with some diminutive of her name (like 'Becky' or 'Bex') and is therefore definitely a posh bird. I am smiling to myself and have just given a little fist salute when the phone beeps again. This time it's a text that's arrived, and I don't need to look at the pop up name to know that it's Katie.

**'You bastard.'**

Oh well, at least I know where I am with that. It's better when they lash out, it removes any feelings of guilt I had over the dumping. Nevermind though, as one door closes, another one opens.

***

I am back at my desk ten minutes later. Ben is studying a holiday brochure, which seems very old-fashioned these days, but he is a regular and the company has taken to sending them to him. He and his wife Mary have two young children and so they go to Majorca every summer. The flight is short and the north of the island is perfect for young families. I went there with Anna many years ago, and I do see the attraction of a quaint, little villa that is half an hour from the beach. It is the big thing that Ben looks forward to every year: fifty weeks of dull toil for two weeks of paradise. I study his face and I can read his concern. He is looking at the price list. Each year the prices have risen far above our inflation linked pay rises, and I know that his one luxury is becoming unaffordable.

He is doing the sums in his head, working out what else could be sacrificed, but his life is austere and there will be few pickings to cut.

I like Ben. He is the person I talk to most in life, but we have such different lives. He had a transitory existence after college and moved around a lot, but has now settled down into a sedentary life of comfortable clothes and weekends at home with the family. His holiday is his one big indulgence and what keeps him going through the tedium of our dead-end jobs. I consider asking him about the brochure but then draw back. I already know the situation and expressing my sympathy won't help. I glance around the office and wonder why we have stayed here so long. Yes, it is an easy and settled life, but it is devoid of challenge or interest. For a moment, I feel that we are all trapped here together, but then my phone vibrates to signal an incoming message and the feeling is forgotten.

## Chapter 3 – Janice

I honestly don't know why we bother with Friday at work. It's a lacklustre day at best with most of the guys trundling in late to do the bare minimum before they push off early. By the time Martin the manager makes it in, I am ploughing through my work as a paragon of productivity. When I started my career, the men (and they were always men) who were in charge were these supermen who had grown up in the companies and knew the products, the markets and the customers intimately. They commanded respect from those they managed through sheer force of personality and the fact that they were always ten steps ahead in any conversation. I have experienced the companies I knew being bought up and absorbed into corporations who prefer their officers to be bland and inoffensive. People who know exactly the appropriate thing to say and yet never really say anything. They are taught a generic toolkit of management skills, unsupported by the experience to make independent decisions without layers of approvals for even the most inconsequential matters. They are drilled in continuous improvement methodology and yet unable to understand how things should work well. Martin is cut exactly from this cloth, for which I have dubbed him the "chocolate teapot" for that is how much practical use he is, as well as "Martin the Martian" as he comes from another planet.

He arrives like clockwork at five minutes to nine, all smiles and nods even to the empty desks as he makes his way to his office. At the start of the week he will make a point of stopping and try to engage us in conversation as per the guidance he was given in a management course on morale and high performing teams. Unfortunately, the only conversation he has is asking us how the weekend went and by Friday that has become stale, so he will rush off to his small office instead. He looks like his mum has dressed him in smart casual clothes that she purchased at discount from a catalogue, complete with grey socks and grim slip-on shoes. He has a haircut every two weeks to keep his hair predictably short. He is pure blandness. Needless to say our American parent company (where the merest hint of a personal life is frowned on) love him. It is hard to pinpoint what his contribution is really. He has a deep love of performance metrics which he generates in complex spreadsheets and has used to minutely record the decline of Chimera in Europe, without ever making a decision which could perhaps slow or maybe even arrest the rot.

I drift back to my work. Now that my evening is organised and I have jettisoned the cargo of last night, I find it easy to crack on. I have had a good week and am pulling together my performance metrics as Friday is reporting time. Well, that and compiling timesheets that are so detailed that one should have a time code assigned for all the time it takes to complete one. I fail to notice that Martin has walked back into the room. He has taken up a central position, leaning on a cupboard and is holding a cup of coffee. He has carefully chosen the position in able to project his voice (learned from a seminar of confidence in public speaking), whilst looking relaxed (picked up from a webinar on leadership behaviours).

"Good morning, team!" he calls out confidently, then waiting for us to look up before counting three seconds and addressing us.

"So… we're on with corporate at three pm," he begins with fake gusto. "That means a team meeting at ten this morning for the dry run! Make sure you have your metrics ready and copied into the presentations beforehand. It's important that you not only know what your information is but that you have some effective commentary on it."

I have already switched off. It's the same speech every Friday and it doesn't get any more interesting. We will go through a lot of effort to present poor performance rather than actually talking about how to fix it. The irony of the fading map of the world behind him showing all the offices is lost on Martin. There was a time when every country in Europe had an office, but one by one all the lights have gone out apart from here in Reading, and our future is not looking that rosy. I remind myself to take a break from the dating sites this weekend and check out the job boards.

***

The video conference starts at three pm sharp with the entire team gathered five minutes beforehand in the meeting room. Chimera spent a small fortune some years ago on dedicated conference facilities as a means to cut down on its travel budget, and the equipment seems out of place in our otherwise second rate offices. Martin lives in terror of this meeting, ever fearful that some misspoken word will curse his career with our corporate masters. However, Nik and Janice are the nicest, least intimidating people you could imagine. The headquarters of Chimera makes no sense, lost in Davenport in the mid-west, and I love listening to their soft accents, an experience only slightly ruined by Janice's propensity to talk entirely in incomprehensible jargon.

"Good morning, guys," says Martin far too brightly. It may be afternoon in the UK but the US is several hours behind and Martin is keen to pander.

"Hey," drawls Nik, raising his massive coffee mug in a half-salute out to the team. The resolution of the conference screen is such that you can nearly read the mug's logo.

"Good afternoon, team!" says Janice.

She has made an effort with her appearance today and looks genuinely pleased to see us. Her replying 'good afternoon' to Martin's 'good morning' (and therefore reversing the time zones) has become a very unfunny in-joke that we all laugh at, despite not finding it amusing. We exchange pleasantries but it is clear that Martin is on edge, and keen to get the meeting moving. He has spent all week crafting his slides and does not want the effort to go unappreciated.

"Why don't we start with repairs?" he says and turns to me with a fake smile.

I watch the body language of Nik and Janice. If I am leading then it means that the sales are bad. They smile at me welcomingly. I put up my slides and run through them robotically, interrupted periodically by Martin who likes to interject to highlight which aspects are particularly good news. However, like with a lot of things in life, my heart is no longer in it. I reach the summary slide with no comments back.

"And so you can see that the repairs revenue has continued to grow modestly, that average repair times are dropping, and the mean time to customer repairs continue to improve," I finish off.

The graphs look good but it hides the underlying story. The product – test equipment for the electronics industry – is rubbish. It has suffered from systematic underinvestment for years from a series of company presidents, all with brilliant white teeth and plastic looking hair. The market has been undercut with cheaper products from Asia, and Chimera's response of cost cutting and re-launches of corporate values have done nothing to slow the demise. I used to design test equipment, it's why I got my current job, and I know rubbish when I see it. The increase in repairs revenue is not a good thing and comes from an aging product that is failing more often as it reaches the end of its life, and the ease of repair comes from the fact that it fails from the same latent faults. This whole situation is due to a botched product and dropping sales.

"Thanks Johnny," says Janice kindly. "The projection of those leading indicators proactively demonstrates the go-forward position."

For those of you that don't speak corporate jargon, she is saying that looking at the trends from the past provides a good idea of the future. It is very flawed logic if one doesn't understand the mechanisms of what is driving those indicators, and the kind of naivety that found itself in the financial markets. I let it go. This is not the time or the place to start challenging the dogma of the corporate world. I wonder if Janice actually believes what she is saying or why she always speaks like this. She is a clever and insightful woman, and a very capable manager, certainly much better than the decaying edifice of Chimera deserves.

"Yeah, great presentation, Johnny," echoes Martin with hollow sincerity. "That is looking really positive. Perhaps Jeff can take us through the sales position?"

I take no satisfaction from his praise. He would have thrown me straight under the bus had there been the slightest hint of disapproval from across the pond, something I am sure that he is about to do to Jeff when he presents another woeful week where we haven't sold anything. Giles the sales manager (who only manages two dysfunctional salesmen) has mastered the art of looking like a rabbit in the headlights and that he is about to permanently soil himself. I have no idea how he got the job, as his previous occupation would seem to have been reciting scripts on cold calls in some call centre before the entire operation was off-shored. His predecessor, a lovable rogue called Matt, saw the writing on the wall two years ago and skipped out to get a job with some prospects.

But I am bored, and my mind has started to wonder. I look at Janice on the conference screen and see that she is staring back at me. I wonder if she is remembering the same thing.

***

I had only been with Chimera a month when we all went over to a big sales conference in Seattle. I was as excited as schoolboy on a school trip, and my enthusiasm must have rubbed off on the others. We were all there: Matt, Ben, Denise (who was a different person back then), Martin, Kevin and nasty Steve. We landed on Sunday morning and ignored the jet lag to explore the town and to do the usual tourist things. We didn't drink much on the first day because we were worn out by the evening and had an early night. The conference didn't start until lunch time the next day and allowed a nice long lie in of nearly twelve hours before we joined the other delegates. Chimera was ninety percent US people, and based in the mid-west so we stuck out like a sore thumb. Our formal clothes and foreign accents provoked a lot of interest and goodwill, proof indeed that Chimera was the multi-national giant it proclaimed in its corporate propaganda. Sorry, marketing.

For those of you who have been to these sorts of shindigs, you'll know that you are compelled to endure the boredom of the days for the networking and partying in the evenings. The senior leadership obviously did not get enough attention as children, and this is their time to be able to perform to a captive audience who is unable to boo. They took it in turns to strut onto the stage accompanied by their individual signature rock track blaring from the speakers, although nothing could be further from rock and roll than the physically unimpressive, badly dressed drones with peculiar voices that made up the executive. Each had some topic or other, all of which translated to something along the lines of "if you would all just work harder and stop raising issues, then everything will be okay." They were interspersed with motivational speakers and psychologists, all of whom seemed to be on a mission to sell their latest self-help books (I actually read a couple of them, and have never been more impressed than seeing someone take a fairly obvious statement and spin several hundred repetitive pages out of it, like 'don't give up too easily' and 'hard work pays off eventually').

There were breakout groups too, where we would divide into teams and go off into separate rooms armed with flip charts and pens with some oh so important problem to brainstorm. We would spend ten minutes gossiping before panicking, and coming up with whatever rubbish we could think of. Each group would elect a representative who had to report our findings to the rest of the conference, while the executives pretended that they were listening to pearls of wisdom. Of course, all these great ideas were forgotten the moment the conference was over (the flip charts covered in post-it notes were just dumped in the recycling) and I'm sure we only went through the motions to stop people getting comfortable and falling asleep.

I knew who Janice was before we went over. She was covering the weekly calls back then, but in a more junior capacity and as part of a much larger team. She had looked like a washed-out mess on the video conferences and the rumour was that she was coming out of a particular messy divorce. By the time I saw her at the conference, she had transformed and stood out from the other delegates both on account of her gender (Chimera has some way to go to establish a diverse workforce) and the fact that she was absolutely, jaw-droppingly stunning in a sea of the overweight and the homely. She was wearing a patterned figure hugging dress which showed a curved but toned body, set-off with her thick, black, curly hair which was cut into a fringe at the front but extended down her back to her hips. She had made a point of seeking us out during registration, worried that we would be uncomfortable in the foreign environment, and then stuck with us ever since. When I met her, my eyes must have betrayed what I was thinking as I was staring dumbly at her, but she just looked calmly back at me. As the three days of the conference passed, the tension between us soared.

There was a reception on the last night. As much free food as you could eat and a bar where everybody had been issued two free drink tokens. Matt had skipped out with his tokens and found a printers, returning with a carrier bag full of copied tokens. Some of our American colleagues had looked appalled but Janice had thrown back her head and laughed, deserting her friends to come and join us. We said that we would eat later as there was an unsightly scrum around the buffet and the barman just rolled his eyes at our blatantly knocked off tokens, before accepting them with a smile. It wasn't his money either way. We were on a mission and were knocking back drinks without regard for the consequences. Some of the other delegates started gathering around the bar and we noticed that they had exhausted the buffet. It was then that Janice suggested we head out to find something to eat, and we agreed, in principle, once we had knocked back a few more for the road. Our American colleagues regarded us with bemusement, a couple joining us on the cocktails but the majority seemed reluctant to let their hair down in front of their peers. They had either a single alcoholic drink or stuck to soft drinks, and some of them offered us their spare tokens to allow us to continue to party as they watched.

We were drunk and it was late when we bailed from the bar and went looking for food. We were literally staggering along the sidewalk singing and shouting when the all-night diner appeared. I don't remember the food, and I don't recall the conversation, but the way that Janice was looking at me is burned into my memory. It had been building all week, the exchanged looks, the way we always ended up sitting together, the way we used every excuse to seek out each other's company. We were crammed onto a table in the dinner and I felt her hand rest on my knee, and then slowly work up the inside of my thigh. It came to rest between my legs and she began to subtly and expertly manipulate me through my trousers. Nobody else was aware. I stopped talking, unable to concentrate but Janice kept chatting and joking as if nothing was happening. I turned to look at her, and she gave me that smile and I knew then what lay ahead.

I walked her back to the hotel as the others remained for coffee. We held hands until we entered the lobby, suddenly concerned that the other delegates would see us but it was now the early hours and deserted. We started kissing as soon as the lift doors were closed, drunken, messy kisses as I pressed her against the lift wall. My hand slipped under her dress and started to return the favour she had paid me in the diner. She held me tight and began gasping audibly through our kisses. We staggered to her room where we had the usual hunt for the key. The door was barely shut when the clothes were off. Janice was long past the point of needing foreplay and shoved me roughly onto the bed, before clambering clumsily on top. She was soaking wet and she put me inside her with a burning urgency and gave a loud cry as she sank on me, sliding down until she hit the root of my penis.

She sat back high on top of me, her eyes closed and her mouth hung open. She rode me hard and without regard for me, taking her pleasure from my body but seemingly oblivious to her partner. She was in a world of her own and I still wonder who or what she was picturing and she brought herself to a loud climax. Only then did she seem to take stock of the situation, her hand pulled her hair back from her face, and she looked down to give me a slightly guilty smile. We held each other to sleep, lust had been the only thing that had kept us awake, and we made love in again in the morning. The second time there was at least a mutual affair, with a searing intimacy than was so at odds with the animal rutting of the night before. We joined the others for breakfast, and with each stolen glance at one another we shared our secret.

The conference ended at lunch and there was a rush to check out and get to the airport. Janice never spoke of what had happened. We sit on the same conference call every week and I am sure that although she has re-married and long since moved on, that in the boredom of the weekly meeting she is also replaying that night in her head. Those occasional times when we catch each other's eyes, it feels no different from the conference. I would love to say that it was just a physical thing but of all the women I have met and dated over the years, she is one of a few that my thoughts return to in the lonely moments.

## Chapter 4 – Rebecca

I hit the gym hard after work, inspired by my arousal from Janice and the prospect of a hot date with a yoga practitioner. It gets crowded fast so it's best to get there early and use the most popular machines first, finishing with the running machine where I run until I am soaking sweaty mess. I always keep my gym stuff in the car with me, as well as a change of clothes in case I manage to wangle a date. I'd be lying if I said that today was an exception but there are a lot of bored singles on the dating sites come Friday night, and it's the perfect time to make last minute plans with those who are looking at another long and boring weekend. I love dating after I've worked out. I feel all pumped and ready to go, whereas otherwise I can barely find the energy to get off the sofa and leave the house. I shower, coat myself in deodorant and cologne, then drop off my car at my house and take a taxi to the bar. The traffic is awful and I am at least twenty minutes late when I arrive.

I have some rules to keep dating as hassle free as possible. One of them is never meet for the first time in a crowded bar, far better to arrange to meet outside where you have a fighting chance of seeing and recognising someone who will look nothing like as good as the photos they have posted. The place is packed with twenty-somethings, a stupid and self-obsessed generation, only good for getting in the way and chronicling their pathetic, pedestrian lives meticulously on social media. Rebecca is stood at the bar and stands out on account of being twenty years older than the demographic and her clothes are not figure clinging and she's not tottering on heels. Her curly, blond hair has been brushed flat, she is wearing a beige, linen shirt that shows off her toned legs but looks like an oversized tea bag with holes cut in it for the head and limbs. She's also wearing flat sandals. I am disappointed. I know one doesn't want to look too keen on the first date but she is a shadow of the woman on her profile.

Rebecca spots me as I make my way through the crowd. She does not look happy, and like most people who are a bit up themselves does not take kindly to being kept waiting. I decide to lie to disarm the situation quickly.

"Oh hi, Rebecca," I gasp feigning being out of breath and adopting an accent several degrees posher than my normal. "Absolute 'mare you wouldn't believe what happened."

Curiosity has got the better of her and she permits a double cheek peck while awaiting my explanation.

"Bloody taxi! The engine warning light only comes on and the driver just stops and lets me walk!" I drawl with a hint of aggrievement. "I had to practically run the rest of the way."

She looks me over. I do not show the slightest trace of having run anywhere but she is convinced anyway. Being let down by one of life's little people plays straight to her prejudices.

"Oh gawd, I hate it when that happens," she gushes, as if this were some regular occurrence. "I mean, we're paying them to drive us, the least they could do is make sure their grotty cars work."

"So," I say. "Tell me about you."

This is a deliberate ploy, not least because people love talking about themselves even if they pretend that they don't, and also the more I know the better I can tailor my own answers to make sure that we get on. I feel slightly smug that this simple ploy has worked so well, including changing the topic so easily.

I order us gin and tonics with named brands for both the gin and the tonic. I am no connoisseur and would drink tramp's piss if everything else was gone but I am trying to impress her, and she takes it all in her stride. Over the next three drinks, she opens up about herself without pause. She is divorced, three kids (Rupert, Jemima and Maximillian, I mean really?), still lives in some style off the alimony of her stock broker ex-husband, has fashionable left wing opinions (but her children are still privately educated. I mean you may be on the side of the common people but you don't really want to associate with them), and is very into everything Oriental (which she believes is more valid than Western culture because it's older).

I order a bottle of Prosecco, which is my first bum note of the evening as she is used to proper champagne only, and we find a table to sit at. As you get older, background noise becomes a real problem if you want to hear what people are saying, but at least it provides an opportunity to lean in close, cheek to cheek. I need to sit down after an hour and the chance comes when a corner table suddenly becomes free. It's quieter here away from the music and the incoherent voices of so many people crushed together. She has started telling me about where she likes to go on holiday when I lean in and rest my knee against hers. No response. Rebecca begins a tedious list of all the places she has visited in recent years, with detailed commentary on the advantages and disadvantages of each, taken from both her perspective and her children. She does not pause once to hear my opinion or if I have some anecdote of my own to share, and only comes to a halt when the last drop of booze is shared.

"What say we grab a bite to eat?" I suggest.

I honestly cannot read how the date is going, which is odd after all the practise I've had. We have been drinking for nearly two hours and Rebecca is still in full flow. This is normally a good sign when a woman opens up about life but I would feel a lot better if there was some sign that she was interested in me. The suggestion of food seems to wake her up and she looks at me in horror.

"Oh, I could never eat at a restaurant here!" she says, full of indignation. "I'm a vegan!"

"Oh I see," I reply.

Vegans are on my list of people to avoid. I am shocked that she has made it two hours without needing to announce her veganism, followed by some small pious lecture about the evils that compelled her to this belief. I really should have been expecting it: right-on opinions, full of herself and self-righteous. I mean all the ingredients are there. I take one look at her leather handbag and bite my tongue but some other piece of information bubbles out of my mouth before I can stop it.

"Didn't you say that you loved Bollinger?" I ask.

"Oh yes, I do love the Bolly," she says with a confused look.

"Oh right," I reply. My brain over-rides my mouth and I do not point out that it is not vegan.

"I mean," Rebecca continues. "It's not just about animal cruelty, it's about protecting the environment. I mean the meat industry is so damaging to carbon dioxide levels."

I stand up to leave. I really need to eat and I can sense that the date is over. I am also unwilling to listen to a lecture on the environment from a woman who drives a diesel Range Rover and clocks up more air miles than most airline pilots. Rebecca gathers her things, checking through her handbag to make sure that nothing is missing, before following me outside through the increasingly packed bar. Our table is taken in seconds. We stand outside in the warm evening sun, allowing our eyes to adjust when Rebecca starts up again. I do not wait for her to get into full flow before I pull her close and kiss her. My arm is around her waist and I work my mouth against hers. I don't normally ever attempt to kiss on an early date but I really want to know where I am. Rebecca does not resist but works her mouth passively against mine. We kiss for several seconds before I break off to look into her eyes. As soon as I stop, she continues talking exactly where she left off.

"...of course, no one says thank you for paying school fees and taking some of the burden off the state system," she declaims.

"Goodnight Rebecca," I say as I walk off.

I would normally walk the lady to a taxi but I have seriously had enough. I do not look back as I weave my way through the evening throng, my mind turns to food.

***

It is too early to go home and there is a place I know that does a plate of noodles for a reasonable amount. You can sit in to eat and it doesn't feel odd to be eating alone on one of the packed together plastic tables. The evening is in full swing and it's a great place for people watching. There is also a pub nearby, a nice quiet one for the older clientele. You can stand at the bar and chat to the other men who seem to prop it up every evening, and there is something relaxing about listening to the wry observations and grumbling of guys, who life has passed by.

The noodles taste bland and I scoff them down quickly before heading to the pub for a couple more drinks. I order a pint of bitter and listen to the locals grumble. Sometimes it's about politics or famous people, other times they put the world to rights, but tonight they are arguing about football. I can't join in but it doesn't stop me from listening to the savage banter of people with too much time on their hands. I have two pints and then feel ready to call it a night. I leave them to their point scoring about players I haven't heard of and teams that I could not care less about.

I drift back outside and stroll back towards the taxis. I am in a world of my own and feeling relaxed when I notice the girl stood recessed a few yards in one of the alleys. She is dressed for a night out but she has clearly been crying for her makeup and eye shadow betray the traces of her tears. She is fixated on her phone, whose screen illuminates her face in the darkness, but whatever she is looking at is no cause for consolation.

"Hey, you ok?" I ask.

She looks up sharply and her face is hostile. I can understand. She is obviously upset and now she is being pestered by some older, creepy guy. I consider just walking off — it's not like she can't call on her friends from her phone — but there is clearly something wrong.

"Rough night?" I ask.

She shrugs, glances back at her phone and then away into the alley.

"Maybe best to call it a night and get a cab home?" I say.

It's getting awkward and I start to walk away when she finally replies.

"I don't have money for a cab," she says.

She makes a small choking noise and I sense that she is close to tears again.

"No one you can call?" I ask.

She shakes her head in a resigned fashion and I guess that she has been abandoned by her friends and does not want to call her parents.

"Look, I can lend you the money," I reply.

"Why would you do that?" she asks suspiciously.

"We've all had a rough night or two," I say with a smile. "I lost my wallet once and had to walk five miles home! But I don't think that I'd want to walk that far in your shoes!"

She can't help but smile. Her shoes may be good for dancing and showing off her legs but not for hiking home in. She walks over to me and we fall into step as we head towards the taxis.

"What's your name?" she asks.

"Johnny," I reply. "What about you?"

"Emma," she says simply.

She is staring at me now, searching my face for something.

"Do you normally rescue distressed maidens?" she teases.

"No," I reply honestly. "Where do you live?"

"Calcot."

I am not in the mood to chat and we arrive at the lead taxi. I open the back for door for her and let her climb in, before closing the door gently. Calcot is a ten pound taxi journey away. I tap on the window and hand the driver a twenty.

"Please can you get this lady back to Calcot safely?" I ask.

The driver gives an impatient nod while Emma winds down the window in the back.

"I can send you the money," she offers.

I shake my head with annoyance and step back as the taxi pulls away. Her eyes track me with genuine curiosity as it departs. I take the next taxi. I just want to get home.

## Chapter 5 – Abigail

"I love you, baby," I hear her mutter in her distinctive Eastern European accent.

I am drifting in that half-awake state early Saturday morning. A surge of contentment floods though my body and I undergo a sudden feeling of well-being. It is like some strange religious experience or happy meditative state. I can smell her natural odour, so arousing and yet comforting. I am home. After all this time, things will finally be okay and I feel pathetically relieved. I reach out to take Anna in my arms and pull her close. My hands slide through the sheets reaching the side of the bed before it dawns on my conscious brain that I am quite alone. The shock wakes me up, the feeling evaporates as I peer through the gloom, and I roll over with a grumpy sigh. I won't go back to sleep now. Those long lie-ins of my youth are a distant memory and now I wake early with an unhappy back, and it's just easier to get up than to struggle through the discomfort for a few more hours.

Anna would smile and tell me that my dreams reflect my unconscious desires but there is something depressingly cruel about being haunted by memories from twenty years ago. It makes no sense, of course. There have been so many women over the years, including a marriage, and yet if my heart were a compass then Anna would be my north star, and wherever I am it points to her. This is why I hate weekend mornings because there is too much time to think. My mind needs to be distracted and not allowed to wallow in the disappointments of the past. I roll over and look at my bedside table. My mobile phone and laptop are both there, and either would serve to connect me back to the world of the lonely searching for redemption. There is a strong possibility that I could waste the whole day on dating sites to distract myself from the crushing boredom of my own company. I pick up my phone and start flicking through the messages. There is one from Katie.

**'I just want to talk. Can I see you today?'**

I am tempted. I really am. I have no interest in taking things any further and although I don't like being berated, it still seems a better alternative that sitting here all day. I keep looking through the messages for a better option. I am not disappointed on one of my dating site accounts.

**'Hey hun x. Are we ever going to meet? We've been talking about it forever!!'**

The message is from Abigail. We've been in contact for a few weeks and things have not progressed beyond an exchange of flirty messages. I note that the message was sent in the early hours, which is not unusual when people have got to the weekend and are drunk and lonely. I am unsure about Abigail as her photos are not that great, there is nothing of interest on her profile, and she is a smoker. I mean, I don't have a problem with smoking per se but there have been better bets to go after. However, I am at a loose end today and the prospect of a weekend entirely alone does not appeal.

**'Hi Abigail. Good to hear from you! Want to meet today?'**

Normally I would play it cooler than that but sometimes the direct approach is the best and I won't exactly be upset if she says no (or suddenly stops replying which is more usual). I swing my feet out of bed, shrug on my dressing gown and pad downstairs to put the coffee machine on. I stop in the hallway to collect my mail (just junk, I can't remember the last time that I had a real letter), and head into the kitchen. The house is not exactly how I imagined it would be when I moved in. I had great plans for all the things I was going to do, but have yet to get around to finishing much of it. I did the kitchen when I first moved in over ten years ago but I didn't have much money then and it is certainly tatty and dated by now. The halls, stairs and landing are all okay. I mean, just a lick of emulsion, some carpets that are slightly worn and a discordant set of pictures that I have collected over the years. There is a small table at the foot of the stairs. On it is the landline telephone, which rings once in a blue moon and is only called by my parents and companies that are trying to scam me for something. There is an old telephone directory underneath, the yellowed paper speaks to its redundancy. My house is tired. It needs a refresh. There are so many things that I need to get around to but I have yet to find a builder or decorator that is willing to put the same dedication into it as I am.

I am waiting for the coffee maker to finish when my phone starts to flash. I have a message. It is from Abigail.

**'Sorry about drunken text. Would like to meet. I am free today. When and where?'**

No matter how many times I have received a similar message, there is a surge of triumph. It would be false modesty to pretend that I do not do well on dates, however the real challenge is persuading women to accept that first meeting. The next steps will follow a well-run pattern that I have perfected over the years. There is a garden centre that I know that is perfect for the first date. It's a few miles outside of Slough and has a nice little coffee shop. You can have a cup of tea and if things are going well, take a small walk and look at the plants. It's as public as you can get and completely unthreatening.

**'Sounds great. What about meeting at Darney's at 2pm?'**

I drop a couple sugars into my fresh coffee and am feeling rather pleased with myself as I look out onto the garden. The driveway runs out at a pile of bricks, which is where the garage should be. I have had a couple of quotes to re-create an extended version of the original structure, which collapsed a long while before I bought the house, but they were eye watering. Better to do it myself when I have a couple of days free. With somewhere to work on it, I'll then be able to buy the E-type that I've always wanted. The smug feeling momentarily dips when I recall first making that promise when I first moved in. My phone starts flashing again. Abigail has replied.

**'Darney's? Wow. What we doing for the second date, a Saga holiday? Erm, okay, see you at two.'**

I smile. I do like her sense of humour. It is the thing that has kept me interested despite the rather unexciting photos on her profile. Two o'clock: time to get myself looking ready.

***

People stress too much about first impressions. The truth is that you either hit it off or you don't and there is no point worrying about it or trying to make the perfect entrance. Most couples shamelessly re-write the narrative of how they met along the lines of "I knew instantly I had met the one" or "I fell in my love with my best friend". Having lived through this myself and seen it countless times in my acquaintances, I can confirm that most meeting stories are complete rubbish. Don't try and create a fairytale for the grandchildren, worry about working out whether you like them enough not to have to find an excuse to bail on them after five minutes in their company. I arrive ten minutes early and make my way to the entrance. I am showered, shaved and covered in enough cologne to ward off mosquitoes. I look pretty fine in my blue shirt and jeans: what mortal woman has a chance? I spot who I think is Abigail sat on a wall next to the entrance. She looks a lot hotter than in the photo. Her brown hair is cut at shoulder length and it frames a face that was made to smile. She is dressed casually: tight jeans, basketball boots and a tight black top, which shows off her flat stomach and firm chest. I find myself starting to like her. When she sees me, she stands up and her smile widens. A flash of perfect enamel makes me realise that I should not be so quick to dismiss those without good photos.

"Johnny?" she asks.

"Abigail?" I reply with a smile.

To hesitate is to make things awkward, so I lean in and kiss her on both cheeks. I am rewarded by that smile.

"So, are all your dates in such exciting places?" she asks.

"Well, let's see if you can deal with this one first," I reply sarcastically.

"A lovely cup of tea and a peruse of the bedding plants? Adventure be my wild mistress!" she replies.

I have no comeback to this so I give her my amused and slightly miffed expression — well practised for those moments when you need to pretend to be annoyed but secretly are amused. We make our way into the garden centre and, to be fair to Abigail, there are an awful lot of retired people milling about.

"Your photos are really good," says Abigail. "Did you get a studio to do them?"

I did. There is no denying that they look good and the lightning was conceived to give every advantage to the more mature gentleman. They look a lot better than the normal selfies and other random snaps that people use. The studio did a good job of capturing me in a range of outfits from smart to casual (a man for all occasions) and they are supported by some older ones of me doing activities to ensure that it comes across that I am fit and sporty. I have a huge selection of photos and was only able to choose the winning five (sometimes less is more) with help from Ben and Denise. I had to devise a complex voting scheme in the end to whittle it down completely but I am happy with the result: a chap who is equal to every occasion and looks damn hot to boot!

"Well, I didn't have many photos of myself," I plead. It's a complete lie because I have hundreds but I wanted to look my best.

"Ah, studio photos! The sign of the dedicated player!" laughs Abigail.

I am annoyed at the hypocrisy because half the women on there have studio photos, most in the same, standard poses, but then again it is expected that women make the effort to look good, whereas for men to do it is vain.

"Oh come on, like you weren't tempted!" I reply.

"Well, you could make do with a simple selfie," she replies.

"I am the wrong generation for that," I dismiss. Another lie since I have taken dozens but I look older than I would like to in them.

"Hmm, I must admit that you are among the more mature of the men I have met off the site," she muses.

"Is that your way of calling me old?" I ask quickly. I'd be lying if I said that I wasn't sensitive to it.

Abigail takes a long hard look at me and makes no secret of the fact that she is checking me out physically.

"Well, you are around fifteen years older than me. That is a fact. But your photos do not lie and you are in good physical condition, plus you are funny and fun to chat to online, so.... It's not a problem at the moment," she says.

I smile inwardly at the compliments but we are close to the coffee shop now and I make a point of opening the door for her.

"As long as this is not some way for you to work through your daddy issues," I reply with a sneer.

Abigail looks at me in shock and explodes with laughter. She has an edgy sense of humour and likes to be shocked. If I can make her laugh like that a few more times then a snog is definitely on the cards. The coffee shop is practically empty. It always is which it what makes it such a good place to talk, especially so with Abigail who has a rather offensive streak to her humour. We order two teas and then take a table in the corner next to the window.

"So, do you come here often?" she asks with a raised eyebrow.

"I do like it here. The tea is okay and there is rarely a queue, plus it's good for people watching," I reply.

Abigail makes a point of taking a long look out of the window. There is no one in view under the age of sixty.

"Well, I can see that. Some of those pensioners are very easy on the eye. One of them has just had a new sexy blue rinse, and another is wearing one of those slimline hearing aids. Phwoar!" she jokes.

"Don't be so prejudiced!" I reply. "Beauty is in the eye of the beholder."

"That is certainly true. Maybe I should set you up with up with my grandmother. She's just had a new hip operation and is looking for someone to go walking with," says Abigail.

I make a point of regarding her before replying.

"Well, sounds like she's in better condition than you are. Probably more fun as well," I say sarcastically.

"Hey!" she says with a large gasp.

She leans over and gives my elbow a playful slap. This is a further good sign.

"So you mentioned that on your profile that you like hiking. Have you been anywhere good around here?" she asks.

I have lost control of the situation and allowed her to start asking the questions. This is very risky since I have not gathered enough information about her likes and dislikes to be able to give the most pleasing answers. Worse still, my mind is completely blank and I have not been hiking since Snowdonia several years ago and that is not exactly local to Slough or Reading. I think furiously while trying to hide my discomfort. The only thing that comes to mind is a walk I did many years ago as a student and like a fool, I clutch at straws.

"There is place I like just north of Brighton. Do you know the Devil's Dyke?"

"Oh right," she says, clearly unimpressed. "I know it. Great place for a family picnic but not exactly a serious hike. Are you still thinking of somewhere to take my gran?"

I laugh like she has made some great joke but inwardly curse the step back.

"Come on then, show off, where do you like hiking?" I ask, trying to regain the initiative.

"My family has a place in the Lake District. I love going there at the weekends. I am trying to hike all the fell tops."

"How many are there?"

"As I recall, around two hundred and fourteen. I have managed over one hundred and fifty."

I am impressed: it explains why she is in such great shape. I am pondering the thought of hiking somewhere so beautiful when Abigail continues.

"I saw a social media photo of you at the Grand Canyon. Was it fun hiking there?"

It's an old photo from when I was married. Karen and I had taken a helicopter tour from Las Vegas, which had flown down to the base of the canyon. The photo is quite a dramatic one looking back up the canyon, and with my walking boots and rucksack one would be forgiven for thinking we were about to start the hike back up. There is no way that Karen could have done it, she complained constantly away from the air-conditioning and would take the car a hundred yards to the shops. It was one of the reasons why her weight ballooned so badly. However, the fact that

Abigail has seen the photo raises another issue.

"Have you been stalking me?" I ask.

"Guilty," she laughs, rocking from side to side in her chair, and I can tell then my faux pas has been forgiven. "But come on, who was she? And what was it like?"

"Well, it was a few years ago now but I guess you can tell that because my hair had not started to go white. She is my ex-wife Karen, and when you ask what was it like, then I assume that you are talking about the canyon and not the marriage?"

"Well, we can talk about your marriage later but I must warn you that I charge fifty pounds an hour for counselling and life coaching," she says.

"So long as those are the only things that you charge by the hour for," I quip back.

I am rewarded with a second slap on the arm but she is clearly waiting for an answer. I am torn between telling her the truth and restoring my prestige as a hiker. Of course, I go for the latter option: I want that snog. I can't remember much about the Grand Canyon to be honest. We took an early morning flight and went for one of the cheaper ones. The helicopter was tiny, cramped and noisy, and it was difficult to see that much from the small windows. The canyon was mostly in shadow early in the morning and the result was an overall disappointment.

"Well, the scenery is breath taking, of course. I mean, I have never seen anything that comes close but it is difficult hiking. It was scorching hot, the paths zigzagged down but were still steep and then there was the change in altitude to contend with," I offer up with false modesty. "And it was difficult carrying all the water you need to avoid dehydration.

"Wow," says Abigail in genuine admiration. "I so want to do that. It's on my bucket list."

I give a small shrug as if to suggest that it was nothing really. The truth is I learned all this from the chatty tour guide cum pilot on the helicopter, while we spent less than twenty minutes on the floor of the canyon. Twenty minutes was quite enough for Karen who had started to sweat profusely, or 'glow' as she called it. She spent the whole way back grumbling about the lack of air-conditioning in the helicopter.

"So did you stay down in the canyon overnight then?"

I happen to know that one is told not to try going down and coming back overnight so I give a little nod. Abigail is suitably impressed. I move quickly to change the subject before I get found out.

"What about you? Where is the most interestingly place you have hiked?" I ask.

Abigail thinks about this for a moment, her face screwed up in concentration. She is kind of cute in an unconventional sort of way. I find myself genuinely liking this girl and make a note to minimise the untruths: I only have to remember them so as not to trip up later.

"Well, outside the UK it's only been the Alps when we were young," she mused. "There are so many places I want to see."

It doesn't matter what age people are, they always want to see more and do more. There are exceptions — the boring and the complacent — but they are best avoided unless you want to spend your years watching repeats on TV and going on package holidays to the same place year after year

(I make an exception for Ben there). However, this is a topic that I have a rehearsed answer for and we discuss locations for long after the tea has been drunk. We break off when Abigail stops to listen to the piped music which is an annoying addition to the coffee shop. It's not as bad as putting TVs everywhere but it is still irritating.

"Hey isn't that the Bee Gees?" she asks.

I listen to the strains of 'You Win Again' and give a wise nod. I am not a big music fan but there certain classics even I recognise.

"Well, it is the music of your generation," she jokes. "I hear that two of them have passed away but I don't know about the third."

"Well, he's 'Staying Alive'," I quip back.

Abigail gives a huge snort and looks at me with her mouth hung open in pretend outrage. Another hurdle crossed and I can almost sense the home stretch, but then she glances at her watch.

"Oh no, listen, it's got late," she says. "I need to go."

"I didn't think you had plans today?" I ask, an unpleasant whine has entered my voice.

She pauses before answering.

“Well, I wasn’t sure how this date would go and after you suggested a garden centre, I didn’t hold out much hope. The girls suggested a night out and it seemed a better prospect than an evening in on my own,” she confesses.

We stand up and make our way back to the car park. It is quite crowded now and we have to meander around the absent minded groups that are wondering around in their own worlds. It makes conversation difficult until we reach her car.

“Well, let me choose somewhere next time,” she says with a bright smile.

I lean in to kiss her, and I mean to kiss her properly and she looks up to me and opens her mouth to receive me. It is then that I smell her breath. It is disgusting. Like something has died and rotted in her mouth. I swerve at the last moment and plant a peck on her cheek before pulling back quickly to get some fresh air. Abigail frowns and then freezes.

“That sounds nice,” I gasp. “Give me a call when you are free.”

She smiles again and climbs into her car. Tonight, she will paint the town red with her friends, and I will get a take out and be back on the dating sites once more on the hunt.

## Chapter 6 – Sarah

I awake early on Sunday. Later I will make myself a full cooked breakfast, washed down with lashings of coffee, but first I will head out cycling before the roads get busy. The south-east is not the best place in the country to be a cyclist but there are some good routes if you know where to go. I used to be part of a club but after a few months I realised that I didn't like any of the other members and would rather cycle alone. Most of them were overweight fathers, who looked ridiculous in tight Lycra and really didn't have much in their lives apart from a love of sport. We had a night out once and they all showed up wearing football shirts (pulled just as tight over their pot bellies as the cycling kit) and then insisted we watch some match that I struggled to feign an interest in. After that, it has been purely solo for me.

I check myself out in the mirror, and admire my shoulders and flattish stomach: quite an achievement for a man nearly at his fiftieth birthday. I push my bike out of the front door and look up optimistically at the bright morning. There is still some residual self-disgust from last night when I had a late night binge of messaging and texting women on the dating site. I have a number of new leads, although some of them are not worth taking further as they just aren't good looking enough, but my ego needed the attention. Abigail also texted me twice. I will reply later as it is best not to appear too keen. I push out onto the road and give Mrs Rogers a wave. She is in her eighties and thoroughly neglected by her family. I mow her lawn and run errands for her. I do worry about her passing away as I'm the only one who would probably notice. She is such a lovely lady, and most weeks she will make me a cup of tea and berate me for not meeting a nice young lady. I think that I may be the only person she has to talk to.

I cycle through the suburbs and then head out into the country lanes, enjoying the speed and the absence of cars. It will not stay like this for long and the sad truth is that it is all but guaranteed that I will have at least one near miss, almost certainly from some idiot driving a BMW or an Audi. I cycle mainly to stay fit but it's also my time for reflection, away from the distractions of the internet and the mobile phone. I will be fifty soon and I'm starting to wonder how I ended up like this. I have started to replay the episodes of my life in my head and try to make sense of where I am going. Why am I still alone? Why am I doing a job that is so beneath my talents it is embarrassing? Why do I never make the time to finish my house? Maybe I would have been happier getting married and having some children? It wasn't always like this and my mind drifts back to the glorious summer when I left college and was looking for my first job.

***

I had a great time in college, perhaps because I didn't spend enough time on my studies and too much playing rugby and chasing girls. When the time came that the final party was over and I was set to face the world in a hot July with a second-class degree, I was at a loss what to do next. My life had been focussed on getting to college and then not flunking out, and I seemed incapable of knowing how to take the next step of growing up and becoming a functioning adult (Ben would add that I am still working on that with his tired, snide voice and I wish I didn't hear him in my head all the time). A friend of my dad had heard that they were looking for engineers at some government agency, and I headed out to an interview, which was organised on my behalf, in my battered Ford Fiesta.

The Agency was called "The Centre for Motor-Vehicular Safety" and was located in an old manor house, with fake roads in a field behind for experimentation. It was beautiful on a summer's day and I had a warm feeling that there were worse places to work. I parked outside and as I made my way in through the porch and to the entrance hall, I was met by a surly girl called Sarah. I was bubbling with excitement and chatting away. Her sullen face seemed to cheer up slightly as I tried to banter with her as she led me down a long corridor and then knocked on a grand looking door. A posh voice called out for us to enter and she opened the door for me but did not enter herself.

I stepped into an office that was so grand it has forever set the bar for my expectations of success. It looked more like a Victorian gentleman's study, with its bay window, large fire place (above which hung a faded portrait of the Queen) and its bookshelves stretching from floor to ceiling. There was a beautiful carved desk in the centre of the room with an old rotary dial phone but no computer, which was noticeable even back then. The metal filing cabinets did not fit in with the general ambience but my attention was soon drawn by Dr Phillips, who was stood with his back to me, staring out of the window. This is the man who I would forever call 'The Patrician' due to his distant, haughty persona and clipped, clear cut accent. His white hair was combed back flat on his head, and a tailored three-piece suit showed off his trim figure. He turned to face me with a gentle smile.

"Ah, you must be Jonathan," he said and walked towards me with his hand extended. I could not remember the last time that someone had used my full name.

"Yes, Dr Philips," I replied.

His grip was both firm and subtle. He gestured towards a small chair in front of his desk while walking back around the other side to an impressive leather throne, where he looked down on me comfortably.

"Perhaps some tea, Sarah?" he asked in his, soft polished accent.

Sarah had been waiting at the door, but she shuffled off with her head down, closing the door silently behind her.

"So Jonathan, are you aware of the work we do here?" he asked, his voice barely above a whisper.

My father wanted me to get this job and he did the homework on my behalf. Being back at home was difficult enough after the freedom of college and I had been drilled every dinner time for a week on what I should say and how I should say it. I was still eighteen in my parents' eyes, and they continued to enforce a curfew when I went out in the evening, without acknowledgement for the fact that I had been independent for three years. It should have been no surprise that they still wanted to set me homework.

"Yes, Dr Phillips. The Agency is responsible for research into various aspects of road safety, including, but not limited to, road surfaces, tyre quality, brakes, steering and road signs and markings," I repeated by rote.

"Exactly, exactly!" he replied with evident pleasure. He had leant back in his chair and was regarding me closely. "Tell me, Jonathan. When you drive your car, do you worry about accidents?"

I was unsure how to answer this but back then I was a more honest person, and so I just shook my head.

"Of course, you don't!" he replied with energy, his voice rising sharply above a whisper.

I had no idea how to respond to this and gave a thoughtful nod. This turned out to be the correct response because he was just getting started and as I would come to know, he hated to be interrupted.

"You do not worry because of the lengths that have been gone to in order to make every aspect as safe as it possibly can be! I make an exception for human error, folly and malign intent, of course – those things are beyond the reach of the work we do here! This Agency is dedicated — and I mean dedicated in its deepest sense — to ensuring that everything is done to optimise every feature of road travel. We look at the best road surfaces, research the effectiveness of every tyre released onto the market: for it is these two things that will govern your stopping distance when the worst happens!" he declaimed.

He paused for effect but it was obvious that there was more to come. Fortunately, Sarah knocked at the door and struggled in with a tray holding a pot of tea, some cups, a jug of milk and a small plate of biscuits. I was unsure whether to help but sat frozen in the awkwardness of the situation. She made her way across the room with a resigned air and set the tray down on the empty table. She worked quickly and diligently to lay the crockery out under the approving gaze of The Patrician. I took the opportunity to check her out. She was wearing a baggy top and a skirt so long that it hid her feet, which conspired to make it difficult to assess her figure but she certainly has an impressive rack and in those days, that was what caught my attention. She had long, perfectly straight, black hair, which she seemed to hide behind, and a very square jaw for a woman. Her face was pretty from some angles, and quite ugly from others, but I did like her mouth with its very red lips.

I was clearly not subtle in my evaluation because she glanced at me askance and gave a tired smile, before finishing off her work and standing back. The Patrician seemed to be in a reverie because it took him a moment to notice.

"Ahhh, thank you, Sarah," he said with a warm glow. "I shall play mother, thank you."

Sarah took these words as her leave and shuffled out of the room. She was very round shouldered and could have done with walking fully upright. The Patrician made a point of slowly pouring out of the tea before a frown crossed his face.

"Oh, I say, do you take sugar?" he asked.

Sarah had neglected to provide the sugar bowl. I didn't drink tea and therefore it made no odds how it is prepared.

"Just with a dash of milk, if I may," I replied in my most well-spoken accent.

The Patrician's smile was restored and he added a small splash of milk to my cup. We both sipped our tea in silence. It felt so relaxed, like visiting an elderly relative who had time on his hands.

"Jonathan, I understand that you are about to make a very important decision, one may even say one of the most important ones of your life: the decision where to invest your efforts in employment. Tell me Jonathan, would you want to join us and help us with this work?"

For the six years I would be employed here, The Patrician always referred to it as "the work" as if we were a cult on some divine mission, or the code breakers at Bletchley Park trying to determine the outcome of a terrible war. It was a grand way to describe the sedate pace of research that was the life at the Agency. A rate of progress that was so gradual that it felt to me like time had slowed down, and looking back that I had come out of the fast lane of college into the slow lane of employment. However, these revelations were all ahead of me at this point in time and I have nothing to compare this strange place to. There are no other offers of employment on the table and part of me is curious to see Sarah again. I had detected some spark of interest and I was drawn to follow up on it.

"Yes, Dr Phillips," I replied in words that my father had drilled into me. "It sounds like a challenging and fascinating opportunity."

Years later, I would joke that I had joined an institution for eccentrics who were unemployable anywhere else. The brief interview gave me no insight into the world I was entering. As befitted somewhere run by a patrician, there was a strict hierarchy. At the top were the researchers, a group of bizarre men who acted as though they were world experts at the Rutherford Laboratory, then the technicians who supported them by developing equipment for their experiments (and this was the role I had been recruited for, even if that was never mentioned until my first day of work), and finally there were the support staff, including the secretaries, administrators and the lone personnel officer.

Most of the names have faded with time but from the twenty or so scientists there are a trio of personalities that I recall even now. There was the incredibly secretive Kenneth (never to be reduced to Ken!) who acted as if our routine work was the secrets of MI5. He was a short man, proudly bald and with a perfectly trimmed, white beard. He had a bizarre habit of glancing left and right before speaking to see who may be listening to the conversation. Every project was assigned some random name in order to protect commercial sensitivities but Kenneth would refuse to mention the name in front of anybody unless they were 'read into' the project, and preferred to refer mysteriously to the 'tests' or the 'application'. I found out years later than he had the reputation for groping women, and was banned from being alone with any of the female staff.

However infuriating Kenneth was, he was a breeze compared to Edmund. He seemed like a quiet if tightly wound chap on first meeting. His appearance would have suited a comic character at six foot four and painfully skinny, with long limbs. He always wore tight suits with white shirts which exaggerated the effect. It was clear that he was tightly wound after two minutes of talking to him, but his explosive and violent outbursts of pure rage were unnerving to behold. I witnessed a couple myself and it left me wondering both how he still had a job and how he coped with everyday life without assaulting some unsuspecting member of the public.

The final member of the impossible trio was Ian, who was permanently crotchety about everything in life. He used to read the tabloids and work himself up about whatever the topic of the day was (immigrants, petrol prices, anything to do with the European Union, government policy, people who claimed the dole, roadworks, rebranding of popular products, motorway services, foreign food, modern music, chewing gum on pavements etc.). He was a rotund man who used to profusely sweat — even on the coldest of days — and would wear badly fitting nylon shirts (I mean, where do you even buy those?) and these awful ties with cartoon characters. The cheery (and sweaty) ensemble did not reflect the bubbling agitation that seemed to power him, and meant that new people misjudged his fantastic tantrums. Despite these personality traits, he was not that hard to work with once one had worked out that one just needed to come up some topic to focus his irritation on so that one did not become the target of it.

On my first day, I was met by the head technician Neil. He was a tall guy with a stooped neck and when he walked, his head bobbed like a chicken pecking at grain. He was a lovely guy with the patience of a saint and always had time to help others. His strong Birmingham accent made him sound a little thick and he had a love of chunky, knitted jumpers and large cups of tea. He led me round the building and introduced me to everyone, who were all very nice apart from Ian. He acted as though we had walked in on him on the toilet and tried to take a photo. Neil seemed oblivious to the tantrum and then led me out of the main building (that lovely Victorian manor) and to the Portakabins behind which is where the technicians had their offices and laboratory. It was a bit of a letdown to go from accommodation straight out of an Arthur Conan Doyle adventure to an oversized box that baked in summer, froze in winter and leaked rainwater in between.

I met the other two technicians, David and Charlie, who seemed to be a matched pair that did everything together. They had done their apprenticeships at the same time and had become best friends even to the point of joint family holidays (always camping trips somewhere in the South of France), but they were a solid pair of lads, even if they were obsessed with motorcycles despite their respective wives refusing to allow them to own one.

There was no internet dating in those days and there was something pathetic about the lonely hearts columns that were to be found in the printed press. My university friends (including the girls I used to hang around with) had scattered to the ends of the country, and although my new colleagues did enjoy the occasional curry, they were all married which meant they were not coming out on the pull with me, and that left Sarah as the sole eligible female for my attentions. I had not bothered to ask about salary and I was overqualified for a technician role, and although I had the benefit of a Civil Service pension, the remuneration was not exactly going to support a playboy lifestyle. I was still living with my parents and although I was a financially independent adult who contributed to the bills, the same rules still existed as when I was a sixth former. None of this added up to an active love life — unlike school or university, there was no immediate, eligible pool of young ladies to fraternise with and just as bad, taking someone back to my single bed in my parent's house was just embarrassing.

It took two years for something to happen with Sarah, which in hindsight seems a long time, especially in light of her situation. She had left school after 'A' levels with no real idea of what to do next and no encouragement from her parents. She had fallen into her job first as a temp, before being offered full-time employment when The Patrician took a shine to her. Her job was unchallenging if very comfortable. She still lived with her parents but her father had been recently laid off and had taken to spirits and daytime television. Her friends had gone to college or university, and there was no one at work who could be considered a peer. All of this made her feel left behind and with a gaping hole where her social life should have been. It was only the creepingly slow pace of the Agency that made something that should have taken a month take nearly two years.

There were not many perks to working at the Agency beyond the pension but the Christmas party was one of them. The final Friday before Christmas would be given over to it and it was the only company financed social of the year. Harriet (Head of Personnel and one of the few women in the Agency) began planning it in October and yet it always followed the same tired format. A bus would collect us from the Agency around midday and drive us to some pub that could accommodate nearly forty people. The drinking began immediately and with a speed that meant most people would be drunk before the shrivelled up turkey with all the trimmings arrived. We would keep drinking throughout the meal and then before the coffee, The Patrician would stand up and give his speech to thank everyone for their efforts and state how important the work was for the people of Britain. It would all be over by three o'clock and then the bus would drop us off in the centre of Slough to continue the drinking, while The Patrician and the more senior researchers all took taxis home.

The evening started with a good vibe. Sarah had made a real effort with her appearance and was wearing a short skirt, which showed her legs off and they weren't at all bad for a larger girl. We had been flirting at work for at least six months and I think we both knew that tonight was going to be the night that something finally happened between us. Ian had adopted a festive tie and for once seemed to be in a happy mood. People started to drop away as the evening continued and the discussion had turned to where we should look to get some food. Curry was the favourite option but Neil said that he wasn't keen on spicy food. As we pondered the other options, I became aware of the conversation between one of the younger researchers and Edmund.

"So where did you go last year then?" asked the young guy.

"I had a few weeks in Thailand, just touring and exploring," replied Edmund.

"Exploring what? The Thai lady boys?" laughed the guy back.

Now this young guy was a bit of a loud mouth knob and he had been drinking for nearly seven hours, and although everyone knew that Edmund was less stable than a bucking bronco, there was a collective gasp of shock as Edmund turned white and then launched himself over the table at this guy. His hands wrapped around his throat as the guy's chair went over backwards and he landed on his back on the floor with Edmund on top of him trying to strangle him. There were shouts across the bar as shocked strangers watched the assault, whereas our party remained frozen. I had a little Dutch courage myself, and I sprang up and grabbed the nearest of Edmund's arms to pull him off. I was twenty years younger than Edmund and was working out a lot then, and yet his arm was like a solid bar of iron that I could not move one inch. The young guy was clearly running out of air as his throat was being crushed and for a horrible moment I thought Edmund would kill him.

One of the doormen sauntered over, observed the situation calmly, and then kicked Edmund from behind between the legs with such power than his entire body — pivoted by his arms around the guy's neck— lifted into the air. Edmund made no sound but his arms went limp and he collapsed to the side like he had lost control of every muscle in his body. The doorman grabbed his ankles and dragged him outside while bantering with the woman behind the bar. I pulled the young guy to his feet but it was clear that the evening was over. I turned to Sarah, filled with the recklessness from a combination of sexual need and booze.

"Let's get out of here," I whispered in her ear.

"Okay," she replied without hesitation.

Thirty seconds later and we were outside the door and heading down the high street. I took her hand — a gesture that has become a common ploy for me in assessing the level of interest of females — and then dragged her into a side alley, pushed her against a wall and gave her a passionate kiss. I had kissed enough women to know that this was an awful kiss. She had the strange technique of opening her mouth as wide as possible and then pulling her lips back to expose her teeth. I could feel her teeth on my lips as we snogged and even in my intoxicated state, I was worried about clashing enamel. My hands were exploring her body while her hands were tracking my movements and pushing them off any of the interesting bits. After thirty seconds, it felt more like we were fighting rather than getting off, but I hadn't seen a lot of action recently and this had been a long time coming.

"I really like you," I gasped.

"I really like you too," she replied, but her hands did not lessen their formidable defence.

I was stuck as to what to do next, since we could not go back to either of our homes with our parents there and suggesting a hotel seemed both rather seedy and was a little beyond the means of my meagre income. The kissing wasn't that great once the initial rush had worn off and we were reduced to finding a park bench to sit on. She sat on my lap, which was a little uncomfortable since she was not a skinny thing, and the great revelation began when we both admitted when we had started liking the other one. Needless to say in our empty lives the attraction had been fairly instant but in retrospect, there was nowhere else for it to be channelled. That night began a relationship that went through two phases and lasted a little over a year and a half.

The first phase was getting Sarah to sleep with me. She was not a virgin and had had a few boyfriends before me and it was more of a case of where to do it rather than any reservation on either side. In the end, we found a quiet place in the woods when the weather warmed up where we made love on a blanket while hoping that no dog walker would trip over us. I was twenty-four and a quick rut in the woods was not where I had seen my life going. We were not sexually compatible in the slightest and to be blunt, I would have had more fun playing solo, but this did not stop a series of rough and unsatisfactory couplings which mostly happened at her parents' house during the lunch hour after her unemployed father got himself onto an alcoholic's recovery programme.

I remember the first time she took me upstairs and showed me her bedroom and I saw her bed drowning in cuddly toys. It was an absolute passion killer but we went through the motions. It did not take me long to realise that this really wasn't for me. Firstly, I really didn't like Sarah that much. We just didn't connect intellectually and she had such a narrow outlook on life, but perhaps the worst aspect was her determination to make herself the victim in any situation. Secondly, the sex was not great and was not getting any better. Thirdly, I had seen the pictures of her mum in the house both as a young woman and more recently, which charted her explosion in size over the years. Sarah was a fat bomb primed to go off sometime around her thirtieth birthday. None of this was a very compelling package.

Sadly, Sarah was of the opposite opinion and suddenly became really keen on me, to the point of being convinced that I was 'the one'. She must have had very poor experiences in previous relationships but seeing as there was nothing else on the horizon, I let it play it out. She sensed my loss of interest and thus began the second phase of the relationship where she went to increasing lengths to keep up the passion levels of the first few months. This began with increasingly daring lingerie, which she took to wearing to work and then describing what was underneath her work clothes to make sure that I accepted the offer of lunch at her parents' house. Her work clothes also transformed to tight fitting blouses, dresses, short skirts and high-heeled boots. She went from being invisible to getting a lot of attention at work, which she clearly revelled in. She would make a point of making sure that I got a flash of a stocking top or a peek of her lacy bra. And once these simple teases lost their effectiveness, she moved onto working through my fantasies in bed. It was effective for a while but at the end of the day, you want to be doing those things with someone you're actually into.

She did not take well to being dumped and got very nasty about it. Computers were starting to make it into the workplace and I recall her emails, which laid out in great detail my many failings as a lover and a human being in general. It made me wonder why she was acting like it was such a loss if I was that dreadful, but as I said:

she always did love to play the victim. It did prove to be the kick up the bum that Sarah needed in life, and she found a college course that interested her (women's studies!) and left the Agency in late August, trading her collection of sexy shoes and tight clothes for the comfortable attire of a student. We never spoke after that, even when we bumped into each other years later in a nightclub in Slough, she just scowled at me and walked out. She had started to pile on the pounds by then and had cut her hair short so there were no feelings of nostalgia on my side.

I lasted another three years in the Agency. It was an argument with Ian that gave me the shove I needed to realise that I was a lot more than a technician, and that there was a whole world of opportunity out there.

***

I return back to the present but the bike ride has done nothing to clear my mind. I'm distracted by a wave of nostalgia and memories that I cannot change, and much that I would rather forget. I shower and then begin cooking my mammoth brunch with all the trimmings. But it fails to distract and when it is ready, I have little appetite for it, and half goes in the bin. Only the coffee seems to raise me back up, but after three mugs I realise that that should be enough caffeine for one day, and it does not take long to come back down. This is why I hate Sundays. Once the papers are read and I have finished my chores (which are now something I enjoy rather than resent as I did as a younger man), I am left with myself and my thoughts, and that is not a good place to be. There is only one sure cure for this: I switch on my laptop.

I have six active profiles on different dating sites, as well as a few that I have allowed to lapse on others. I took the tag "Johnny1969" because it has the year of my birth, but there have been times that people have assumed that I was going somewhere else with that number. I log onto each one in turn, sort through the pages of female profiles and look for options. It is a quiet day with few new arrivals (or 'fresh meat' as I refer to them) and far too many older faces or accounts that appear to be neglected. I fire off a few messages but don't feel hopeful. I turn to my phone instead.

**'So that is it? You not man enough to even reply?'**

Katie sounds angry. I would have thought that a couple of days would have been enough to get over it but maybe she did like me a bit. I delete the message. I don't need her dragging me down. I have enough of my own stuff going on. Instead of replying, I send a message to Abigail.

**'Hope you had a good night yesterday! It was good to meet up at last. Do you want to get a drink sometime?'**

I turn my attention back to the last of the dating sites but am distracted by the warming buzz of my phone. It is Rebecca.

**'Hi. How are you?'**

I may not like the woman that much but part of me loves this: messages coming in from different women. Somehow I am no longer some sad guy on his own but am connected to so many people. It temporarily stops my thoughts returning to those dark places. I bash out a quick reply to keep my options open with her but then Abigail responds.

**'Definitely up for that drink mid-week! Let me know what works for you.'**

I offer Tuesday and she accepts. I experience a rush at the positive response and can't help doing a happy dance. However, nostalgia is not fully dispelled and I fire up my social media and stalk Sarah. Her security settings are set high on her account but there are some pictures of her wedding from a decade ago. She looks enormous and the wedding looks cheap. No pictures from the Honeymoon. She probably stayed in a caravan somewhere awful. I dodged a bullet there.

My parents used to complain when I was growing up about people squandering their lives watching television. They had not encountered then the power of social media and the internet for wasting life on unproductive activities. I know that tomorrow I will look back on the weekend and be disgusted with how I have idled away my precious free time when there are so many things I could be doing. It makes no difference though as I spend the next few hours scanning through the same, tired dating profiles and imagining what those women could be like and what I would say to them. Maybe Ben is right and this is a full-on addiction. It is only the need to eat dinner that breaks me away from the screen, and after I have eaten it is time for me to iron my shirts and prepare for the week of work ahead. The day is gone and I have nothing to show for it.

I remember to ring my parents.

## Chapter 7 – Sharon

Every Monday follows the same repetitive routine. The pace of my life seems to have accelerated as I have grown older, with each year passing faster than the last. It seemed not long ago that I was celebrating my fortieth birthday, and I sometimes wake up from vivid dreams where it takes me a few moments to realise that I'm not still working at Hamiltons with a bright future ahead of me (the dream about Anna was a good example, and sadly not untypical). The alarm goes off early and then I hit snooze a total of three times before forcing myself out of bed. I shower and dress with the clothes I laid out the night before, and then it's out the door to brave the morning traffic. If I am honest, there may be five minutes of checking my phone for messages but I never answer them. There will be plenty of time to do that at work and it allows me to consider my replies on the drive in.

I park up and head into the office exactly as I do every working day. Ben and Denise are both at their desks but appear in very different moods. Ben is actually humming (on a Monday!) and is emanating a sense of smugness that only settled people with families can seem to manage. Denise is leant over her desk, a pen in her hand, and staring at the calendar.

"Morning, Ben," I say cheerily although my body is calling out to be back in bed.

"Alright, mate?" replies Ben with a wave. "Good weekend?"

This simple greeting is the lead-in to the interrogation about my love life. I am not falling for it. I may normally enjoy being centre of attention in the office but I am worried about Denise. There is not long before her operation and I can tell that it is occupying her thoughts. It wasn't always like this with Ben. When we first met, we hit it off and used to put the world to rights on every topic you could imagine. Friday afternoons were a time for us to sit back and chat after the weekly call to the US, and we lost hours in animated conversation. As the years have passed, that wealth of topics has dwindled down to a single interest in my love life.

"Coffee, mate?" I ask to Ben.

He gives me a nod and an approving expression. I have no idea where this calling each other "mate" has come from, we're both far too middle class for that. I accelerate towards the kitchen but then detour to Denise. She does not notice me until I am right next to her and then she gives me a startled jump and a nervous smile. She has not been sleeping and there are large, purple bags under her eyes. Her hair is pulled back in a bun — a sign that she overslept and did not shower this morning. She is also devoid of any makeup, which is out of character for someone who is a perfectionist about her appearance.

"Hey you, you okay?" I say gently.

I like Denise and I am concerned but I also don't want her welling up on me here in the office. I am not good at dealing with emotions from colleagues or how to handle sympathy with people you work with. When

Ben's mum died, I avoided him for a week. When it comes to drama at work, I am a firm believer in being part of the audience and not part of the show.

"I didn't sleep much over the weekend," replies Denise.

She looks exhausted but she doesn't need to expand on why. I scan the countdown calendar and can see that she has until next Wednesday before the hospital admission. She has been waiting for two years for this but now that the moment is closing in, I can see that she is terrified.

"Did you see your mum?" I ask.

She nods her head but I can tell that simple distraction is not going to work here. She is close to her mother, in fact they seem to spend every weekend together going shopping and eating in nice restaurants. Denise has a lowly administrative role in reality and I have no idea how she affords all the stuff that she buys. I have never seen her wear the same clothes twice and her array of shoes is bewildering. However, her life has been on hold for a while and I have no doubt when she has recuperated from her operation that she'll be onto bigger and better things. She has mentioned night school and finding a job that actually excites her, as well as covering a whole list of places she wants to see on her bucket list.

"Didn't feel like doing much this weekend," she mutters.

"Look, why don't we all go out this week? We haven't done it since Christmas. Have a few drinks, try and take your mind of things," I ask.

It's a poor suggestion but it elicits a tired smile.

"Okay, Johnny, that sounds nice. What about Wednesday?" she says.

"I'll have to check with Mary," chimes in Ben, who was been listening shamelessly to our conversation.

I hate it when he does that. Mary is not some controlling harridan and would be delighted for him to go out with friends.

"Why don't you ask her too?" I shoot back at him. "I'm sure you can get a babysitter."

"Oh yes, that would be nice," added Denise.

Ben pulls his 'I don't think it's very likely face' but I know if he mentions it to Mary, she'll be glad to have an evening of grown-up company. She adores their children to bits but a five-year-old and a two-year-old can make for tiring conversation after a while. My social work is done for the moment and I move off to boil the kettle and confirm my personal plans for the week. I am considering follow-on dates with both Abigail and Rebecca, and there are a couple of other opportunities brewing as well. It would be nice to get them moved on to the next stage as well. Best to keep the pipeline full, so to speak.

I get to my desk and fire up my computer. It takes a few minutes to get going and it seems to be slowing down as it gets older but I suppose there is no equivalent of coffee for computers. I pretend to be busy until I can log in and access my emails. The news is not good: a wealth of return notices have arrived from late Friday, with a cluster from one of a few remaining volume customers. I scan through these, noting when the equipment is due to be returned, but there is also a lone email from Janice. Accounting for the time zone difference she must have sent it late Friday evening. There is no auto-signature on the bottom so I know that it must have come from her phone and been sent outside of office hours.

**'Please can we talk soon? Can we set a time? I will ring you. J.'**

I am curious on a number of levels and I cannot deny that I still harbour some feelings for her. I would love to see her again but I also know that what happened between us was a one-time thing and she is happily settled in her new life. Her message will pick at me until I chose to do something about it but I need time to work out what the right things is, so instead I switch my head back to my mundane, repetitive job and start ploughing through the "to do" list. As I am diligently giving my work the attention it doesn't deserve, Ben saunters over with the dregs of his coffee in his mug. I can tell that he wants to talk, well really to pry, about my weekend.

"Soo…," he begins in a rather unsubtle gambit. "Get up to much over the weekend?"

This is the point that we normally cover off the latest developments in my love life. They are absolutely fascinated by it but love to judge, and everything I tell them will be met with eye rolling and loud tutting. It bothers me that Ben, a colleague with whom I socialise occasionally, is actually one of the few people who is interested in my life. My need to talk to someone means that I massively over share in work, which is not exactly a professional way to behave. I reflect back on the gangs of male friends that I used to have, and which I have somehow contrived to all lose over the years.

"Yeah, it was okay," I reply nonchalantly. "Bit quiet. Did some cycling."

"Sounds nice," replies Ben, which is a blatant lie as he is digging for gossip. "It's good to relax a bit."

I don't want to tell him anything more, and certainly not about Abigail, who I am starting to like even after a single date. Denise has started to listen in but so far there is nothing to attract her attention.

"No hot dates then?" he pushes.

I sit back in my desk, torn between telling him about this nice, funny girl and knowing that it really is better to keep your personal stuff out of the workplace (although to be fair I have never managed to do that).

"I did see someone," I confess in spite of my better instincts.

"Oh yes!" says Ben. "Do tell!"

Now Denise is interested too, turning her chair round so that she is looking in my direction. She exchanges an amused glance with Ben: the soap opera is on!

"Well, I did have a first date with a girl that I met on a dating site," I admit.

"And…? What was she like? Are you seeing her again?" pushes Ben.

Denise is grinning, which will only egg Ben on further, and he could not be more pushy if he tried.

"She was nice," I confess. "Nice looking, great sense of humour. I liked her."

"Ker-ching!" booms Ben. "So tell me more! How old is she?"

"I am not sure. Thirty maybe?" I reply.

"Ooh, a younger lady!" says Ben loudly in an annoying camp accent.

I hate it when he does this, like some game show from a previous era camping it up for the amusement of the audience. Denise is enjoying every minute of it and I could imagine her having a drink and some popcorn as she listens.

"Will there be a second date?" he asks.

"Yeah, we're going to meet up this week with her friends, and then go to a comedy night," I reply.

"Meeting her friends so soon?" says Ben, without the teasing tone. "Wow, that's moving quickly. The date must have gone well."

"Yeah, it was okay. We laughed a lot. We have the same sense of humour."

"So you like this one?" snaps Denise.

I meet her eyes and give her a nod. I can tell that she wants to say something cutting but that would be churlish. I wish Martin would get in so that they would both go back to work, but in the silence I return to my computer screen and ignore them as I make myself busy.

It is two hours later when Denise takes a call. She looks over at me with a smile that is unpleasant. She hangs up and then strides over purposefully.

"Say Johnny," she says. "Would you consider yourself to be single at this moment in time?"

"I suppose," I reply, pretending to be buried in my work.

"Good, because Sharon is here," she says as she moves off to the reception.

Now, I know that women have been exposed to creepy, over-familiar men since the beginning of time. You know the kind: average looking under-achievers who are convinced that they are lotharios to the females of the world and most likely drive a car that tries to compensate for their failings. I suppose that it is only fair that with increasing equality that men are also subject to the attention of such loathsome specimens. Sharon must be over forty years old and, to her credit, is incredibly well maintained. She is maybe five foot tall but her most noticeable characteristic is the fact that she looks like a low resolution computer rendering of a person with straight lines. She has very square shoulders and her torso runs directly straight down to her feet, with no curvature over the waist or along her legs. She is proud of her chest but even this looks too rectangular. Ben once described her as looking that she was made out of Lego bricks and the image has never left my mind, especially with her hair cut like a German helmet from the Second World War.

Denise moves off to let Sharon in from reception and I groan inwardly. I could go and hide in the lab but Sharon will just follow me in and then I would be cornered. At least in the open office her behaviour will be moderated by other people but then I have the public embarrassment of her attention. I bury myself in my work — something I do every time she visits — safe in the knowledge that it won't make any difference.

"Good morning, people," booms Sharon as she struts in the office.

"Morning," replies Ben.

Sharon ignores him and heads straight towards me. I do not look up but out of the corner of my eye, I can see her peculiar gait with her legs swinging out to the side as she walks. Denise follows behind with an evil grin on her face. She is loving this and looking forward to the spectacle.

"Hello, Johnny," she says and then sits down next to me on the desk.

She is sat on my desk with her legs inelegantly apart. Her dress has a split up the front and I can see a generous amount of thigh. I know she has done this deliberately and there is nothing erotic about it. She is in my personal space and I am not comfortable with it. The smell of her perfume is overpowering, as though she has taken a bath in it. I slowly push my chair back to give me some room, and Sharon shamelessly leans over and reads my email inbox.

"Oh dear, oh dear," she says as she scan reads the subjects of the emails and notices that they are all work related. "All work and no play makes Johnny a dull boy."

If this is supposed to be some sort of chat up line then it really isn't working. I give a shrug and look away, hoping that she will take the hint.

"Denise, how about that cup of tea? I'm gasping here," she commands before turning her attention back to me. "So, you still looking for love on those dating sights?"

"He is!" shouts Denise over her shoulder.

I hate her a little for that. She knows how uncomfortable this is for me and yet it seems to bring out her sadistic side.

"Oh dear, babe, still?" says Sharon, her voice filled with fake sympathy.

I give another shrug. I have learned that it is best to engage as little as possible. Sharon, however, is on a mission, she has thought this through in advance. She has made a special effort with her appearance, and is wearing a very tight grey and black striped dress. Her foot reaches over and subtly touches my calf.

"I don't know why you waste your time on those computer sites anyway! I mean they are all desperate fakers on there!"

"Thanks," I reply, twisting the comment into a dig at me.

"You know what I mean! Anyway, you don't need the hassle of all that. Look, why don't we go out for a drink sometime?" she says.

Finally, after all these months of her hints and innuendo, she has publically asked me out on a date. Denise is returning with a cup of tea and has a grin so wide that it must be uncomfortable. Ben has put his face in his hands so that I cannot see his amusement. The rest of the office is listening.

"No, you're alright," I reply.

"Why not?" she pushes.

I should have told her that I was seeing someone: it's the only lie that can get you out of these situations without causing offence. Instead all I can muster is a shrug and pull an unhappy face. Denise pops the mug of tea down next to Sharon and retreats to a safe distance. I do not want to have this conversation in public and certainly not at work. I do not want to be laughed at for weeks at every coffee break. I have had a few workplace romances, that is true, but they were long ago and handled discretely.

"Look, babe," she pushes. "You can see that I am the full package!"

She has leant forward and pushed her chest out. I see Ben's shoulders heave and fall in silent laughter and I cannot bring myself to look at Denise. I push my chair back further until it hits the desk behind. The refusal has not deterred Sharon one bit and she continues to rub my calf with her foot, a gesture that is now blatantly visible to the rest of the office.

"I'm the kind of girl you can take anywhere! I love to travel, I'm good fun, I look good and believe me, when it comes to the bedroom, then I know how to take care of a man!" she explains without hint of embarrassment. "So what's your problem? Worried that you can't handle this much woman? Don't worry, babe, I'll break you in easily."

I finally bring myself to look at her. I feel myself becoming angry and the only words that are filling my head are cutting ones. She is loud, she is dreadful, she is shallow, she is ignorant and she needs to learn to take no for an answer. The situation is saved by Martin striding over from his office. His expression is displeased and I am grateful for his appearance.

"Good morning, Sharon," he says. "I am slightly surprised to see you after I explained on your last visit that we have no budget left for capital procurements."

His voice is professional but lacks the gravitas to easily master the situation. Sharon glances in his direction but only as if it is an unwarranted annoyance rather than any shame at being called out. Her face shows her anger with me and it is twisted into an ugly visage, and I know that if I did entertain a relationship, I would be seeing this a lot.

"More of a social visit if I'm honest," replies Sharon dismissively. "Just catching up with old friends."

"Well, I am afraid that will need to wait. We have quite a backlog of work we need to get through this week," said Martin.

For a moment, I think that Sharon will tell him to get lost and continue pushing for a date, but Martin is still the manager even if he lacks much personal presence. Sharon reluctantly stands up from my desk and I give an internal sigh of relief.

"Right then, people," she announces grandly. "I need to be getting on. Keep in touch, won't you?"

This last comment is aimed at me but I am looking away and wishing her gone forever. Denise rushes over to escort her out, and Martin gives a satisfied nod. When she is out of hearing, he turns to me.

"I don't want your personal relations spilling over into this office, yeah?" he says.

This may be blatantly unfair but I am too relieved to care.

"Yes, boss," I reply and turn back to my computer.

***

"Thank you for calling," intones Janice. "It is appreciated."

Her voice is so distant and formal but I love her accent. I came home early and phoned her sat on my bed, with a cup of coffee beside me. There was a tingling in my stomach as I was dialling her number, and my heart raced as I listened to the dialling tone waiting for her to answer. My mind has run a thousand scenarios of why she wants to speak to me outside of work, but they always come back to the same one of her visiting the UK and us carrying on where we left off all those years ago. I can still remember the scent of her skin and the texture of her hair.

"No problem at all, Janice," I blurt. "How have you been?"

I can sense her smiling and then listen to her sigh before she answers. I know then that this call is not driven by feelings of nostalgia.

"I am well, thank you Johnny," she replies. "Things were not good for me when we met over here, but they have settled down now. I am happy."

"I am glad for you," I reply.

I am lying. I am bitterly disappointed. I want to hook up with this amazing woman and repeat the evening we had together over and over.

"I guess you are wondering why I asked you to call?" she says with a hint of teasing.

"Yes, I am."

I hear the sound of my own voice: closed and guarded.

"Look, I won't deny that I have always been fond of you; what happened between us was because of that."

"I've always had feelings for you," I exclaim.

"Yes, I've known that too. And that is why I need to say something to you."

"Okay."

"I never knew why you stuck with Chimera in a dead end job for so long. It's obvious to everyone that you could do so much more. I've never known how to broach that with you since it's none of my business. There is no hiding that Chimera is not doing well and to be blunt, there is no sign of it turning around."

My mind is racing ahead. I already know what she is going to say. The writing has been on the wall for so long that the uncertainty has become a fact of life. I don't interrupt as she carries on.

"The decision has been made to withdraw from our European offices completely. We will support spares and repairs directly from the US with a call centre in India."

"I see."

"The announcement will be made on Friday but I wanted to warn you. You must not mention this to anyone else but you need to start looking for another job."

She pauses. I don't care for my job. I know I should have found something else long ago but this still comes as a shock. I feel paralysed.

"Johnny," she continues with sudden urgency. "You need to see this as a good thing. You have been stuck in this job for too long and it's not a career. This is a chance to get your life moving again. I know you still haven't settled down, and I think that's part of feeling stuck. A new job with new challenges is just what you need, and once you start moving forward again, then all the other things may just fall into place. You deserve better than Chimera and you deserve to be happy."

My heart is racing. The disappointment is crushing me. Deep down, I wanted her to be my way out of this. I would move to the US in a heartbeat if she had asked. The emotion is too strong and I hang up the phone without replying. I wonder how long it had taken her to prepare that speech. I will be made redundant. I will need to find something else quickly or not be able to pay the mortgage. The idea of eating into my savings terrifies me. However, none of this really matters. I don't care about Chimera. I will find another job. I will never see Janice again and I can't stand the thought. It has been a long time since anybody has made me feel like this: that sickening mixture of upset and despair.

## Chapter 8 – Hamiltons

It all started with an argument. Sarah had been the only thing that had made the Agency bearable, not so much in her company as rather a distraction from what was a slow and tedious job in an organisation where I had friendly colleagues, but no actual friends. My salary had edged slightly up with Civil Service inflation linked pay rises, but it was clear that this was not going anywhere as a career. Even the promise of a final salary pension was not that compelling when your remuneration was not exactly a passport to the world and what it had to offer. The sense of superiority of the scientist grades towards the technicians was the catalyst but the real reason was boredom from a lack of intellectual challenge. Ian's temper may have been intimidating when I was new starter but I rapidly outgrew the point where I was going to take it from a person who was physically pathetic and an intellectually inferior idiot. I suppose we had some level of informal truce but a clash was inevitable when we were both having a bad day.

Ian was verbally haranguing Neil because his latest trials had failed due to the wrong measuring equipment being used, making the results worthless. It was entirely Ian's fault that he had picked up the wrong stuff and then completely failed to notice during the trials. He was incompetent but worse, his feelings of superiority meant that he was going to take it out on someone more junior. And that meant that Neil was getting an ear-bashing, even though he knew nothing about the trial, and being the quiet guy he was, made no attempt to protect himself. I was in a bad mood that morning and in no way willing to let it go unchallenged. I was ready for a fight and marched into his office and over to his desk, interrupting his outburst at Neil.

"What is your problem, you fat fuck?" I snarled.

Now if Ian routinely lost his temper to gain control of a situation and belittle other people, he had never seen me lose my rag. My face was twisted in fury, completely out of control, and ready to kick seven shades of crap out of him. Such aggression would never be tolerated in the office now, and even back then it was sailing close to the wind (even with The Patrician's laissez-faire management style).

"What did you call me?" he shouted back.

I could see the fear in his eyes. He was a petulant, little bully and not up to someone actually talking back to him.

"You deaf, you rancid lard bucket?" I bellowed back.

"You can't speak to me like that," he complained, looking to Neil for support.

Neil was staring at the floor, wanting no part of this confrontation, but I was here for a fight and ready to take it up a level. I reached over his desk and dragged all his books across the desk and deposited them on the floor. I placed both hands on the desk and leant forward, staring at him in fury.

"What you going to do about it, fat fuck? We going to step outside and sort this out?" I spat.

"Don't speak to me like that! You are just a technician and I am a scientist!" he said back.

"You, a scientist?" I said with a laugh. "Have you ever done any actual science? When, for that matter, have you ever had a single new idea? You do the same, tired experiments over and over, and yet never come to any real conclusions!"

"At least I have a degree," shouted Ian.

"We both have degrees, idiot," I spat back.

"No, I have a degree from a proper university. You have a piece of paper from some technical college that no one has ever heard of," he replied.

It was a good return; I have to give him that. Hidden behind his desk he felt safe from any physical threat and by using his advantage in education, he could maintain his superiority. But I had learned a thing or two about arguing from an older sister.

"And what an embarrassment you must be to that university! A pathetic, underachiever hidden away in some dead-end organisation who will never accomplish anything," I said, faking genuine sympathy.

"Well, you'll never get a job anywhere else either!"

Ian was looking defeated now, his eyes drawn to the doorway which was packed with his peers all watching his humiliation. I could feel the rage draining out of me.

"Twat," I muttered and turned to leave.

Neil fell in dutifully behind me and we made our way out of the main building and back to the

Portakabins, where we would inevitably have a cup of tea.

"You should just ignore him, you know," said Neil.

In reality, I look back and thank Ian for the impetus he gave me. I read the local paper over that cup of tea and saw an advert for a local electronics manufacturer that was looking to hire people with just the skills that the Agency had given me. Even back then, long before the age of internet job sites, there was something quaint about advertising a skilled job in the local paper. I phoned the number and spoke to a rude receptionist, but ten minutes later I had a job interview setup for a lunchtime in a pub. The company was called Hamiltons and I had never heard of it.

***

I wake up on Tuesday to a text from Abigail.

**'Hi. Hope you're ok. Looking forward to tonight. X'**

It makes me smile as I lie there waiting for the five minute snooze on the alarm to go off. I normally don't respond to texts immediately; it is far better to consider your response carefully but this one has put me in a happy mood.

**'Hey Abi. Tonight will be fun. Hope you have a great day. X'**

I don't know why I suddenly truncate her name down to Abi. It is an intimate thing to do with someone who I have only met once but it feels right. I am still reeling from Janice's warning, but somehow I feel more positive knowing that the axe will finally fall. It is similar to that argument with Ian all those years ago; it is the kick that I needed to sort my life out. I don't wait for the alarm and swing myself out of bed to get started with the day. I feel a wave of happiness and the resolution that I can get the job hunting underway and finish the day with a hot date. It doesn't get much better than that!

I get to work full of energy like I have not felt since my twenties. I am the first into the office for once and waste no time in dusting down my CV. It has been a few years since I have given it any attention and the depressing fact is that not much has changed in my life in that time. By the time Denise and Ben arrive, I have updated it and posted onto the job boards of three websites. I take the chance to see what roles are currently being posted and am not disappointed to spot a number of things that I could do. None of them are a step forward from what I am currently doing but I am in survival mode, rather than career progression.

I sit back with my second cup of coffee of the day and take a few minutes to contemplate the next steps. A slight feeling of guilt makes me open my email inbox and glance through what has come in overnight. There are the usual raft of enquiries, some asking for progress on returned equipment, others new requests for help with failures, but all of it seems so pointless suddenly. On Friday, I will be called to a meeting and given the news that my role is under consideration for redundancy, so who cares if my metrics fall off a cliff? It will make no difference to my severance package and faithful service will have no consideration when I am exited from Chimera by some faceless contract HR drone. One email stands out: an unsolicited message from a company that re-sells bankrupt test equipment. Normally I delete these without a second thought but an uncomfortable premonition makes me open it. I don't know if I'm expecting to see an advanced notice of Chimera equipment going onto the market but as I read through the information and note the address, it affects me far worse: it is the sell-off of the remains of Hamiltons.

My old company has been preying on my mind a lot these days. It is a strangling nostalgia that I cannot let go of as I approach the big five zero. The news of its final demise shakes me more than it should and far worse than my own impending redundancy. I read and re-read the email, searching for every clue or insight, my mind pondering the fate of the community that I had so loved. I don't hear Denise walk in and put her things down and when she speaks to me, I practically jump out of my chair.

"So what is the plan for tomorrow?" she asks.

I look at her in bewilderment as my distracted brain fails to process what she is asking me. The grey pallor of her skin and visible bags under her eyes show her exhaustion. I know that it is worry that is keeping her awake with less than a week to the operation. She has called me heartless before because of the women I have dumped, but she is still looking to me for one night of drunken distraction.

"Right!" I reply as my brain moves into gear. "Thought we'd start with a few cheeky ones at the Kings Arms before taking in a few places along the Kings Road. There's a new Italian place on the High Street which should be good to try for dinner before we find a club."

"Ohh, then I need to dress for clubbing?" she asks eagerly.

"That's right," I reply and can even feel myself getting excited.

"And Ben is up for this?" she pushes.

"Of course," I say carelessly, even though I have just made this up.

We break off chatting when Martin arrives as he disapproves of idle conversation in the office. He won't actually say anything but will come and stand next to you until it gets really awkward. I am not sure which management seminar teaches these techniques, but they are oddly effective. I stand up quickly and follow him into his office.

"Morning Martin," I say with a quick knock on the open door. "Sorry to ambush you when you have just got in but may I have a word?"

"Sure," replies Martin.

He actually freezes halfway through taking his laptop out of his oversized briefcase and stares at me. I am least twenty years his senior and have always been sure never to give him any problems. I am a solid, independent worker and I have learned over the years how to anticipate my manager's needs well enough to be appreciated. I can see that my approach has genuinely wrong footed him.

"Look, I know that our capital expenditure has been slashed these last few years and that has left us exposed with our aging test infrastructure," I begin, turning on the corporate bullshit. "But I've just had notice of a company closure — a developer of test equipment no less — and I think we should take a quick look to see if there are any bargains before the local vultures swoop."

Martin stares at me in relief. I wonder if he has got wind of the imminent demise of our office and is on edge.

"Good idea," he replies. "You need anyone to help?"

"No, I've got this covered," I dismiss casually.

I head back to my desk with a smile. I'll call the agent and make an appointment to pick over the bones of my former company. My head and heart are reeling.

***

I recall my interview for Hamiltons so clearly. Dad had always told me to invest in a good suit from a tailor that was both timeless and well cut. I looked good by my own admission as I stepped out of my car in the car park of the Nag's Head all those years ago, having spent the morning grooming myself and ensuring that my shirt and tie looked as good as my suit. I had glanced around and the collection of rusting, old bangers told me that I massively over-dressed, even if this was supposed to be an interview. I had explored the area the night before, a quick reconnaissance so that there were no surprises, and had found the ugly 1950s block that was Hamiltons, which you could make out through the trees from the pub. I was ten minutes early but I did not feel comfortable lingering in the car park, lest someone try and sell me a stolen car radio or some drugs. Instead I made my way towards the bar to get myself a drink, under the hostile eyes of the men who were smoking outside. It was a decade before the smoking ban came in, but there were those who liked some fresh air with their nicotine back then.

It is hard to convey my initial image of the inside of the Nag's Head. My eyes struggled to adjust to the dim interior, the noise of so many people drinking and shouting was disconcerting, and the air was thick with cigarette smoke. The furniture was chipped and tatty, the horse brasses looked ridiculous in a town pub, and the almost entirely male clientele was dressed in styles and materials from a previous generation. Mum would have dismissed it in a single word: grotty. A group of locals, all drinking beer and with their shirt sleeves rolled up, stopped talking to glare at me. I felt uncomfortable and very out of place. The landlord seemed no less pleased to see me. I froze my expression to hide what I was really thinking and headed towards him.

"What will it be?" he asked, clearly not caring either way.

I was about to order a coke when as fortune would have it, I hesitated as I realised that would make me the only person in the pub having a soft drink. Instead, I made a point of studying the selection of bitters when a voice called out my name.

"Johnny!"

I did not recognise the man who was pushing his way through the patrons to come and shake my hand, but there was a change in the demeanour of the locals who suddenly relaxed and went back to their conversation, as well as the landlord who all of a sudden started smiling.

"Hi there, our kid, lovely to meet you," he said. "Call me, Ken. Now then, let me get this, what you having?"

Ken was variously described as looking like a South American dictator, a porn star and a drug smuggler. He was of middling height with tanned skin, and had a distinctive moustache and chaotic hair combed over his bald spot. He had an energetic smile and the ability to make anyone feel the most special person in the world. His clothes were directly out of a 1970s sitcom and his teeth were deeply stained by tobacco.

"I was thinking of the Pale Ale," I volunteered.

"Good choice, lad," replied Ken and he gave me a happy slap on the back to show I had made the right selection. "Best make it a round, Dave."

The landlord gave an impressed nod and began to pump out the ale. He had started to smile amiably and I was left wondering at the strangeness of a city pub that seemed to only want locals.

"Shall I put these on account, Ken?" he asked.

"If you would be so kind, Dave, and could you chuck us over a few menus?"

"Right you are," replied Dave.

He handed me my pint first and I made a point of wishing them both good health before taking a sip. It was warm and frothy but it was well kept. Dave handed Ken a few tatty menus which had obviously been typed on a typewriter some time ago (and to be clear, a typewriter was an anachronism even back then) and the prices whited out with Tipp-ex and then handwritten over multiple times as the years had passed. I took a quick glance down the offerings: it was basically either white bread sandwiches or anything you could deep fat fry with chips. That was the way of things back then.

"You are a gentleman, sir," Ken said to the landlord with a deep bow.

"Always a pleasure, Ken! Why don't I bring your beers over when I'm done?"

Ken ushered me through the pub, with the locals standing aside and nodding at him in recognition. I had my trusty faux leather folder (the one that my father had given me for my first interview at the Agency) in one hand and my beer in the other. Ken led me over to a table where two other people were waiting, and who had pretty much drained their first round of drinks. Now I was no stranger to a lunchtime drink but this was going at a pace before one had eaten. The man was thin and wiry and in his mid-fifties. He had a pencil moustache, which looked a bit pathetic compared to Ken's bush, and an expression so worried that one would think he was the one being interviewed and had needed to stock up on Dutch courage. The woman sat next to him was of a similar age but was dressed like she was twenty years younger in a way that my mother would have described as 'a bit tarty'. She had dyed platinum blond hair, blood red lipstick and a short skirt that showed off her long, trim legs. I must admit it was a look that worked for me.

"Right you two," shouted Ken, even though we were right next to them. "This is Johnny! Johnny let me introduce Stephen, our Technical Director, and Jenny, who is Head of Personnel."

"Hello," I said nervously and put my pint down so that I could shake hands.

Beer had slopped down the side of the glass and I wiped my hand on the side of my trousers before reaching for the handshake, which looked a little bit like the sort of thing that a grubby schoolboy might do.

"Pleased to meet you, my name is Stephen. I am the Technical Director for Hamiltons."

He tried to squeeze my hand hard to show his dominance but there was not much to him in terms of muscles. I squeezed back harder and he was compelled to break the handshake.

"And I'm Jenny," said Jenny.

She took my hand and held it as she held my eyes. It was a much nicer sensation.

"Well, sit down before you fall down," said Ken, pulling over another chair for me.

I sat down, unzipped my folder and passed out copies of my CV to all three of them. I had starting using word processers in school, so to me there was nothing that impressive about the document but it provoked more comment than I was expecting.

"Ooh very la-dee-da," sneered Stephen, despite being clearly impressed.

He held the document close to his eyes and read it in what seemed to be mounting horror before putting it down on the table and finishing what was left of his pint in one gulp. The table was damp from the condensation of the glasses and I watched as it soaked into the paper.

"Did you get these done professionally?" asked Jenny.

"No, I did it myself on my computer," I replied.

"That's right impressive, that is," said Ken with a deep nod.

There was no doubt then that he was on my side from the off, but I was less sure of the technical director. Dave arrived with a fresh round of drinks and we broke off speaking. Ken ran through the menu, asking us what we wanted and then relaying it slowly to Dave so there would be no mistakes. Dave did not write it down so I was convinced he would get it wrong anyway.

"You really done all those things?" blurted out Stephen.

I had been worried how impressive my CV would actually be. The job at the Agency had been like a playground and I had found the time to experiment in a lot of different areas, and the ability to buy things and play with them without any oversight. I had learned to properly program, to design all types of electronics, and got them to work practically. I had written the business cases for the latest and greatest design tools and then had the luxury of having the time to learn them well. I was not an expert in anything but a sound generalist who could turn his hand to most things.

"Well yes," I replied, making no effort to hide the confusion in my voice. "We were always trying to keep ahead of the curve to make sure that the science team had the best support for their experiments. We sold some of the equipment too so I had a lot of experience in type approval and release to market."

To say that I had a lot of experience was a bit much as I had done it once, but it had made me want to make products and see them sell. It seemed far more exciting than creating things that then rotted on some shelf until the next clear out. There was no doubt that what I had written on the form must have been complete gibberish to Ken but he was shaking his head in wonder.

"Amazing," he said.

"And you have experience of managing teams?" asked Jenny.

I had drunk half my pint quickly and could feel it going to my head. I also felt her hand give my knee a squeeze under the table. I looked at her and she smiled at me with an amused twitch of her eyebrows.

"A little," I reply. "But that is an area in which I am looking to gain some experience. There isn't a lot of that in my current role."

The food arrived with worrying haste, and we switched away from interview topics. Ken regaled us with stories and a second pint arrived for me. I had ordered chicken in a basket, which for those of you who never suffered pub food back then, was literally a lump of fried chicken on soggy chips in a basket. The chicken was like rubber and the chips were cold and soggy. Lucky then that there was beer to wash it down with. However, Ken was too much of a nice man to be anything other than effusive in his praise.

"Dave!" he bellowed. "My compliments to the Chef! Another great feast!"

No one contradicted him and the landlord was quite happy to accept the compliment as he tidied away the fat-soaked baskets, which no doubt he intended to re-use. I had nearly finished my second pint and was feeling quite drunk, while hoping that Ken would not order a third round. Instead he called for coffee while he and Stephen disappeared into the rear of the pub. It felt so awkward being left with the woman who had groped me minutes earlier.

"How long have you worked at Hamiltons?" I asked.

Jenny leant back in her chair, smiled and took her time in answering.

"At least twenty years!" she said. "It does make me wonder where the years went. Mind you, I know everything and everyone at Hamiltons. The stories I could tell you!"

"So you would recommend it as a place to work?"

"Johnny, you will love it. It's a great place to be or I would not have stayed for so long."

I had run dry of questions and Jenny seemed happy to finish off her wine. Ken reappeared and waved me over to the back of a pub. I made my apologies to Jenny who gave me a wink, and then turned her attention to regarding the rest of the people in the pub. I followed Ken who suddenly seemed filled with a sense of urgency.

"This way Johnny," he said. "We don't want to keep the Old Man waiting."

There was a private room at the back of the pub and it would have come as no surprise had there been a bouncer on the door. Ken knocked on the door, hesitated and then we ducked inside. There was Arthur Hamilton, sat in a leather wingback armchair like a king on his throne. His immaculately cut, three-piece suit could not disguise his prize fighter physique, with his barrel chest and gorilla arms. His head and face were brutish, there were large golden rings on his fingers, and his expression was one of disdainful fury. A cigar burned slowly in his right hand and the room was heavy with its smoke. Ken scuttled forward to make the introductions and I took a moment to notice that Steve was stood at the right hand of his master, and that there was a second gaunt, wraith-like man stood by the open window. They were the courtiers to their King.

"Arthur, this is Johnny who we were telling you about," said Ken.

I heard how nervous his voice seemed, all humour and charm stripped bare. I stepped forward to shake hands but Arthur made no movement and I froze after the first step under his unhurried gaze. My CV was resting on a small table to the side of his chair alongside a tumbler of whiskey.

"Why are you looking to leave your current job?" he demanded.

I had told Jenny about my desire to manage teams but there was something about his direct gaze that ripped the truth out of me.

"I am sick of designing things that are used once and then rot on a shelf. I want to make products that people actually want to buy. Something that really feels like it has a purpose," I replied bluntly.

I knew instinctively that I had given the right answer. Arthur took a long drag on his cigar and then watched the smoke curl towards the ceiling. He picked up my CV and ran his eyes down my list of capabilities.

"You have some good skills."

It was an observation, not a compliment and required no reply.

"You're asking a lot though," he continued.

I had taken a look at the trade press for roles with my experience and taken an average. It surprised me to hear this called a lot of money and my mouth spoke before my brain had a chance to stop it.

"You get what you pay for."

Arthur gave an involuntary chuckle and then smiled at me.

"Give us a moment," he dismissed.

I stepped back outside and then hovered around awkwardly. I did not want to go back and sit with Jenny, but I felt so conspicuous in a pub full of people who all knew each other. It was only a few minutes before Ken came bouncing over, and shook my hand with genuine joy.

"You did it, Johnny! You are in!" he laughed and then gave me a hug.

So that was how it worked. I was given a job rather than offered, and my acceptance taken as read. I was about to join a company in decline, somewhere that had lost its way and was stuck in the past in a world that was changing. However, it was not a company in the modern sense but a community that I was enlisting to help save: a mad, dysfunctional family. People may curse political correctness but Hamiltons was a place rife with casual racism, homophobia and misogyny. If one challenged these prejudices, one would be dismissed as a poofter. To be accepted into the social fabric of the company meant a ready set of friends who genuinely cared about each other, and made going to work on a Monday something to look forward to. However, in order to survive, it was going to need to change beyond recognition and no matter how much Arthur loved his company and its people, he knew that he needed fresh blood if his legacy was going to survive.

***

"Wow, you must be having a productive day!" beamed Denise at me.

It was true that as my mind wandered through the memories of happier years, I had blitzed through my daily work list systematically. It should have worried me that I could do ninety percent of my job without concentrating. Having completed the open jobs, I had cleaned out my email box and was now scratching around for things to do.

"Yeah, I think so," I reply.

She looks happier today; still tired around the eyes but somehow her face was radiant. I realise how much our planned night out means to her. Her job is not challenging enough to keep her distracted and the constant worry eats at her.

"I told mum about it!" she continues. "If she was a few years younger, then she would want to come to!"

Her mum has had both hips replaced so her dancing days are over but the thought makes me smile. Sometimes, I really think that Denise needs to cut the apron strings, but then I also envy the relationship she has with her mum, especially when she is going through a lot. I have never had such a bond with my parents and I feel a little jealous.

"We going straight from work?" I ask.

We used to do this in the old days. Somehow it was always more exciting getting changed in the work toilets, leaving our cars at work and taking a joint taxi to wherever we were starting the mayhem. It has been a few years since we've done that and some months since we last all went out together.

"Yes!" she enthuses and claps her hand together in genuine excitement. "I'll bring my clothes and makeup and we can go direct. So much better than meeting up later."

I do agree with the last point as once I've gone home and had a sit down, it becomes increasingly hard to go out again. A lot of my relationships have failed because after the initial excitement, I have found I just can't be bothered with the effort of seeing them. I know that sounds awful, but it's the truth.

"Right then, from work it is!" I smile.

Denise is grinning at me. It is nice for her to be looking at me with joy rather than the disdain for a male chauvinist pig. Our relationship is a strange one. She does genuinely like me and enjoys my company but my love life has provoked accusations that I just use women for my own gratification. She may love to hear about my exploits but there is a thin line between her amusement and her anger. I suppose from her perspective it must be one of those 'love the sinner, hate the sin' things. However, tomorrow is another day. I turn off my computer and my mind is already on this evening's date. I am excited. And it has been a while since I felt that way.

***

The plan is less than ideal. I am meeting Abigail in a student pub and, even worse, have agreed to meet inside. It is a beginner's mistake to try and meet somewhere crowded, wandering around and trying to work out which one is your actual date when they look nothing like their pictures. At least I have met Abigail before but I am rather put out that we are not meeting outside. The other issue is what to wear. It's difficult for men of a certain age to do "smart casual" well, since we either look too smart, too relaxed or get accused of trying to dress like a younger man. I have had a lot of practise over the last few years and still struggle with it. I am fan of double-cuffed shirts as cufflinks are one of the few ways that a chap can add a bit of flair to his work attire. I transform my work shirt into a casual one by untucking it from my trousers, removing the cufflinks and folding the cuffs half-way back up my elbows. There was a time that I was fonder of leaving my shirt tucked in to show off my flat stomach but that has softened up over the last few years, despite a hundred sit-ups every morning.

I arrive bang on time and begin trawling around the venue to find Abigail. I had hoped that there would quite a diverse range of age groups but the place is crammed with students, who, to be fair, seem to treat me with a certain air of deference and move out of my way as I squeeze through. It occurs to me that I must be the same age as their fathers. It is not a good thought. Needless to say, I have made nearly a full revolution of the venue and failed to see her when I hear my name shouted out.

"Johnny!"

Abigail moves effortlessly through the crowd and then stands awkwardly in front of me. I lean in and kiss her cheek and she gives me a half-hug. It is not a good start.

"We're sat over here," she says. "We got a table."

She then takes my hand and leads me to a table against the wall where her three friends are sitting. There is no spare chair at the table and looking around, there are none to be seen at any of the other tables. I like holding her hand though: it is a sweet gesture.

"Hey guys," she shouts to her friends. "This is Johnny."

All three are engrossed on their smartphones, hypnotised by the warmth of the glowing screens. There are three of them and I immediately give them nicknames: hottie, grumpy and pigface. This is a real problem of mine since I never then make the effort to remember their real names. Abigail continues with her artificially happy voice to introduce them all.

"So, this is Tricia, Mel and Steph," she says.

"Hey guys," I say and give a little wave.

They barely glance up from their phones, which I find quite cutting. Only Steph with her porcine face regards me with a sneer.

"You were right, he is old," she says and looks back down to her phone.

Abigail blushes at the rudeness and I suppress my urge to tell her how ugly she is. Instead I try and rise above it.

"Would anyone like a drink?" I ask.

They are sharing a bottle of Prosecco but all their glasses are full. Perhaps it was a naïve question but it only seemed polite to ask.

"You timed that right," sneers Steph without looking up from her phone.

I take a deep breath but only Abigail notices. I can tell she is uncomfortable: this is not how she imagined things going. I weave my way to the bar and it takes a long five minutes to get served. Normally I would want to share a bottle of something with my date (it helps to bond) but this time I order a pint of bitter and then make my way back. There is no chance of getting another chair and I end up stood by the wall, nursing my pint. Since Abigail would have needed to talk through Steph to exchange anything with me, she gives me a smile, but the group remains silent.

I take a dislike to the comedian as soon as he starts his act. He is clearly far too full of himself, and he has an annoying habit of pulling his long, black hair from his face and smirking whenever he hits a punch line. His jokes start off with some popular culture references, and sound like he has lifted them off some website. The crowd are here to be amused and indulge him with some chuckles, but he is struggling to get the theme of his act established, and then twenty minutes in he changes approach. One of the spectators heckles him, and the comedian responds by turning his attention to the audience and begins picking targets. He starts with the heckler himself, who is a little on the large side, and starts asking him about Weight Watchers. He then turns on a guy with a shaved head and asks him how much he saves on shampoo, which falls flat. I then see him scanning the room for his next victim and his eyes fall on me.

"Oh no," he shouts and points at me. "Granddad has escaped from the home! Someone give them a call."

I suppose that being stood up against the wall was one way to be conspicuous, but it is uncomfortable to feel every eye in the room turn on me. Abigail's friends are loving it and I can hear them scream with laughter, suddenly delighted to be part of the show.

"You alight there, Granddad?" continues the comedian. "You enjoying your pint?"

Buying a pint rather than, say, a bottled larger or maybe even a glass of gin and tonic suddenly doesn't seem like such a good idea.

"It's outrageous!" he continues. "Young people today! Making an old man stand? Were they brought up with no manners?"

Steph makes a point of offering me her chair, her face is even uglier when twisted in laughter. I am not upset or offended, and it is hard to explain exactly how I feel. One part of it is boredom, but I just don't want to be here. These people are not my friends. I am not enjoying the evening. I would rather be home. I put the pint down on the table, give the comedian a smile and a small bow, and walk out. As I approach the exit, the doorman, who looks like a seasoned bruiser of the same age as me, opens the door and speaks quietly.

"That guy is an arsehole," he growls, angry on behalf of us older men.

I reward him with a smile as my feet carry me towards the taxi ramp.

Abigail does not follow me.

## Chapter 9 – Stanley

I awake early and feel strangely fresh. There are a couple of messages on my phone from Abigail but I am not interested. I roll out of bed and pack a small bag of clothes for the evening and then get ready for work. I flick open my dating app as I am cleaning my teeth and see that I have a few messages there too; I have been rather neglecting it for the last few days. I am excited and it has nothing to do with the prospect of a night out with my colleagues. It is Hamiltons. I dreamt about it in the night and I now have a burning need to return to the place where I spent my happiest days, and where the future still seemed bright and full of opportunity. I find myself taking my time over my appearance, much as I did for the first interview all those years ago, even though I know the building will be empty and my former colleagues long gone. However, I can't help it. I need to look good.

I drive to work following my normal routine, parking in my normal place and drop my bag under my desk for later. I work until ten o'clock without pause or break and I can feel the slowness of time as each minute crawls past. It has been a long time since I felt this kind of energy and excitement, and I can even remember clearly exactly when that was. I was a younger man then, excited by the prospect of a crusade where Ken and I were going to save Hamiltons, and where I had the perfect woman in Anna who was head over heels in love with me. I stand up at ten on the dot and am straight out of the door without even as much as a sideways glance to my confused colleagues. Hamiltons is about thirty minutes away and despite the passing of the time, the route is etched into my brain.

It is a sunny, clear day and the traffic is light so I arrive exactly half an hour later. I have the day planned in my mind. It won't take more than an hour to pick over the bones of my former employer and to indulge my nostalgia, and then a slap up lunch at the Nag's Head. I pull into the car park of Hamiltons and my mind works hard to process every small detail. The ugly 1950s building looks even worse today, with its stained brick and concrete and those small windows that were neither practical nor aesthetic. The flower beds, once the pride and joy of the Old Man and brimming with beautiful roses, are now a tangle of weeds. We were forbidden from reversing into the parking spaces near them in case the car exhaust damaged their delicate petals. The name of the company has been removed from over the reception, although the individual letters can still be made out as the bricks behind them are unweathered. Despite the effects of age, this is still the same company that I joined, and I can feel butterflies in my stomach.

I park up the car, open the back door to recover my jacket off the back seat (I stow it there to avoid creases) and take a moment to let it all sink in. It had been a cold morning in October when I had started here. Ken had told me to get here early and I had been dutifully stood at the locked reception door at eight o'clock. I noticed one of the factory workers head in by a side door to the right, and I walked around to investigate. That is when I encountered a furious man guarding the entrance. He was thin but well-muscled, with regimental tattoos on his arms, and his white hair was cut close to his scalp. He positioned himself in the doorway so that I would be unable to pass.

"Who are you?" he snapped. His arms were folded across his chest and there was a faint air that violence was a possibility.

"Good morning," I replied politely, determined to make a good impression on the first day. "My name is Johnny. It is my first day today and I was expecting to meet up with Ken. Is he around?"

"I never heard of you," replied the aggressive guardian.

He looked through me and off to the side, pulling an unimpressed face. There was no way he was going to let me in or even try and find Ken. I remained where I was, watching him, curious how he thought that it would work out. I supposed he wanted me to ask him again in order to show who had the power, but I was in no hurry and folded my arms behind my back like I was standing at ease on a parade ground and just waited. He was not expecting this and began to twitch. The impasse was broken by the sudden appearance of Ken who came bustling down the corridor.

"Hi there, our kid," he shouted and there was no hiding how pleased he was to see me. "Come in, come in! Now then Stanley, this is Johnny. I was telling you about him."

Stanley had just been caught out in a lie and although part of me wanted to call him out on it, that was my first day and I needed to behave. He did at least have the decency to blush and step aside, although from anger or embarrassment I could not tell.

"Morning, Ken," I replied with gusto and reached out to shake his hand.

I was chivvied into the bowels of the building, past offices and workshops. The whole place smelt of metal filings and coffee and was every bit as tatty as the Nag's Head where I had my interview. There was a notice board packed with old bits of paper, yellowed and curled at the edges, aging thank you cards, and sign up notices for various social events. I could smell the canteen before we got there, the odour of burned toast and fried eggs getting thicker as we approached, and my stomach gave a happy rumble in expectation of breakfast.

"Right, here we are!" said Ken, and ushered me in like we had arrived at a posh restaurant and were in for a treat. "Bacon and egg, Johnny, bacon and egg!"

It was a canteen in the old fashioned sense of the word, packed with long tables and mismatched chairs. There was a stainless steel counter where all the ingredients for a cooked breakfast were curling up under heatlamps, a self-service toaster and a pile of cheap, white bread, plus urns of tea and coffee beside a collection of chipped mugs. Ken handed me a tray and then took the lead to show me how it was done.

"Right then, Carol," he said to the long-suffering cook. "The full trimmings and a cup of cha."

Carol gave me a long look, silently questioning why Ken did this, before picking up a plate and then dolling out a breakfast that a giant would have struggled with. I asked for something more modest, and then helped myself to a cup of lukewarm coffee from the urn. The whole meal cost one pound, which was nothing even back then. I revelled in this as I turned round to see where Ken had gone. The room was filled with happy laughter and chatter. It felt nice and homely. Ken found us a place on our own so that we could talk, but there was no hiding the natural curiosity of the people who were regarding me with interest. I caught the eye of a pretty girl, the one who would always be the pretty girl to me even after all these years, staring at me. She smiled when our eyes made contact and the hairs rose up on my back. She had long, black hair tied in a ponytail, bright eyes and elfin features. I hoped desperately that she was single. I made my way towards Ken treading very carefully. I did not want to fall over with everyone watching me.

"I said you would love it here," enthused Ken when I sat down. "Bacon and egg to start the day!"

"It's great Ken," I replied.

And it was. This is not the stuffy, cold world of the Agency. It was like being adopted into a loud, friendly family.

"Now, the Old Man wants to see you at nine, so that gives me a little time to show you around and get you introduced."

I glanced over my shoulder and saw the pretty girl watching me. She looked back down at her food and then smiled to herself. There was only one person I wanted to be introduced to.

***

I come back to the present with a start. I pull on my jacket and lock the car. The wind is cold and cuts straight through my business clothes. I start towards reception but it is clear that it is locked and the lights are off. There is a heavy chain with a padlock on the outer door handles. I don't break step but swerve towards the side entrance as I had all those years ago, only to freeze in horror. For a moment I think that it's a trick of memory, or I have gone mad, or it is a ghost, or even that I have travelled back in time all those years. The side door is open and the angry visage of Stanley is staring at me. He has got older and certainly thinner. His face is pinched and the muscles of his arms have wasted away, leaving his wrinkled skin obscuring his tattoos. His impassive face betrays no surprise and it is only when he speaks that I can start moving again.

"So you finally came back then?" he asks. "I always knew you would but they all thought you'd come back and save them."

There is something quite cathartic about the rebuke. It stings me to the core but it is what I have been saying to myself since about a month after I left. I feel I deserve it, and perhaps that is one reason why I have come back: to face up to my part in the failure of this company. I had always imagined that it is what Anna would have said, or maybe even Ken, although he always wanted to see the best in people. I know now how much I hurt them both when I walked out, and it is only now that I can look back and face up to what happened. Stanley watches my face closely and reads my emotions well. He gives an angry snort and a wave of the head to beckon me out of the wind.

"The vultures have all been," he says shortly as he locks the side door behind us. "There's not much left."

I never thought that there would be but it is telling that Stanley had not told the agent this when he was told that I was coming by. He never liked me and I am sure was delighted when I left, but he is all alone now in this prison to the past, and the company of someone with the same memories is not to be declined easily. I never knew exactly what Stanley's exact role was in the company, but then Arthur had seemed to collect strays. He had acted as a sort of caretaker, security man, driver and general dogsbody. It comes as no surprise to still find him here, the last man standing from the scattered community.

"I'll show you what there is though," he continues.

I have yet to speak but Stanley does not seem to mind. The old smells of the building are gone and I can just detect damp and mildew. The paint of the corridor walls is peeling, there is water damage apparent on the roof tiles, and the floor is missing some plastic tiles. I follow him in the footsteps of my first day. The workshops are bare. The offices have a few pieces of broken furniture and piles of old paper. The notice boards are long gone from the walls but one can make out from the paint where they were. I feel that I have stepped into the scene of a low-budget horror film, but cannot back out now. We pass the canteen, now left completely bare, turn the corner through the internal fire doors and then past the registry where Anna used to work with Edith. The filing cabinets are all gone, and with them the history of every design and product record of everything that had ever left the factory. Edith was in her sixtieth year when I joined the company, and yet she had an encyclopaedic memory of every piece of paper that had entered her realm. Never once did she falter to remember where some forgotten record had been stashed. She was the reason that Hamiltons had never needed a computer database. I slow for a moment and my eyes loiter on the room so long that Stanley notices. He thinks I am remembering Anna.

"She went back home in the end," he says bluntly. "Mind you, she looked like a ghost of herself after you left. All pale and red eyes and couldn't concentrate. When the new management came in, it was only a matter of time before she was asked to leave. She helped get the records computerised after Edith had her turn but then she went. We never heard from her again either. She disappeared just like you did. I suppose she must be married now with kids."

There are so many questions I want to ask about Anna, but I know that Stanley will not have remained in contact. Anna always thought him an idiot who was too full of himself. However, her name is enough to make me dizzy with longing and regret. Edith having a stroke was another sin to be laid at my door. I had heard some rumour through one of my contractor friends but it was hard to hear it confirmed. She had been such a lovely woman with the solitary flaw of her cigarettes, which she needed about every thirty minutes to stay functioning.

"Edith passed?" I ask.

"Stroke killed her straight out. I guess that's a mercy," replied Stanley, before turning away and moving on.

"What about the Old Man?" I ask.

Stanley stops. The name of his former master still resonates with him. He does not turn but his voice carries over his shoulder.

"We buried him six months after Edith. It was just before the redundancies started in earnest and the last time we were all together. They all thought you would at least come back for that. He believed in you."

I feel a little sick. I should have been there at those funerals. I thought that I could put this place and its people behind me, and I had done well but each lost moment feels magnified by time and I am overwhelmed. I force myself to follow Stanley. The stairs take us up to the cramped second floor, and past the managers' offices. It had been a sign of status in the company to have one's own office, but they were small and poorly lit, and most could barely accommodate a full-sized desk. I pass mine but the lights are off and there is so little natural light that it is hard to see inside. I do not resist the impulse to open the door and look inside. A solitary old computer monitor is shoved in the corner but there is nothing left that is familiar, and in my current state that is a blessing.

"In here," calls Stanley, his voice carries down the corridor.

I set this lab up after I first joined, converting it from a store room into somewhere proper we could do our work. The workshops downstairs were filthy and not suited for electronics. I get a jolt as I walk in. The metal racking is still screwed into the walls, stretching from floor to ceiling and still containing some of the detritus of the past. The component drawers are still there, each lovingly labelled but the cardboard is brown and the ink faded. The benches are gone along with the stools, but some large cardboard boxes have been turned upside down to make a table and some of the old equipment has been laid out for sale.

It is, of course, complete junk. I look in it at wonder since most of it was old when I first joined the company, and every piece brings back memories of my time here. Only a scrap merchant would hold any interest in the broken oscilloscopes and power supplies that would not meet modern safety standards. That does not stop me walking over and inspecting it, picking up items and examining them closely. I flip one over and see my name still written on it in indelible pen (the only way to avoid your equipment reappearing somewhere else in the building) and I recall buying it from the catalogue. This place is like picking through my memories: a museum to the best part of my life.

"What do you think?" asks Stanley but he already knows the answer.

"There is nothing here that we can use, I'm afraid," I reply politely.

My attention is drawn to the racking and I wander over, having seen something hidden behind one of the boxes. I shove the box aside and am rewarded with a Daedalus 100. It is the thing that I designed that I believed would keep the company safe and revive its fortunes. There was going to be a whole family of them, all based on a common design and easy for the production teams to churn out. I pick it up gently and even now I marvel at how good it looks. The lid is not fixed down, and I slide it off and examine the interior. My eyes seek out the circuit board I designed, and I can see where I put my name etched into the copper, along with a smiling face. It was how I autographed the things I designed, and it amused me to know that for years there would be products out there with my name on them.

"You gave us a few years, I will give you that," muttered Stanley, but from his tone I cannot tell if this was cruelty or kindness. "Why don't you take it with you?"

I am tempted but I know that this will lead to madness. The past belongs in the past, and keepsakes will not bring those times back nor keep the lost people close. I don't want to come to terms with my time here: I want to forget it. I put the box back.

"No, thanks," I reply curtly. "It was a long time ago now."

He gives a small grunt and continues his unwavering vigil of my every movement.

"Do you still keep in contact with any of them?" I ask, although not sure if I wish to hear the answer.

"Nah, not anymore," he replies and then stops. He does not expand on the answer and I realise that it was too long ago now, there is no way to make up what happened.

I have had enough of this mausoleum. It has not been a pleasant wander down memory lane but a humiliating reminder of my failures. Sometimes, when I dwell on why my life has turned out in the disappointing way that it has, I always come back to this place and wonder if I deserve it. I don't wait for Stanley but start making my way back the way we came. Every corner of Hamiltons is full of recollections but I can stand no more. We move quickly back out of the building without pause until we come back to the locked side door. Only there do I have to wait to allow Stanley to let me out.

"I was going to get some lunch at the Nag's," I venture. "Would you like to come? My treat."

I have no idea why I asked him. He takes a long hard look at me, and I can see the tears forming in his eyes.

"No, best not," he answers. "I need to look after things here."

He waves his hand behind him to the cold, damp building and what little junk remains. Part of me is glad because it would make lunch awkward but on the other hand, he is one of the few people I could talk to about what happened. He is clearly no more over the past than I am but the moment passes quickly. Stanley gives a final nod and locks the door. I wonder what else there is for him in life and what will happen to him. I have a flashing image of his lonely funeral, the community that once would have looked after him now scattered or dead. I walk to the car and don't look back.

I had considered leaving my car and walking to the pub but that would mean having to walk back to the old building, and I do not wish to face that. In twelve months, the old building will be gone and a new housing estate will be built on the site. The only remainder of that close community will be in people's memories.

***

The car park of the Nag's Head is nearly empty when I park up. The outside of the pub has been completely renovated, and looks very nice. There is a large, faux old-fashioned sign outside and there are fancy metal railings around the car park, which have been made to look Victorian. The pub has been gutted inside, and I find myself in an airy, open place with heavy old tables and comfortable leather chairs. I am met by a polite server who leads me to a table by the window, and takes my order for a pint of bitter. I have long since given up on the pleasures of lunchtime drinking but today it feels right, and anyway, with the impending closure of Chimera, I am feeling reckless. The menu is nice, if rather generic, and when the server returns I order the pork belly on a bed of mash. How different from the old-fashioned pub grub of Dave's day!

The server takes my order on her tablet, struggling to find her way through the options. She has the adorable habit of tucking a curl of hair behind her ear every time she gets stuck, and rewards me with a warm smile when I tease her about it. I notice the name on her badge but then instantly forget it again. There is no point trying to flirt with her as she must be half my age, but this does not prevent me from checking out her posterior when she walked to the kitchens. She is wearing tight black trousers which show off a delightful backside, all done with the intention of making sure she gets the maximum possible tips from lecherous old men like me.

The beer is cold, which I still find odd with bitter, but it is strangely refreshing and I allow my mind to wander. I wonder if Ben is right and this is a mid-life crisis, suddenly torn apart with the decisions I made so long ago and now powerless to change them. But then again, even if those choices had been different, would my life be any happier? I pull out my phone, still ignoring the texts from Abigail, and seek out the comfort of a dating site. I have never found any other activity that can distract me in quite the same way. But this time my mind refuses to be fobbed off and the recollections of Hamiltons come thick and fast.

I had been working there for a month when the Old Man summoned me to his office for a second time. His secretary Elaine came to find me. She was a thin-lipped woman who clipped up and down the building in her high heels, and had the mannerisms of some predatory bird. A summons to see the Old Man was like being called to the Headmaster's office, and was met with dread by most people. I was expecting the call, and moreover was looking forward to being able to present my findings. I was sat in the lab with Mike and Tim, two of the worst engineers I have ever worked with. These were the sort of amateur, bodge-it merchants who you would not trust to rewire a plug, never mind design the next generation of product. I had spent the last few weeks working my way in horror through their designs, finally realising why nothing moved easily through the factory. The two engineers looked at me with concern when they heard the summons, expecting that it meant I was to be fired, but I calmly picked up a circuit board and a wiring harness, tucked them in my jacket pockets, and followed Elaine.

It was like a scene from a film where the condemned man is being led to execution. People gawped at me in concern. I may have been new but I had worked hard to fit in and switched my charm into overdrive, and to be fair it had worked. The company had an active social calendar and I had been to every karaoke night, curry night and five-a-side practise. I bumped into Anna, who clutched a folder to her chest and gave me a brave smile. I had finally learned her name rather than just calling her the Pretty Girl, and she was starting to occupy my thoughts far more than someone who I had exchanged barely a few sentences with should. I returned a nonchalant grin back and headed up the stairs, taking the folder from her hands as I passed, much to her confusion. I was already hooked by her looks and her Czech accent, and delighted in any opportunity to interact with her.

We arrived at the Old Man's office. Elaine opened the door and nodded for me to go in. Arthur Hamilton was sat back in his armchair glowering at the latest balance sheet in one hand and an unlit cigar in the other. The room was dark, the windows were just too small, and he did not like artificial light. The odour of tobacco was strong, the furniture expensive but worn, and the walls were covered in framed clippings of the glory days, when he was a younger man in his prime staring out at the world confidently.

"Coffee," he snapped at Elaine, who was hovering by the door.

It was perhaps half ten in the morning, and if it were after four pm then it would have been whiskey from the decanter on the drinks stand. I advanced into the centre of the room and stood at ease with my hands holding the folder behind my back. It made the Old Man smile and he pointed his cigar at the empty chair opposite. I took my place quietly, laying the folder across my lap. He laid the balance sheet down and took a moment to compose his thoughts, as if steeling himself for a difficult conversation.

"So what do you think?" he asked.

It was more of an order than a question. I made a point of hesitating before I answered.

"Honestly?" I asked back.

"Honestly," he replied.

He already knew the answer, of course. He was a clever and capable man who built the company in a time when he understood the technology and his personal relationships with other local companies had secured orders. But his whole organisation and his principal officers had not kept up with the world.

"We have two problems that are basically linked. We are selling the wrong products and we are selling into the wrong markets," I replied humbly.

I waited for the answer, unsure of what response it would provoke. He liked straight talking but then his directors were all basically sycophants, men who would have struggled outside the safe bubble of Hamiltons.

"Go on," he said.

"I'll start with the easy one. Our traditional customers are in decline. They are just not where the growth is and we have hitched ourselves to their demise. Even if our products were brilliant we would be struggling, and things will only get worse because most of them won't be here in five years," I offered.

These were not my observations. A drunken Ken had poured all this out over too many beers one night, and his views had been echoed by the rest of the sales team. Their Director must have known too but it was clear that this message had been filtered on its way up.

"So where should we be playing then?" said the Old Man.

He was staring towards the window and he was not attempting to hide how upset he was.

"Mobile Communications," I said with the certainty of someone who has never failed on a large scale. "There are dozens of companies starting up around here and that's where the money is. But that leads me onto the second problem."

Everyone takes the mobile phone revolution for granted these days and cannot imagine coping without their smartphone, but I remember when the plague first started spreading and every braying, loudmouth idiot suddenly had a new way to annoy those around him.

"What's the second problem?" he asked, his eyes never leaving the window.

"Your engineers can't design for toffee. It is why the current products are rubbish," I continued.

That got his attention and he swivelled his furious eyes onto me. There was a flash of anger in his cheeks. He may have known this deep down to be the truth but this went against the myth of Hamiltons providing high quality goods made by craftsmen, and the message was doubly unsavoury from the new boy. I reached into my left pocket and lifted out the cable harness. I unfolded it on the desk in front of him. They were notoriously delicate and easy to damage and laid out it looked like a rat nest of wires, like some modern day Gordian Knot.

"It takes two days to make one of these, another day to test it, and then a further day to de-bug it. It practically constrains your production line to one unit per week per person. It is the limiting factor of our productivity. Add to that, they are delicate and unreliable and why we see so many coming back for repairs within warranty," I stated calmly.

I had attacked the whole culture of the place: the overtime and the heroics to get these out of the door on time. It was a common theme that got the supervisors to rally their teams to hit the production targets every month through weekends and evenings. It was the feeling of them fighting together to protect their jobs and families, and it ran deep into heart of the place. There was no hiding, however, that the orders were declining and every year when new functions were added to the equipment it became even more of a mess and even harder to make, resulting in more heroics to make fewer products. The balance sheet that Arthur was looking at was telling him the same message, and as he pondered my words I opened up the folder that I had taken from Anna and laid it out.

"These are the schematics from the registry for the latest product. Look: they are hand drawn and full of corrections! I have no idea what exactly is attached to what and in the end, each production operative ends up making his or her own variant that will finally get through test. It also makes it so hard for the repairs team," I said with my voice gaining emotion.

"So what? That's how we have always done things like that," he replied defensively.

He knew why, of course. It was the reason he was willing to pay me the market rate for coming in. The Old Man would have done anything to protect his extended family. I didn't reply but reached into my right hand pocket, took out the circuit board and placed it to the left of the loom. It was perhaps half the area, and a fraction of the volume. The little silver tracks gleamed in the dull light, making for hypnotic patterns.

"I have corrected the schematics and got them into electronic format. The tools will check for a lot of the design errors that we've been seeing. I used them to create a Printed Circuit Board. These cost about a tenner each, and take less than half an hour to solder into the product. They are solid, will come in without errors, and will transform the reliability of the current products," I said.

"You did all that in a month?" he asked but then remembered himself. "So you want to buy these in from outside and then what? Lay off two-thirds of the production force?"

"Not at all, but if they cost a fraction to make then we can make more in the same time and drop the price," I countered.

"You said it was a declining market!" he snapped.

"It is. But it stops any competition in our current market as we carve out the next," I said firmly.

I had prepared this conversation over and over in my own time. I had gone to sleep rehearsing it. I had practised it in the mirror as I shaved. I had spoken it aloud on the drive into work. Whenever I had been alone in the last few weeks, I had been preparing for this.

"So how are you going to get into this new market?" he replied warily.

"There is a big conference next week, and test equipment is one of the topics. I was going to ask to go along and talk to some of the engineers. It will allow me to find out what they will really buy and how much they will pay for it," I said.

He stood up quickly and I could see the excitement in his face. I understood how he had been fighting with this very conundrum for years, how it had eaten away at him as he had seen the end of the road coming closer. Life had made him hard and cynical, but not too cynical to not grasp at the straw I had offered.

"Take Ken with you to the conference," he ordered.

He had walked over to the window and was continuing that thousand yard stare into the distance. I packed the folder back up as it gave me an excuse to go down to the registry to see Anna. I left the loom and circuit board for him to ponder on, and as I let myself out of his office I remembered that the coffee never arrived. Elaine was a rubbish secretary and another example of the sentiment that the Old Man had for those in his company.

I come back to the present with a jolt as the waitress leans over me, her face betraying concern.

"I said, would you like anything else?" she asks kindly.

I finished my meal ten minutes ago and have been staring into space, much as the Old Man used to. It is something that I have been doing a lot of recently. It is late and I need to get back to the office before Martin gets annoyed and gives me one of his ineffectual frowns. It won't matter soon with Chimera disappearing like many so many of the companies I have worked for, but I still feel guilty.

"Sorry about that," I reply with a smile. "I was in a world of my own."

"Still remembering your old company?" she asks with genuine interest.

"Yes, I was. It was a different world back then. Companies were like extended families complete with the crazy uncle. People still moved from place to place, but many people would work out their career in the same place, from apprentice to retirement," I say.

I am babbling, like one of those old people driven crazed by loneliness, and I can't stop myself. She looks at me and then around the pub.

"I cannot imagine working in the same place my whole career," she replies with a hint of concern.

"Like I said, it was a different world," I continue but I have recovered myself. "And one I won't bore you with! I am running a little late so just the bill please."

"You certainly weren't boring me," she says with a hint of reproach, but returns quickly with my bill and the card machine.

I give her a generous tip and for some mad, impulsive reason I slip her my business card. I can't help myself.

***

It is two o'clock by the time I get back. The traffic was bad and there was nowhere to park. Well, that's just life in the south-east but I still hate it. Maybe it's time to move somewhere quieter and enjoy a better standard of living. It has put me in a foul mood and a long way from where I need to be if I'm going to be the life and soul later. Martin is mulling around in the office and has obviously been waiting for me to get back.

"How did you get on?" he asks.

I can tell that he isn't that interested. He has a print out of an email in his hand and I know that it is what is really on his mind. We walk to the coffee area together.

"I am afraid that it was a complete waste of time," I reply honestly. "The good stuff had long been stripped and there is only junk left. It was just a shell of a building. The sooner they send in the bulldozers the better."

Martin gives a distracted laugh but I can tell that he's not listening. I put the kettle on and take two mugs off the drying board ready to make some instant coffees, and watch him askance. He is ambitious beyond his meagre talents and this job was only ever going to be the next rung on the ladder. I know that he'll never do well at a senior level, lacking the ability of charm to go any further. He wears cheap, short-sleeved shirts with a pocket on the breast. It was probably a pack of five matching shirts bought in a sale, but they have been ironed too often and the cotton is becoming transparent. He brings his sandwiches — always processed ham on processed white bread — into work every day in a Tupperware box. This is not a man on the fast track.

"Hey listen," he says looking down at his paper. "Corporate has cancelled the team call on Friday: they only want me to dial in."

He is terrified. I can feel it. He has come to me because he sees me as the most senior after him and he needs to confide in someone. He is worried that they are going to dismiss him. He needs this job because there aren't that many companies with low enough expectations from their managers. He is thinking about his mortgage and what he is going to say to his wife in their identikit housing estate home. I could tell him the truth but I cannot bring myself to be cruel.

"Oh, I see," I find myself saying. "Corporate is probably going through its periodic re-organisation and they want to take the managers through it so you can brief the staff later when the announcement is formally made."

His relief is apparent and colour rushes back into his face. I can watch his emotions shift. His body language is so transparent, which is another reason why he will never do well in corporate politics. He then flusters as he feels foolish for thinking the worst, but most of all he feels gratitude to me for dispelling the dark clouds. It won't last. Gratitude never does and can turn quickly to resentment in the petty minded, and so I make a note to take advantage of it while it lasts. The kettle has boiled and since I like my coffee to stay hot, I use the first of the water to pre-heat the mugs before throwing it away and making two strong cups of instant coffee. I hand one to Martin.

"Thanks, mate," he says and I can sense that he will now sleep tonight.

"You coming out with us later?" I ask. "Should be a good one."

"Sorry, I can't tonight," he offers and turns away back to his office without further explanation.

I knew there was no chance of that. It is best not to fraternise with the staff as it undermines managerial objectivity, and anyway he knows that no one likes him. I walk back to my desk to use the time to accelerate my hunt for a new job. Janice had been telling the truth: the axe is about to fall on Friday.

## Chapter 10 – Big Night Out

I have three emails from recruitment agents wanting to represent me with great opportunities in my area. It reminds me of the adverts on my dating sites for all the amazing singles in my area. I agree to all three despite the fact that they are probably the same opportunities. There has been a lot of consolidation in the industry and there is no longer the number of companies that there used to be. They all ping back in the hour asking for telephone interviews to get a better understanding of what exactly I'm after, which translates as what dead-end job can they palm off on me to take their commission fee. I don't care. I have had a quick look at the job boards and Janice was right: there is a lot more that I could do. It is time to get back in a managerial role and move at least my professional career forward. I wish that I could do the same with my personal life but one battle at a time.

I don't have that much to do in the afternoon as I am so far ahead of my workload that I am in danger of running dry by Friday. I take my time, idling in recollections of the past and imagining future career choices. It gets to five o'clock and Denise makes a point of standing up, collecting her bag and heading towards the toilets. She ensures that Ben and I notice, with her big smile as she happily bounces out of the office. I turn my attention back to my monitor, scanning reviews of local companies to help me better know my future options. I will also need to get ready myself for tonight but I need to give Denise at least a half hour's head start or I will be sat twiddling my thumbs when I am glammed up. It has been an intense day for me and the thought of a few drinks is more compelling than it should be on a school night.

I can resist no longer and finally open up my texts and see there is one from Rebecca and about four from Abigail. I am torn between wishing she had got the message and being slightly flattered that I am worth the effort of chasing. She is cute, but she also has awful breath. I read Rebecca's.

**'Hi. Are you free Friday? I have found a nice restaurant we can try. R x'**

I am hoping that it is not some vegan restaurant full of vacuous, self-opinionated idiots. I know that sounds bad and I'm not saying that all vegans are like that (am I veganist?) but I know she will be drawn to pretentious places where one has to pay over the odds for badly cooked vegetables. I have no idea why I am even considering seeing someone I cannot picture any future with or even really like for that matter. However, I have had enough lonely self-reflection to know that it is physical. I am drawn to that yoga toned body, and I will happily lead someone on to feel those long legs wrapped around me even once. That leaves Abigail. Like the girl. Hate her friends.

**'Look I am sorry about last night. Steph was out of order and I am sorry what happened. Message me. Abi x'**

**'Hi. You're very quiet. Everything ok?'**

**'Are you just not talking to me?'**

I know how this trail will turn out if I don't reply. It may start with pleading but it will soon turn to upset and then anger. It is a smallish dating pool around Reading and I have run into a couple of women I've dated and received verbal harangues at least twice for cutting people off. I bash out a quick reply.

**'Hi. Yes, was quite upset. This is not what I'm looking for.'**

It is a reply I have used on a number of occasions to give people the brush off. It is important to make yourself the victim quickly and firmly so as to have the moral high ground. If they don't get the message and keep pushing with an apology, then play for time. It's never a straight rejection but a case for asking for time to get over it. A month does the trick. Both sides will have moved on by then. This brings me back to Rebecca, who is truly dreadful but also quite physically attractive. I am past the point of lying to myself about my motivations: they are physical and short term. I quickly knock out a suitable, gushy message.

**'It sounds perfect! So much to catch up on. Definitely need to get a date in the diary.'**

The possibility of me getting into the afterlife has just shrunk a little smaller, but I cannot help myself. I can't bear another Friday evening on my own, only warmed by the glow of the computer monitor, scrolling through the profiles on dating sites. I am about to put my phone away when a further text pings in.

**'Meet me. I will make it up to you.'**

Ok. That stops me in my tracks. There is the promise that I am looking for. She is an attractive girl and suddenly I have a second chance if things don't go well on Friday. We get on. She is funny. Her breath smells, but that has to be fixable. Maybe she was dehydrated. Maybe mouthwash. Either way, it was worth taking a chance. I cannot prevent myself from replying.

**'How?'**

I do not have to wait long for the answer, which means she is sat there waiting for mine.

**'I have two tickets for the Reading gin festival. Meet me for a quick drink this week and you can have one.'**

Two tickets. That means that her stupid friends won't be there. And gin. I love gin. There was a time that it was seen as the preferred tipple of the vaguely disreputable middle classes, never quite losing the reputation of mother's ruin. It may have been colonised by the emerging trendies, but I do enjoy it. A drunken afternoon of gin makes evening sex a distinct possibility. I am in but I must hide how keen I am. Best keep it simple and cool.

**'Ok.'**

I glance at my watch: it is approaching half past five and I need to get ready. I stash my phone in my pocket and reach for my bag. I do not take as long as Denise, but I will need some time to get ready. Ben gives me a happy nod as I head off to the toilets but makes no move to follow me. He is quite happy to remain comfortably dressed.

***

I am looking into the mirror critically. I am not a young man and there is no hiding it in my reflection. I know that I still look good for a man of my age, but the kicker is in the last bit: for a man of my age. My hair is silver and thinning, and no amount of hair product can restore the texture or the volume. My midriff has started to soften and the tight shirts I have always worn to show off my shoulders and arms, are starting to look unflattering from some angles. It is better when I am stood up with my back straight, but if I sit down and lean forward a distinct paunch will appear, which tight clothing will mercilessly betray. My shirt is a casual one, one that doesn't need to be ironed, and is white with a blue pattern. It hangs loose of my jeans, which set off my handmade leather shoes. I look good — but I can't help feeling that my mother would call me mutton dressed as lamb. I splash on a generous amount of cologne, pack my work clothes in my bag and make my way back to the office.

Denise and Ben are waiting for me, with Denise sat on Ben's desk swinging her feet backwards and forwards. She is wearing a short, red dress with matching heels and they show her legs a treat. She is grinning like a maniac, her hair is pinned up and she has large hooped earrings. I wish that even a fraction of my dates looked this good.

"Wow, you look alright for an old fart," she laughs.

Ben gives a happy chuckle. He is wearing jeans and a tight-fitted, woollen pullover which is not flattering to his beer belly. I cannot believe that he thought the comment was funny but I suppose I do come across a bit vain.

"You look good," I reply.

"Obviously, granddad," she dismisses. "You ready? Because I want to party!"

That is the second time that I have been called that recently and it hits home hard. I wince inwardly but Denise is oblivious. She jumps off the desk and strides towards the door, making sure to swing her hips provocatively. Ben and I exchange a look, and he raises his eyebrows, but we follow obediently out of the office to the waiting taxi.

The evening starts with gins and tonics, which we knock back quickly followed by a second round to make sure that the buzz hits sooner rather than later. We arrive at Antonio's before seven pm and are seated in what is essentially an empty restaurant. It is the kind of place that my parents would have loved and would have been thought sophisticated in the 1970s, when Italian food was still exotic to the humdrum British palate. We order starters and red wine, our voices uncomfortably loud in the silence. It is a long time since I felt this level of excitement on a night out, like being a young guy out for fun and a wealth of possibilities ahead of me. We are talking rubbish about work, doing impressions of Martin, and reminiscing about the few social events we have enjoyed together on Chimera.

The starters arrive and we order our mains. The proprietor offers pepper and Denise agrees, only for him to return with a massive grinder which he proffers in a slightly phallic manner. Denise blushes and giggles at the show. I roll my eyes and tut as soon as he is gone, but she just gives a shrug. The wine is evaporating at a fast pace and we order a second bottle. We are happily merry but pacing ourselves from getting drunk. I tell them about my trip back to Hamiltons and the memories it stirred up, which moves Denise close to tears so I make a point of laughing it off. She isn't fooled for a moment but the conversation moves quickly on with Ben talking about his first job and some exaggerated tales of what a mess he made of things. This is classic Ben: telling stories of his mistakes and general incompetence, as if trying to lower people's expectations of him. I don't know if it is insecurity, or a way to make people feel unthreatened by him. I have heard most of the stories before but I chuckle along at his anecdotes.

We break off when the mains arrive and dig into them greedily. We are on the third bottle now and without something to line the stomachs, we'll be wiped out in another hour. The food is okay. It has the feel of "heated meals for one" rather than authentically cooked cuisine, but it's good enough, even if Denise insists on going through the whole pepper grinder charade again. However, I can see how happy she is. She hasn't looked like this in a while: her face lit up and radiant. Tomorrow, she will wake up with the knowledge that the operation is one day closer but for the moment, this is not hanging over her. I wish that I could take all the fear and apprehension away from her, but this is the best we can do.

"Phew, that was good!" says Denise, as she empties her plate. "But I don't want to stick around for afters, we need to go dancing!"

"Right, I'll call for the bill," I say, and wave to the nearest waiter.

He knows exactly what I want and gives a tired nod.

"Ohh, ever the man," teases Denise.

Ben leans back in his chair, rubs his stomach and gives a happy, little burp.

"Charming," laughs Denise. "What is it with your gender?"

"Hey!" replies Ben good naturedly. "Happy tummy means happy person!"

"Yeah, that may work on your kids but you're with adults now!" says Denise.

"Where?" I ask and make a point of looking around.

It is a particularly weak joke but it is received warmly by my happy companions. I pretend that I'm going to the loo and nip over and pay the bill at the bar. The waiter is running at a snail's pace and we are on a mission. I make my way back to the table.

"Okay, all done. Let's go!" I say.

"You paid?" asked Denise.

I give a dismissive shrug, and she is caught between gratitude to my generosity and annoyance at my presumption. The former wins out and she stands up, kisses me on the cheek and allows me to help her on with her coat. She is not the only woman I know who struggles between her feminist principles and enjoying the attention.

"Ta, mate," says Ben.

He gives me a pat on the stomach as he heads towards the door. His lips are stained red by the wine and he looks half cut already. I had forgotten that he doesn't drink that much since having kids.

It is dark outside and the cold air wakes us up. We head into the nearest pub to get a cheeky round in, before making our way to the dilapidated charms of Revlon. It is a themed club from the golden age of disco and the perfect place for the music we grew up with. It is popular with the older revellers and, for some strange reason, hen nights. There is no need to queue mid-week, and we pay our entrance fees to a tired looking woman in a grotty cubicle before making our way upstairs. The walls have the faded images of bands, stars and films from the 1970s and 1980s, and the main dance floor has a huge disco ball circling slowly overhead. It is perfect for a trip down memory lane.

I am not a fan of clubs but I love this one. It is like going to a wedding where an old-fashioned DJ is committed to making even the eldest guests get up and dance. The hits from yesterday pour out thick and fast, and although we buy drinks, they are rapidly abandoned as we hit the dance floor. We joke about "Dad dancing" in the office but Ben embraces it with a passion, right down to the thumbs up pose and facial gurning. Denise enters her own world, oblivious to everything, and spins round and round on her heels. I feel a surge of self-satisfaction to see the evening working out so well. It helps with the guilt of knowing that we'll all be put at risk on Friday. At least this way, we'll have some good memories to look back on.

The DJ finally strikes a bum note on the music choice, which is a blessing in disguise, and we make our way back to our drinks. We are all out of breath and can feel the beginnings of being foot sore.

"Hey, I'll get some water," I say to the others.

The music is not deafening here and they respond with nods and thumbs up. The bar is uncrowded and I get served quickly and head back clutching three bottles of chilled water. My heart stops as I watch trouble unfolding in front of me. I have not seen Steve in three years since he was fired from Chimera for bullying and harassment. It would appear that he has not forgotten it either as he is marching towards Denise with two of his ugly mates in tow. There is a half-finished pint of larger in his hand, and his brutish face broadcasts hateful anger. I accelerate my pace to head him off but I can see that there is no way to get there in time. Denise was watching me but she sees my expression change and follows my eye line. She practically reels in shock when she sees her former tormentor bearing down on her, and this sign of weakness will only provoke Steve further. I arrive just as they confront each other.

"It should be fucking illegal to allow trannies in here," spits Steve.

"Hey," says Ben.

He sounds half-hearted but as much as he hated Steve, he was never one for confrontation.

"Shut up, you fat bastard," snarls Steve.

Steve is not an impressive figure to look at, skinny arms and a paunch forcing against his cheap, nylon shirt. He has cropped his hair close to his head and a thin moustache haunts his upper lip. There was always some deep insecurity in him, which manifested itself in a hatred of anything that was different. He despised women generally, and the concept that a man may identify as a woman provoked wrath. He was nasty enough to Dennis when he thought he was homosexual but the day that she began her journey to becoming Denise was too much. The snide comments became pure, open bile in the workplace, and to be fair to Martin's predecessor, he fired Steve without hesitation. I know that in Steve's mind he is the victim of the situation, that his prejudice is perfectly truthful and that the pernicious forces of political correctness conspired against him.

"Look at you, you disgusting pervert!" he continues to attack Denise. "Lucky your Dad is dead. Saved him seeing what his only son turned into."

Denise has wilted under the verbal assault and it is only shock that is holding back the tears. He must have been storing this up for years, and the outburst is shocking.

"That'll do, Steve," I state firmly.

His small eyes swivel on me and, for a moment, he hesitates. He has ten years on me but I am bigger and in a lot better condition, but his two friends are behind him and my hands are holding three plastic bottles.

"What's the problem, Johnny?" he asks. "Bored of shagging all the real women in the area and have now moved onto this tranny?"

There are so many things I could say to this but life has taught me that we are far beyond the point of reason. I drop the bottles to the floor, step forward and give Steve a huge, double handed shove backwards. He flies backward in a shower of cheap lager, his friends step aside making no attempt to save him from hitting the floor hard. I consider putting the boot in for good measure but there is no need, as Steve is clearly unable to get back up. His friends scarper at the first sign of trouble. I grab Denise with both hands and bundle her towards the door, knowing that the bouncers may already be heading over. Ben grabs her other side and between us we charge out of the hall, down the steps and out the front door.

"Where now?" asks Ben.

"Taxi ramp," I reply.

I have no idea where this certainty has come from. I cannot remember the last time I got into a brawl, but when I was a young man on the town and before the advent of CCTV and smartphones, a punch up was always on the cards. I am sure that's why people were more polite back then. Maybe that's rose-tinted glasses.

Maybe it's that I don't go out to many clubs. Maybe the young brawlers see me as too old to take a swing at.

As we approach the taxis, we let go of Denise who is now sobbing deeply. Her face is a mass of tears, snot and running makeup. One of my girlfriends once told me never trust a woman who can cry prettily, that they are just crocodile tears for effect, and that genuinely upset women look a mess. I pull out a tissue from my pocket and offer it to her. It's a futile gesture and seems to provoke another bout of crying. I know that we can't put her in a taxi like this and Ben and I stand there awkwardly until she is finally able to speak. I keep looking back up the road but I have no idea who I am expecting to see. There is no way Steve is in pursuit and the chances that the club called the police are very slim.

"Why did he have to be here?" asks Denise. "Of all the people that we could have bumped into, why him?"

Ben and I have no answer. There is nothing in this dreadful situation that can make things better.

"Why does he hate me so much? Why does he not understand?" she asks, before falling silent.

Denise begins to clear her face up with the tissue. She reaches into her handbag to find a mirror and some proper wipes. It takes a few minutes to clear the worst of it up but when she is finished she looks exhausted and ready for bed.

"I'm going home," she says simply.

"Don't worry about Steve. He was a nasty piece of work," I say sympathetically but I am concerned about starting the water works again.

"There has always been someone like him though," she replies with a heave of the shoulders. "Thank you for sticking up for me. In a few weeks the operation will be over and no one can call me that again. I will see you in work tomorrow."

I freeze rather than say anything and watch as she gets into the taxi. Work is her safe place now but soon that will be gone too. She doesn't really have anyone apart from her mum and us, and we're not exactly close.

"Night Denise," says Ben. "Sleep well and we'll talk tomorrow."

"You've finally learned to speak then?" I snap at him when the taxi pulls away.

"I didn't know what to say and anyway, you're supposed to be the smooth one," he counters. "Look Johnny, we'll try again in a few months when everything has settled down."

I know that his home is calling. He has not had a good night and all that remains is for him to head back to his family. But I am not ready to turn in so early. I won't sleep anyway with this much adrenaline pumping through my veins.

"I'll see you tomorrow, mate," I reply.

"Yeah, night," he says.

He climbs in the next taxi and I am already walking into the backstreets looking for somewhere quiet to have a drink. I scan my phone and to my surprise see that

Emma (the waitress from earlier) has messaged me. I bash out a long reply giving a quick summary of the evening. I have made it to the bar and ordered a whiskey when my phone buzzes.

**'Sounds like an awful night. I am out too. Want some company?**

The message is a lot more abrupt than I was expecting. I reply where I am, which is busy but not packed. I cannot believe that she seems keen to see me, and I shake my head. This is not going to happen. Moments later she replies.

**'Coming.'**

I feel something that I have not felt in a long time: excitement. My stomach starts to churn and my mouth suddenly feels dry. I don't know whether to knock back my drink for courage or to ask for water so that my breath smells less of alcohol. I try and work out how long she is likely to be. Do I have time to pop to the loo? Where should I stand so that she can see me? Will I even recognise her when she arrives? Will she recognise me?

I stand frozen by the bar and even several drinks over the evening cannot take off the slow trudge of time. There is no issue of recognising her when she comes into the bar, a young lady in a bar full of old men. Everyone is staring at her but she is oblivious: she has locked onto me and drunkenly weaves her way over. She looks good. I mean really good. A little black dress that shows off her long legs and knee high boots. Her hair swings loose and her makeup sets off her cheekbones. She looks so different to the girl I had exchanged a few words with earlier. She also shows no sign of nervousness as she strides over, places a steadying hand on my shoulder and kisses me gently on the cheek.

"Hi there," she says.

I am trying to work out how drunk she is, and why she is alone.

"Hello, thanks for coming over," I reply. Her hand is still on my shoulder and my heart is racing. "May I buy you a drink?"

"Well, I shouldn't really," she says with a laugh. "I am already flying and I don't want to do anything that I may regret!"

"That's a shame," I reply without thinking.

I can smell her perfume and she smells as good as she looks. It has been a long time since I have felt so electrified like this. I lean in and kiss her on the mouth, gently at first on the lips and then with my tongue. My arms pull her close and she melts against me, kissing me back with passion. We stay locked like that until we come up for air. This really isn't the place to be behaving like this.

"That was nice," she says, still smiling. "I guess I will have a drink after all."

I order her a Prosecco without asking and she seems fine with that. We have our arms around each other's waists and it feels strangely comfortable. My head is reeling: things just don't happen this fast.

"So you know about my evening, how did yours go?" I ask.

It's a lame thing to come out with but my head is scrambled. I learned a long time ago that you don't need anything too profound to say on a date, you just need to find a topic of conversation that keeps the evening moving.

She gives a big shrug and I worry then and there that things are going to get awkward pretty quickly. This has always been the big issue for men my age: go for younger women and enjoy their firm, toned bodies or go for women of my own age and appreciate the experience and conversation. I have never expressed that out loud even in my heart to hearts with Ben. He would tear into me for it.

"I met up with friends… but you know… it's the same boring stuff over and over. And all the drama," she slurs. She really is quite drunk.

"Drama?" I ask in spite of myself. Like Denise, I do love a bit of soap opera if I am not involved.

"Well, Kelly just split up with Matt and they did it in front of everyone. I don't want to hear that when I'm out. And it's always the same: on their phones having some drama or other," she says.

"They split up in front of you? This evening?" I ask.

"I know," she mutters with a far-away look and a shake of a head. "That's why I don't like guys my age. They are so immature and don't know what they want."

She gives me a look and suddenly everything makes sense. I have been here before and it has never gone well. She is not the first woman I have dated with daddy issues and I really should be running a mile, and certainly not leading her on. I have smudged her lipstick and I am aching for her, my entire body fired up.

"Want to come home with me?" I ask.

"Sure," she replies and drains her glass.

# Chapter 11 – Hangover

"You're late," says Martin.

I am. It has gone nine o'clock and I have just arrived at work. I don't think that I have ever been in this late, and it's not even *that* late, it's just very out of character.

"I had trouble parking," I reply.

It's a poor excuse but it is all I can come up with on the spur of the moment.

"What happened last night?" he pushes. "Denise rang in ill this morning."

"We ran into Steve. He had a go at her."

Martin freezes and then gives me a nod to signal that I should follow him to his office. I follow him two steps behind, passing Ben, who has his head down. The office is practically empty today with the sales guys out on the road and it feels uncomfortably quiet. My head is still reeling for Emma. I can't believe that it came to pass and my mind keeps re-running what happened after we got home last night. Work is just an annoying interruption at the moment. Martin is oblivious to my distraction and closes his office door behind us. The office is small and feels very cramped with the door closed. I know that he has worked hard to escape the open-plan office but he must feel disappointed in his prize.

"Steve was there? What did he say?" demands Martin.

I had assumed that Ben would have spilled the beans already but he is quick to distance himself from anything controversial. Much as I like him, he can be such a coward.

"Well, not much. Just called her a few names. He was really aggressive though, like he still hates her," I reply.

"I had hoped that he would have put this behind himself and moved on," says Martin grandly. The episode was before his time but I know that it is all over the personnel records, and anyway, the whole office knows the story.

"Well, he blames her for losing his job. I don't think he will get over that any time soon."

Martin is a great believer in therapy and confronting emotional issues. He can't seem to understand that is not how everybody's minds work, especially those who need to work through their issues the most. He once hinted that I should talk to someone about my dating habits but then back tracked quickly when he realised that he had crossed the line between professional and personal spheres. On reflection, he may have had a point though.

"What a mess! I mean, corporate are acting all weird and now we are a member of staff down because of ancient history. She goes off next week for medical reasons and I could have done with her clearing the decks before she left," he rants.

This is the closest he gets to losing his temper. I am unsure whether he blames me for what happened.

Martin has a strange view towards work socialising; he recognises the benefits of teamwork but lives in terror of personal issues becoming problems in the work place. There are just some things that those management seminars don't address well enough. I know that it is best just to distract him.

"Why is corporate acting all weird?" I ask, with my best concerned voice.

He falls for the bait easily. He may be genuinely concerned about Denise but he needs this job, his mortgage is relying on it.

"I have no idea but they have been cancelling meetings left, right and centre. It is like I am no longer in the loop for anything! I sent in the weekly based on Friday's meeting and there wasn't even an acknowledgment! Can you imagine?"

"And you said that this weekly was re-purposed?"

I can't help myself. I mean I know that he's in shock and denial but the writing is very clearly written on the wall. The more time that it has to sink in, then the easier it will be tomorrow. He's going to have to look for another job.

"Yes. I don't know what to read into that," he says.

Really, he knows exactly what to make of that. I feel guilty that I already have three interviews lined up and a pay-off may be the thing that allows me to get the house sorted.

"I'll make us some coffee," I say.

"Thanks," he dismisses.

I can't even concentrate on the conversation. Emma is occupying my mind.

***

Emma had cuddled into me in the taxi, her head nestling on my shoulder and with my lips pressed to her forehead, which I would occasionally kiss as we talked in whispers. She squeezed my arm each time in return. I have no recollection of what we were talking about, but it was sweet and intimate and for once I was unworried about missing out on something better. I paid the driver, fumbled for the keys and let us in. Emma seemed so confident as she strolled into the hallway and kicked her boots off. She was a lot shorter without heels.

"Water," she said.

She followed me into the kitchen and accepted a glass of tap water, before regarding me as she drank it.

"You don't remember me, do you?"

The question caught me off guard as we had discussed where she works, Hamiltons and what it was like before the pub was re-fitted.

"What do you mean?"

"It surprised me when you came in for lunch. For a moment, I thought you were stalking me but then it was obvious that you didn't recognise me as you stared off in a world of your own. It was clear that you have all your own stuff going on but when it mattered, you still helped me."

I had no idea what she was talking about, but her voice is certain and I really didn't know what to say.

"You gave me taxi money home when I was stranded."

My face must have betrayed everything because she rolled her head back in uncontrolled laughter. She had to put the glass down to prevent from dropping it and she smiled with an indulgence that is moving. Suddenly, my brain kicks into gear and I remember her.

"It was you!"

"Yes, it was me. You helped me and without wanting anything back from me. That is very remarkable. I couldn't stop thinking about you and I was shocked when you showed up again! I was so happy when you gave me your number: it meant you liked me!"

The truth is that I had not placed her as the girl who I helped with the taxi and, even worse, I just randomly hand out my details to practically anyone I like the look of in the hope that I get a date. In her mind, she has made this something special and I know that I will disappoint her.

"You looked very different that night," I said weakly.

"If you say that my makeup made me look like the Joker, then I am getting right back in the taxi," she laughs but there is hardness to her tone.

"I wasn't going to say that."

"Good," she said with a smile and extending her hand, "then take me upstairs."

We held hands up the stairs and at the top, I indicated the bedroom. She strode in purposefully, turned to face me with a lopsided smile, and then stripped off her dress in one, fluid movement. I was struggling to take her in: smooth skin, firm breasts and a flat stomach. I wanted to say something nice but my mind was busy trying to remember where I left the condoms. She was only wearing a lacy thong and she took that off next and dropped it on her dress. I pushed the door closed behind me and moved quickly to remove my shirt and trousers, before pushing her back gently onto the bed and climbing on top of her.

The first thing I noticed was how good her skin smelt and I inhaled deeply pressed into her neck, and then we were kissing and our hands feeling around each other bodies. I lifted myself off her and then slowly worked my mouth down her body, kissing, licking and nuzzling her from her neck to her navel. I paused my mouth between her thighs and she widened her legs in anticipation, her hands slipping behind my head and pulling me close. My palms caressed the tops of her thighs, stroking and massaging, as my tongue first danced across her lips before plunging deep inside her. I heard her groan and felt her hands pull my head forward to push my tongue deeper.

***

"You seem distant. Still upset about last night?" asks Ben.

I give a start and look up to see Ben stood over my desk. I have been so deep in my thoughts that I have no idea how long he has been there. I have not done much productive all morning and I am sure that the guilt is written across my face. The truth is that I have not spared a single thought for poor Denise but have been lost in the memories of Emma. It has been a long time since I felt this way about anyone.

"No, I'm fine," I reply too quickly. "Have you heard from Denise?"

"She has not replied to my texts and I guess that since you asked that, she has not been replying to yours either," he says.

I have not texted Denise. I really should do. I do worry about her. She is so fragile. I have been thinking what to say to Emma. I want to see her again but I worry that we won't feel the same magic and intense connection the second time. I glance at my watch, remembering that I have the first phone interview in an hour. I need to be re-reading my CV and preparing myself for all the obvious questions. I am caught between knowing that I need to get myself together and a strange apathy that none of it really matters. I will find another pointless job to keep a roof over my head, but it's not something that will make me happy.

"Did you go straight home last night?" he asks.

"No, I had another drink or two," I add.

I want to tell him about what happened, about an amazing night of sex and waking up in the arms of someone I really like. I want to tell him to make it feel real.

"I can't believe that we ran into Steve," continues Ben. "He is such a nasty piece of work."

I know that Ben feels guilty for not having stood up for Denise, for once again just watching as she was bullied in front of him.

"That guy needs help," I reply.

"Well that shove you gave him seemed to help!" laughs Ben.

"That's not the kind of help I meant," I reply. "I mean, don't you ever wonder what happened to him to make him like that?"

"You think he was abused?"

"Well, maybe not abused. But what was his childhood like to make him so full of anger and hate? And what makes him target it at people like Denise?" I wonder aloud.

And it does bother me what makes people like that and why they target the weak so readily. I can still see his face so twisted by hatred. It can't be good for you to live like that, driven by antipathy towards others. But his face is soon replaced by Emma's and I can see her once more, as she rode me rhythmically and looked down into my eyes with such tenderness.

"Should I call her?" asked Ben, referring to Denise.

"No, not yet," I dismiss. "Let her get her head together first."

Ben gives a nod at the wisdom of this and wanders off. I look at my phone. Nothing from Emma. I am itching to message her but I don't know if that seems too keen, or whether she regrets this morning what she did. I wonder if she is looking at her phone thinking of me. I give my head a shake to clear my thoughts: I need to get my brain in gear for the interview.

***

There is a meeting room that I use for the first interview, while pretending that I am on a customer call. The company is called Synagistics and it appears to be one of those large companies that seems to do everything. The local headquarters is in Reading and is a modern looking building: all metal, glass and carefully branded logos. I hate it on sight and I know that I will never be happy in such an environment, but I am strangely drawn to it. The interview takes less than an hour and the questions are so pathetically generic that it makes me annoyed that the manager and the HR business partner could not put a bit more effort in. I engage with a calm humour, giving solid personal examples of all the situations they outline, and even making sure I add a few more they don't ask about just to make sure I give a fully-rounded appearance. I do brilliantly. I have so much experience making myself sound good on a date that an interview is a breeze.

"Well, I can say that we are both genuinely impressed!" gushes Helen the HR woman. "We would like to move quickly to the next stage for you to come in to meet us and see a little more of what we do here at Synagistics."

"Wow, that is excellent news!" I gush back with faux sincerity. "I mean, Synagistics has been on the radar as a company where I'd like to work for a while and this opportunity seemed too good to be true!"

"We're going to email through some times for next week, let us know which of the options suits you best!"

"That's perfect! I'll get right back to you!"

"Well, I think that's all from us, Johnny. Thank you for your time today."

"Oh, thank you so much. Goodbye!"

"Goodbye," they chime in unison. They have obviously done a lot of interviews together.

I feel a real surge of elation as I hang up the phone. They are keen. I have done some interviewing myself and I know how hard it is to find good people. I will be even better in the face-to-face interview. I sit back and relax and suddenly all the concerns about the demise of Chimera are gone. I can take the pay out and sail into my next job. I am smiling in smug satisfaction when my mind once more drifts back to Emma. I should message her. I give in. I don't care if it's cool or not. My phone is in front of me on the desk.

**'Hey. How are you?'**

It's a rubbish message, but if she wants to hear from me then it will be enough, and if there is no response, then so be it, onto the next one and don't look back. I look at my watch. I have another telephone interview with Socratech this afternoon.

***

His name was Arif and he had been given a job at Hamiltons because his father knew Arthur. He was a painfully shy introvert, even by the standards of engineers and I have honestly no idea what he did all day because we had no products that called on his skills as a trained mechanical engineer. The Old Man had made it clear that any racist comments were not going to be tolerated, so Arif was generally left alone. There was some story floating around of the Old Man punching a guy out in a pub for calling someone a Paki. It was a different world back then, what can I say?

"I need you to design a proper mechanical enclosure," I said to Arif.

We hadn't spoken that much and I knew that he must be bored out of his mind with his job. He gave me a searching look, perhaps trying to work out if this was genuine or a joke. I sat down next to him at his spacious desk, which was hidden away in one of the many concealed alcoves in the rabbit warren of a building. Arif had a modern computer workstation — one of the few in the building to do so— and the latest CAD software. He had supported marketing in drawing up some brochures but apart from that, this colossal investment had gone to waste. I unfolded my hand drawings of the new product, which I had called Daedalus in acknowledgement of my classical education.

"I had some ideas but I am an electronic designer, not a mechanical guy," I began with an excuse.

Arif started looking through my designs, mentally checking out the sizes and dimensions.

"You want me to draw this up?" he asked quietly.

"No, I need you to design it. I mean, it needs to be lightweight and keep the electronics cool. Plus we'll need to get it through EMC testing."

"What material do you want it made from?"

"I don't know! Metal?"

Arif gave a soft laugh. His guard dropped and he then opened up.

"Well, how do you want it to be manufactured?"

"Easily," I replied.

He laughed again and I could tell that he was interested. I would come to appreciate him as one of the most diligent designers I would ever work with, but right now he was just another member of the Old Man's dysfunctional family. He worked his way through the drawings, slowly pondering each one, before finally asking a question.

"Have you already designed the boards that will go inside it?"

"Yes," I said.

I had already worked out how it was all going to go together, but I was realising that it may have been better to ask someone who knew what they were doing. I had a vision of a product that would snap together like a Lego kit.

"If you make a few changes to the boards, it'll be a lot easier to make and assemble," he added.

"Can you design it?" I asked.

There must have been a hint of desperation in my voice but I needed not to have worried. He looked at me with pure relief as I had finally given him a challenge to dispel months of boredom. He smiled and gave a small nod.

"When do you think that you will have something to see?" I asked.

I couldn't help myself from pushing. The product had become all-consuming to me. I had pretty much finished the remainder of the design in my weekends and evenings. It had been barely a month since my last conversation with the Old Man, but I didn't want to lose momentum. I needed this to work.

"Tomorrow," he replied.

I had expected that it would take weeks but I was not going to argue. Ken and I were off to a conference in a few days and it would have been perfect to have a concept to show people. Ken was as excited as a small child and kept talking about us "going on the road" like we were some rock band on a comeback tour. I had found the excitement infectious and his enthusiasm had melted away my cynicism, but I was also terrified of the concept floundering at the first hurdle.

***

**'Hi. Was worried that you were so quiet x'**

It's a bit rich coming from Emma but I am just glad that she has replied. I should have guessed that she was feeling a bit exposed after putting herself out there last night. I want to see her again, the impulse is overwhelming. I know that there are rules to dating, and one of them is not to put the other person off by being too keen, but I don't care. It is so rare to connect with someone like this.

**'Meet me for a drink tonight?'**

A perfect example of being too keen but I feel confident. She told me no less than three times that she was tired of people playing games and just wanted to be straight with her how they felt. She is half my age and yet so mature. I don't have to wait long for a reply.

**'Didn't get enough of me, huh?'**

I can't help but smile. She wants to see me otherwise she would have made some excuse up. She likes me and she wants me to show that I like her too.

**'No. I didn't. So drink?'**

I want to close this down. I cannot think about anything else and keep staring at my phone, willing for the messages to arrive. She keeps me hanging for four long minutes before my phone vibrates reassuringly. I snatch it up to read the message. It is lucky that Denise isn't here or she would have picked straight up on that.

**'Three Brewers. Half six. Coming straight from work.'**

I am happy. A drink that early means that dinner is a strong possibility, and that means hopefully that we can carry on directly from where we left off this morning. I may not have the stamina that I once did, but she certainly makes me feel like a younger man.

***

There was a technical meeting every Thursday morning at Hamiltons. It was an informal affair where people stood or sat around the lab, and we all took turns to say we were up to during the week. There were no minutes written or actions taken, and I think that just tradition had kept it going over the years (plus it was a good chance to complain about stuff with a captive audience). The technical director was supposed to chair the meeting but Steve had no presence at all, and few people gave him any attention. I used this forum as the opportunity to present the new product launch for Daedalus. They all listened in silence until I finished.

"So the Old Man gave you his full support?" asked Steve.

He was supposed to be the technical director but has not had an original idea since he joined. I didn't know if he was angry that the project had the only backing that counted in the company, or whether he felt that the pressure was off him to produce something. I nodded to his question to dismiss it, as well as him, and then moved on quickly.

"We're going to cut metal next week, and the electronics boards should arrive a week later. It won't take me long to test them on the bench and then we can start integrating them," I replied.

"Wow, that fast," said one of the technicians, called Tony.

"No point hanging around," I said in a voice that is far too macho to be mine, and would make sense for the lead character of a 1980s action show. "Ken and I will be at the conference next week, and if there is interest, then we'll need something to demonstrate quickly."

I ran my hands over the schematics and drawings to flatten them out. All the engineers and technicians crowded around to scan over them: they had been drawn up on CAD and looked professional.

"If," replied Steve.

I was not in the mood to challenge him yet. I was terrified that next week would be a flop. I was not sure how I would cope with coming back to work with my tail between my legs. It had made me quiet and withdrawn, so far from my usual chatty self. The team had seen this as a new gravitas rather than nervousness, and they had started to act like I am their leader.

"This is great!" said Tony. "It will look amazing — just what the company needs!"

There was a chorus of agreement from the rest of the team. Even Tim and Mike, the useless twins, were nodding along happily. Tony opened up the tool locker to get a metal ruler to better help him understand the true size of the new product. He opened the doors wide, revealing the multitude of cut out page three nudes on the inside.

"Those are going to have to go," I said.

He followed my eyeline to the pictures, his face the very image of dismay.

"Why?" he asked.

"That's not the company we're going to be anymore," I said flatly.

A week earlier he would have argued, or even told me where to go if he was feeling brave enough. There was something about my new authority that just made him accept it. I said it was a hierarchical company.

"Ok," he replied and obediently began to take them down.

I felt suddenly restless and got up to leave.

"Mark the drawings up if you have any concerns," I said over my shoulder.

I almost walked into Anna, who has been watching from the door the entire time. She was smiling at me in admiration and my heart gave a skip. I realised then that if the new product fails, the thing that will humiliate me most was this girl, who I barely knew, thinking that I had failed.

"You made them take them down," she stated in her seductive accent, with a wave towards the tool locker.

"Yes," I replied.

My heart was racing but my brain was frozen. I had pre-arranged so many conversations with her in my head, but now it was happening I am lost for words. I liked everything about her, although I barely knew her. Eastern Europe was still another world to me and I used to daydream about the two of us going on a roadtrip to explore.

"Good," she replied.

Anna had not moved to the side and was looking at me in expectation. I knew she liked me, and it was not like I didn't know how to talk with women, but I had never liked one this much before.

"Are you going out for curry tonight?" I said. It was really was the best I could muster.

"I don't know," she said with a frown. "Why?"

"Well, I am going and I was hoping that you would come too," I replied.

"Ok," she said, the frown back to a smile. "I see you later."

And with that she was off, her hips gyrating and her ponytail swinging. Suddenly, it felt that all aspects of my life may be coming together. I was scared, I was happy, but most of all I was excited.

***

I work late and then go to meet Emma directly from the office. On reflection, that is not entirely true. I stay late at work but achieve absolutely nothing. I compile my weekly report for Friday, even though I know that it will never be needed, however not doing it may suggest that I already know that it is entirely superfluous. It is something to kill the time which allows my mind to wander freely. I love the invention of computers: they have allowed people to look busy when they have absolutely nothing of merit to do. Amazing. I have no idea how people managed to waste time so easily before them.

I still get to the pub early and order a soft drink. It'll hide if my breath is stale and I want a kiss without smelling like something has died in my mouth. It's a strange choice for her, more like the kind of place that I would rather go since it is quiet, sells a range of draught ales, and one does not need to queue for a drink. I wait at the bar and feel slightly nervous, but nothing like I had the previous evening. Emma arrives at least ten minutes late and looks exhausted. She has not changed since work — flat shoes and black trousers — and no makeup. She has freckles, which I hadn't noticed before, and her hair is pulled back into a ponytail. She smiles when she sees me and heads over.

"Hey you," I say and give her a hug.

She looks up to me for a kiss — her forehead barely reaches my chin — and I give her a slow kiss on the mouth.

"How was your day?" she asks.

"Well, let me get you a drink and I will tell you," I say. "But I thought about you a lot."

"I thought about you too," she says, her cheeks flushed.

I wave to the barman and Emma orders herself a vodka and coke. We take our drinks to a small table away from other people. I imagine that we are about to have the conversation where we both confess to liking each other and I would rather not have an audience for that.

"So what happened today?" she asks.

"Well, Denise did not come in at all after what happened last night and I know that we are going to be put at risk tomorrow," I confide.

"Put at risk? What does that mean?" she questions.

"Chimera will be closing its UK office and we will all be made redundant," I say quietly.

Emma gasps and reaches out to take my hand. I realise that the way I have presented it makes it sound far more dramatic than it is.

"Oh, that is awful! What are you going to do?"

"Hey, it's not that bad. I got a tip off from an old friend in the US office and I have lined up some interviews. It will be okay, this is not the first time that I have been through this. Chimera has become a depressing place to work anyway and so it's time to move on. Plus I will get a pay-off, which is always nice," I explain, trying to make it sound like nothing.

"I don't know what I'd do if I lost my job. I would not be able to pay the rent," she says.

"You'd find another one quickly enough," I reply easily. "Anyway, how was your day?"

"Long and boring," she confides. "I mean, carrying food from the kitchen to the table and then carrying empty plates back is not exactly going to set the world on fire."

I laugh at this. It occurs to me that she is far too bright to be doing this forever, but it is too soon in our relationship to start dispensing career advice.

"I wandered over to that place where you used to work, was it Hamiltons? It is so depressing to see a rotting old building and imagine that it was this happy company once upon a time."

This takes me by surprise. The only reason she would do that is because of a desire to be closer to me, to understand me from my past. She will also have searched me out on social media, and if she is suspicious, on the local dating sites as well. Hamiltons was a happy place for all its problems, with everyone feeling a shared responsibility for each other and the company. I loved it because, for a while, when I was at the centre of things,

I enjoyed all the attention and a feeling of importance. No other job has ever come close to that and I doubt ever will. No amount of seminars on building effective teams can ever match what the Old Man had achieved so effortlessly.

"I don't think I will go back again. It depressed the hell out of me," I admit. "And as you are no doubt about to say, one cannot keep looking back."

"I was thinking that."

"I know. But sometimes it is good to learn from the past as well," I admit.

I don't want to have this discussion at all. I spend so much of my time wading through the past, and it is not good for me. I make a conscious effort to move the conversation on.

"Hey, are you busy this weekend?" I ask.

She pauses for a moment, looking genuinely uncomfortable, and for a moment I think she is about to let me down easily.

"My parents have rented a cottage in Devon. We're heading down tomorrow afternoon and getting back on Sunday. I mean, I would invite you as well, but we're only just a thing and I haven't even mentioned you to my parents."

Emma looks seriously embarrassed and I am reeling from the revelations in what she said. We were not a one-night stand but the start of something. I like that. The thought of meeting her parents scares me, because we must be close in age, and that is something that will need careful handling. Of course, this leaves a long and lonely weekend ahead of me, which I hate but maybe it will do me some good. My expression must have betrayed me because she leans over again, kisses my cheek and puts her hand on my thigh.

"Hey, don't look like that," she says. "You can still take me home tonight and do whatever you want to me!"

Her bawdy humour makes me laugh, and although I am slightly shocked by the directness of it, it is just want I need to shake my morass moods.

"Listen, there is something I need to tell you."

"What is it?" she blurts and for the first time, I hear concern in her voice.

"I just need to be straight with you," I say carefully. "This has happened really fast and I just need to sort a few things out. I've been on a few dating sites for a while, and I need to suspend those activities, plus I have seen this girl for a couple of dates and I need to let her down nicely."

Sometimes, honesty is the best policy. Emma squeezes my thigh before leaning back to take a deep swig of her drink.

"I love it that you're straight with me, I really appreciate that. I told you that I can't stand silly games. Everyone has a history and we can be open with each other when the time comes. Now, drink up and take me home."

I do exactly as she says.

***

I still remember that fateful curry night at Hamiltons all those year ago. My happiness and excitement had given me a feeling of pure elation. The afternoon had gone brilliantly and I was left feeling invincible. I had taken the same drawings I had shown the engineers and technicians to the Old Man. His office was dark and murky in the late afternoon, with the ever present cigar aroma and a half-drunk glass of Scotch on his desk. He had asked no one else to the meeting, which was unusual, and my initial nervousness at taking him through the concept soon evaporated as I got into my stride. I started with the intended market, talked about the growth of mobile handsets, moved onto the needs of testing the devices, and then finally onto the product and what it would do. The Old Man asked no questions throughout, but picked up each drawing and rendering of what the product would look like and examined them minutely. I sat down at the end and waited for his response.

"You cannot imagine how long I have waited for this," he said.

There were tears in the corners of his eyes. He had watched the decline of his company powerlessly. The promise I had made a month ago now looked like a silver bullet. Everything would depend on the conference next week.

"How soon can we enter production?" he demanded.

"Well, there is still some tooling we would need to makeup, write up the work instructions and then train the operators. Probably about two months away."

"How is Ken getting on?"

"He has worked up a marketing campaign," I said, knowing that such a concept was as alien as so many others I had introduced. "We shall be handing out fliers next week at the conference and then hit the trade press with adverts."

"We're gambling the company on this," he said.

"It's a good product," I replied.

"I can see that. It's the best we've ever come up with," he acknowledged. "I know you get it, that you feel the same as me. We're only here to look after the others, keep their jobs safe and allow them to look after their kids. That's what we do: we look after others."

I gave a nod. I got that entirely, and at that moment, I believed it completely. The afternoon meeting with the Old Man had been quite cathartic and by the evening I was drinking and laughing with abandon. We had occupied the window seats at the Alehouse in Reading, and the drinks were flowing. Ken had brought over a tray crowded with pints of beer, and was rewarded with a colossal drunken roar. We passed the drinks out, toasted him and then started to down them.

"Hey look at that!" shouted Tony, indicating an obese family leaving the KFC across the road. "KFC? Kid Fattening Centre more like!"

In a more enlightened time, such humour may be deemed offensive but back then, we exploded with laughter and drank faster. Even amid the noise and merriment, I noticed Anna askance as soon as she entered the pub. She walked towards the table but was intercepted by Ken, who gave her a big hug and insisted on buying her a drink. She endured the hug and accepted the offer of a drink and then came over to sit opposite me. She looked nice. She used to tie her hair up, which exposed her lovely neck. She was dressed in denim and basketball boots, a casual look, which suited her down to the ground.

"You made it," I said.

"I see you have already started! How many drinks have you had?" she asked with a smile.

"Not sure. A Couple. I lost count," I replied. I was deliberately exaggerating because I thought it would make me sound more fun.

"You lost count after only a couple? I don't think so," she dismissed but she looked amused.

I gave her a smile and a shrug. The corners of her mouth twitched but she fought the impulse to smile back.

"I hope I don't have to carry you home," she stated, her tone still flat.

"Aww," I replied. "Would you look after me?"

"Would you like me to?" she shot back.

Her tone was not joking and she was looking deep into my eyes. I realised that she was not talking about just when I was drunk. My heart leapt but I was left speechless. It was only Ken arriving with Anna's drink that broke the intense deadlock. She sipped her drink delicately as she regarded me. Our knees touched under the table and we both left them there, a response more profound than any words we could have said.

## Chapter 12 – Redundancy

I don't sleep at all on Thursday evening. A part of that is Emma pressing into my shoulder and snoring gently in my ear. The warmth of her body makes me overheat and I have to kick the duvet back to expose my legs and half of my body in order to retain some equilibrium. However, it is something else that pushes my mind into a furious race that does not release until an hour or so before I am due to wake. There is something about Emma that has brought back all those feelings I have worked hard to suppress: all those memories and the poor decisions of my life. I am terrified that maybe Emma is a final chance for me to find the stability that has eluded me for so long. She reminds me of Anna, that same infectious optimism for the future, the same belief that everything happens for a reason. I am scared that she will discover the dark and pessimistic cynicism that has eaten me up inside so long ago.

That night in the Alehouse, Anna and I crossed the line and never looked back. We had tried talking before, but we had both been so nervous that conversation had been stilted and difficult. It had meant that we had a host of things that we wanted to know about one another, and the alcohol seemed to unlock it all. I am not sure that I spoke to anyone else after Anna arrived. We poured out our lives to each other, through rounds of drinks and a cheap curry, and when the evening came to an end, we walked off to find a petrol station. Anna was an occasional smoker and pretended she wanted some cigarettes but it was just a ruse for us to be alone. We walked together and I took her hand. She giggled and squeezed my hand tightly; I knew then how much she wanted this. The petrol station was closed when we got there and we stood outside just looking at each other. We didn't speak but I pulled her to me and kissed her gently. I felt her arms pull me close as my hands worked under her jacket and blouse, to gently explore her. I could feel her grinning as we kissed, and when we finally broke for air, there was no hiding how happy she was.

"Do you like?" she said, glancing down.

She was asking whether I found her body nice to the touch. And I did. A perfectly flat, toned stomach and gently curved hips. I wondered why this woman was still single. Age has not changed my observation that there are so few women that are beautiful, sane and not a bitch. If I could tell my younger self one thing, it would be if you find one and can capture her heart, then keep her no matter what.

"Yes," I replied and then decided to be cheeky. "I mean, you have a nice body under those boyish clothes."

Her mouth twisted in pretend annoyance, and she gave me a soft punch in the arm.

"You want me to dress more ladylike?" she asked.

I pulled her close and we kissed for long minutes. She was amazing. A car passed and beeped its horn in support, and we suddenly felt conspicuous.

"We could go back to yours," she said.

But I didn't want to at that point. Even drunk and aroused, I knew how much this girl was likely to mean to me and I didn't want to rush anything. I shook my head. I was also embarrassed to bring her back to a dingy room in a grimy shared flat, with the stench of damp and washing up piled high in the kitchen sink.

"I don't want to rush this," I replied.

There was a flash of disappointment, but then she seemed to consider whether this was a good thing. We walked back towards town holding hands. I wanted this moment to last. I was scared that tomorrow would feel awkward and embarrassing. Everyone had seen us head off together, and it would be all around Hamiltons in the morning.

"I'll get you a taxi home," I said.

We arrived at the taxi ramp about ten minutes later, having stopped periodically to kiss again. I loaded her into a taxi and paid the driver. I will never forget her watching me and waving as the taxi pulled away. The parallels with the first night I met Emma are worrying.

***

The alarm is like a siren going off and I leap awake with an intense sense of disorientation. Emma gives a groan and pulls into me. She feels good and had I slept properly, then I would make love to her one more time before we have to separate. She doesn't start her shift until eleven o'clock and the thought of staying with her is overpowering, but I know today is the day. Martin will be informed later that Chimera is closing and that our jobs are all at risk. Plus Denise will be back, and I know that this is not the day to be out. I kiss Emma, our lips lingering on each other, before heading for the shower. I run through my morning regime and she is still unconscious when I am ready to leave. I reach down, stroke her hair and feel her stir awake.

"Hey, it's okay," I say. "You can let yourself out when you are ready."

She smiles up at me. Some women are a fright in the morning, looking like one of the undead without their hair brushed and their layer of makeup, but Emma looks cute and inviting. I lean down and kiss her again on the mouth.

"I haven't cleaned my teeth," she mumbles.

I kiss her again and she lets me.

"I don't care," I reply. "It's going to be hard not seeing you for an entire weekend."

"Will you miss me?" she asks.

"Yes," I state simply.

She smiles and her cheeks flush. It was obviously the right answer.

"Will you text me over the weekend?"

"Only once every five minutes," I reply. "I promise."

I make a gesture that crosses my heart and give her my wide-eyed look, which I save for moments of maximum manipulation. She giggles happily and I know that this is my cue to leave. I sweep downstairs to my car and for once, the commute to work passes in a happy daze as I sing along to songs on the radio. You know that you are trouble when pop lyrics sound meaningful.

***

"Denise doesn't look good," mutters Ben.

He has followed me over to the kitchen to make coffee. I give a nod. I am debating whether to make her a tea — I learned long ago exactly how she likes it — but am caught between a sympathetic gesture and not wanting her to cry in the office. Ben is correct. She has black bags under her eyes and I guess that she has been crying a lot over the last couple days. There are people who would have just shrugged off what happened but Denise is not like that. When someone beeped at her last month when she drifted lanes in her car, she was shaken by it for days. She is so emotionally fragile and I keep thinking about how her colleagues are part of her support network. When the office closes, we will be gone and she will have to start again with a group of strangers, always with the worry that her new team will have another Steve in it.

"I'll make her a cup of tea," I say for my own benefit as my internal thought processes reach a slow conclusion.

"Well, that's very British. You feel bullied and humiliated, but a lovely cup of tea will do the trick," replies Ben.

"Do you have a better suggestion?"

"Oh no, I wasn't being horrid. It's just that as a nation that seems all we can do."

I hand Ben his coffee and then head towards Denise. She is sat at her desk and staring vacantly into the distance. Her computer is still off and I notice that her mobile phone is not on her desk in its usual spot.

"Morning, you," I say in my friendliest voice. "Made you some tea."

She looks up at me and I must confess that the power of her stare is unnerving. It is an odd sensation as I watch her face change, like she is an old person finally recognising me.

"Oh Johnny, that's sweet. Thank you," she says.

Her mouth lights up in that famous smile with her perfect teeth but her eyes do not smile. It does not reassure me that she is okay but is more like she is bearing her teeth at a threat.

"No problem. I know that you've had a rough time over the last few weeks."

"It has not been the best of times," she replies. "And listen, I meant to say that it was appreciated the way that you stood up for me. I don't know what I would have done had you not been there. I mean, he was so aggressive that he could have hit me."

Denise breaks off and shakes her head as her minds races through the possibilities. I know that this is the dangerous time for her to break down on me. I hate myself for wishing that she just keeps it together. It feels like I have been flying this morning and just being near her is bringing me down. I don't want to wallow in the spitefulness and ignorance of other people, I want to re-run through every moment that I have spent with Emma. However, Denise recovers herself and when her eyes meet mine again, she gives a careless shrug.

"Hey, you know that Ben and I will always look out for you," I offer.

"I know. And like I said: it is appreciated."

Her voice has a final tone to it and I know that the conversation is over. I give her a small nod and walk back to my desk. The office is as full as it gets. The entire sales team are in, along with Alison who is part time and works from home one day a week. There is a concerned feel to the office with people huddled together and murmuring: they know something is wrong. I have another problem entirely in that my phone is burning a hole in my pocket and I have the need to keep checking it to see if Emma has messaged me, while fighting the sensation to send her some banal message. I am missing her.

I sit down at my desk and pretend to start working.

***

There used to be a French themed restaurant in the centre of Reading called "La brassiere Toulouse". The menu was in French and there were paintings of famous French landmarks on the walls, as well as a huge wine rack in the windows which was full of empty bottles. The serving staff were smartly dressed and the brilliant white tablecloths gave it a hint of sophistication. I chose it for my second date with Anna because I hoped that it would impress her, and I get there early to make sure that I get a good table. There was one in particular that I liked, which had a good view onto the road and was perfect for people watching. I felt smug when I was able to persuade a tired looking waiter to give me the table I wanted, and sat there drinking a gin and tonic while stewing internally about seeing her again. It had been two days since we kissed and I had this huge sense of unfinished business, which was only slightly mitigated by the occasional, knowing smiles we had been exchanging at work.

Anna arrived ten minutes early, which caught me by surprise as I was still preparing myself, and she looked amazing. Her tight blue dress showed off her shoulders, clinging to her torso and then flaring off at her hips. She was wearing a black choker and her hair was up to show off her long neck. She walked seductively in heels, her hips giving a distinctive flick with each step. I noticed that she had attracted every eye in the restaurant, male and female, and she lent that tired establishment a far more chic air than any of its faux ornaments and decorations. I stood up to greet her and I could see her smiling at my astonishment. She offered a cheek for a kiss, but I turned her chin with my hand and kissed her firmly on the mouth at the risk of smudging her bold, red lipstick.

"So am I feminine enough for you?" she asked mischievously.

"You look amazing," I said with a nod. "I mean, completely stunning."

This was good enough for her and she moved to sit down. A waiter pulled her chair out for her and she seated herself gracefully. The waiter handed her a menu before moving off, and Anna gave a frown and ran her hand across the tops of her thigh.

"Are you okay?" I asked.

"I think my stocking has come loose," she replied.

She was watching my reaction and laughed when I blushed. Later on, she would tell me that she did this to make sure she could seduce me. She had already decided that I was a keeper and was keen to move things on. She had a very practical view and any good mannered prevarication on my part used to drive her to distraction. I smiled back at her and made an effort to rise above it.

"What would you like to drink?" I asked.

I used to drink almost exclusively beer back then, but this would not set the tone I wanted now. I really needed to impress her, and the more she seemed to like me, the more I needed to be worthy of her regard. Therefore, I had already researched some good wine choices and run them by Ken, who, despite living off an exclusive diet of fried food, used to fancy himself as a bit of a connoisseur.

"I don't know," replied Anna. "What do you have there?"

The gin and tonic had gone to my head quickly and I do not want another. I had known enough friends make an idiot of themselves on a date, and that was not something I intended to do with Anna. I choose not to answer her directly.

"They have a wine here I like, would you like to share a bottle?"

"Of course," she replied.

The answer seemed to delight her and I suddenly felt that I was clearing every hurdle of her expectations easily. I gave the waiter a discrete signal and pointed out the bottle. He pretended to be impressed with the choice and I inwardly winced at the price.

"I like this place," said Anna, as she surveyed it.

"Have you been here before?"

"This is not a place that my ex-boyfriends would bring me," she laughed.

I failed to guard the hurt that the mention of her previous lovers caused me. She noticed my expression change and leant over to squeeze my hand.

"Hey, I am sorry. Everyone has a history, you know, and you are so much better than anyone else I have dated," she said. "I have already told my mother about you."

I loved the fact that she was trying to reassure me even though I had no reason to be so sensitive. I squeezed her hand back, not wanting her to let go.

"What did your mother say?"

"She thinks that I am in love," she replied.

Her voice was quiet but once again, she was regarding me closely to see my reaction. She had a wicked smile and one eyebrow rose provocatively. I was learning quickly to deal with her teasing, and this time I kept my eyes fixed on hers.

"And are you?"

She laughed again but this time in embarrassment and looked away. It took some moments before she replied.

"Maybe."

The wine arrived and the waiter performed the uncorking ceremony (in a time where wine bottles all came with corks) and then allowed me to taste it, and sentence its suitability. I gave a nod to show that I was content and he poured us both half a glass, placed the wine in a cooler and then disappeared. We raised our glasses and we looked at each other and sipped our wines. I loved how the moment felt, no one had ever made me feel so good, and the last time I felt this way was as a child.

"I like you too," I said.

She blew air from her cheeks and rolled her eyes in mock exasperation.

"Oh, you like me, do you?" she said. "Although not enough to take me home the other evening?"

My brain switched abruptly to deep seriousness. I frowned intensely and put my wine glass down. She was sensitive to the change and listened carefully.

"Listen, I need to be honest with you. Don't be upset that I didn't want to take you home on Tuesday but I meant what I said about not rushing this. I really like you and I have done since I first saw you in the canteen."

"I remember!" exclaimed Anna, unable to help herself from interrupting.

"So, I do want to take this slowly and make it work because you are so amazing, and I don't think that I will find anyone else like you easily. But there are some things you need to know about me."

I broke off and took another sip of wine and I could tell from her expression she was thinking whether I was about to let her down easily or not.

"My life is a bit of a mess. I stayed too long in a dead-end job and that really didn't help me get my life in order. One of the reasons that I didn't want to take you home is that I have a grotty bedroom in a shared house. It's not exactly the sort of place to impress anyone."

"You don't need to impress me."

"But I want to."

"I know, and I want you to like everything about me too but we need to be honest with each other. And anyway, I am glad that I have found you at this part of your life. Your career is taking off and now you are thinking about getting your own place to live. I have had some bad times too in my life and I know I would find it easier if I had someone to share these problems with."

"There is so much going on at the moment," I said.

I ran out of words. There were a million things rushing around my mind about the future, and so much of it seemed good, but deep down there was the feeling that it was all a mirage in the distance that will be cruelly snatched away. Anna seemed to know all this instinctively on some level.

"You have a big week next week. The entire future of the company is resting on you, and I can imagine how that must feel. Arthur believes in you though. It is clear to everyone, and I am certain that you will do brilliantly for all of us."

I had to look away as my eyes welled up. Not even my parents had ever shown this much faith in me and it was hard to deal with. Anna saw this and it seemed to melt her heart. She leant forward over the table and her expression was intense.

"Whatever happens next week, remember that there will be two of us now to face it."

***

I take a break at lunch time to get a sandwich. There is a food wagon ten minutes' walk away on the industrial estate. Normally, I don't have the patience to queue up for food, especially as some of the idiots will have been waiting a while before their turn and only decide what they want when asked. I hate people sometimes, but most of all when they are in their own little world with no regard for others. It's one of the reasons that I despise the rise of the modern smartphone, despite being addicted to my own. I consider asking Ben and Denise to join me for company but then selfishly acknowledge that I would rather be on my own.

The fresh air is welcome. It is a warm enough day for the time of year with no cloud in the sky. I weave my way between the atrociously parked cars that litter every available space and piece of grass on the estate. That is another thing that I hate: people believing that car parking is a fundamental human right and leaving their vehicles wherever they please. It makes me wonder if Ben is correct and that I should go off and live on a small island somewhere. I would certainly be less angry that way. There are moments where I have started to catalogue those things that bring me to rage, and it is a worryingly long list.

The real reason of not wanting any company this morning is so I can check my phone. There have been a dozen messages from Emma already, ranging from the slightly mad to the downright flirty. I have taken my time before replying to make sure that what I say will make her smile. I am slightly depressed at the thought of her being away for the entire weekend. The usual escape of trawling dating sites do not appeal as I seem to have developed a mild addiction to her company. I am eating my sandwich on a damp bench when my phone vibrates and I check it to see a message from Abigail.

**'Hi. Do you want to get that drink tonight? X'**

I know that I should tell her that I am seeing someone else but the weekend stretches long and lonely in front of me. I convince myself that I should let her down face-to-face rather than a heartless text, but I know in my heart that I don't want to be alone this evening. The string of texts from Emma has dried up and I need the fix of the warm buzz and flashing light of an incoming message from someone else. She warned me that she wouldn't be able to text much over the weekend as she is with her family, and I know that will leave me in a vacuum for longer than I can bear. Plus Abigail did say that she had some tickets for a gin festival.

**'Ok. When and where?'**

I put the wrapping of my sandwich into the bin and start the walk back to the office. I am halfway back when I feel the reassuring vibration once more.

**'The Foresters Arms at six?'**

I analyse the five words. It is a nice, old fashioned pub, which serves ale and she knows that it will appeal to me. A drink at six means that an impromptu meal and more drinks are on the cards. I read all of this as positive interest and type a quick response.

**'See you there.'**

My reply is deliberately terse. I want her to feel that she is making all the running here. I am enjoying the heading euphoria of attention when I arrive back at the office. I fail to notice the tense atmosphere for a few minutes until Ben seeks me out. He looks terrified.

"Have you seen the message from corporate? We have all been called to a team meeting after Martin has the afternoon call."

I notice that most of the office is watching my reaction and I feign concern. My heart is stone cold towards the situation and the feelings of my colleagues. The demise of Chimera is an opportunity for me and it is time for me to move on. I can't bring myself to say anything and make do with a worried shake of the head. Ben drifts off and the others return to their desks. My mind switches back to Emma, and the distraction of Abigail. Nothing has changed for me.

***

There are those people you will always look back on and see them as beacons in your life; whose positive influence you remember and make you feel that there is genuine good in the world. Jeff was the opposite. He was poison, a hardened cynic who oozed resentment at other people's happiness, and revelled in seeing people fail. Despite this, he was also the person that allowed me to succeed at Hamiltons, and because of that it took me a long time to see him for what he was. The weird thing was that we were friends and even genuinely liked one another. He was obsessed with horror films (and I mean really unpleasant ones) and martial arts, although I never saw him train. He also had an opinion on everything and everyone, and it was rarely a positive one.

I met Jeff at the trade fair for the mobile phone industry. Ken and I had been doing the rounds passing out leaflets on our new product. It was obvious that we did not belong. The whole market was going crazy and money was being thrown at the industry. A small company like Hamiltons had no place there, where we stared in bewilderment at company stands, which had been fine polished by the best marketing agencies. We were out of place: small, scruffy and irrelevant. Most of the people on the stands had no real idea what their products did or whether they worked, but were there to raise the awareness of their brands, as stunning choreographed films played in the background. I had some small success with the few engineers I met, but most of them looked as uncomfortable in this environment as we were.

It was the afternoon of the second day and I was foot sore from wondering around and mostly discouraged. I had watched the natural excitement slowly drain out of Ken. He had been like a hyperactive puppy at the start, rhapsodising about the cheap transit hotel we were staying in, and behaving as though the carvery pub we ate in was the definition of luxury. He had started off like we were on a mission and I liked him so much that I could only indulge his good humour, and it was awful to watch it drain away.

I was tired and had found one of the many bars at the conference centre. The larger ones had been full of braying business development characters quaffing warm sparkling wine and boasting about themselves. This one was mostly quiet with only a scattering of the lonely, but sat at the corner of the bar were two guys. I had clocked them as I made my approach and noticed how they were failing to engage a clearly bored barmaid. One was slightly aggressive looking, broad shoulders but more meat than muscle, with a ton of hair gel to maintain his spiked look. His friend was best described as a gangly, spotty teenager who had grown up but whose cheeks still bore the signs of the battle with acne. I arrived at the bar exactly as the barmaid chose to disappear into the back.

"Fuck," I muttered rather loudly.

I hate deliberate rudeness, especially from strangers. It makes me want to hurt people. I was less than a metre from the two guys, who laughed when they heard me. It was not for their benefit but I was too angry to be embarrassed.

"Bad day?" asked the spikey hair guy.

"You could say that," I replied. "And then I can't even get a drink when I need one."

"She's a lazy cow. She will come back when she thinks you've gone. We should try being quiet for a bit."

The skinny friend threw his head and laughed with false enthusiasm, and a speck of spit landed on the shiny bar. I knew immediately who the less dominant one in the friendship was. I couldn't help but smile since it was exactly what I was thinking. The barmaid was still within earshot from her hiding place and gave a cough to show she could hear us. It made us all roar with laughter.

"Who you with?" asked the spikey hair guy.

"A small company called Hamiltons," I ventured.

He gave a dismissive snort and a shake of a head. I hadn't expected him to know the company but there was something else in my answer that he didn't agree with.

"Who you guys with?" I asked back.

"We work for ourselves. No fat corporation is going to bleed us for our hard work!" sneered spikey hair. "I am Jeff by the way, and this is Chris."

He shook his head as he spoke, his eyes fixed into the distance, and his skinny companion gave a nervous laugh and nodded at the profound wisdom of the statement. We did not shake hands.

"Oh right," I replied. "Well, pleased to meet you. I am Johnny. So you have your own company then?"

"Well, we do for tax purposes, but we are contractors. We go where the work is and get paid appropriately for it. We don't have to buy into all that corporate bullshit that modern companies seem to love. We do what we do best and move on to the next job."

I am now older and wiser, and would dismiss anyone who came out with this kind of rubbish as a bit of a tosser, but back then it seemed to resonate. I admired the approach and the sound of independence; so far from my own situation of being married to Hamiltons. I just gave Jeff a nod but couldn't think of anything to say. It was hot and my collar felt tight. I unbuttoned it and loosened my tie, I could feel myself getting angry: I just wanted a drink.

"You don't have to bother dressing like that," said Jeff. "This is a technology show and it's a bit old school. It's only the corporate tarts who need to make the effort. It hides their lack of any skills."

Jeff was a deeply cynical and nasty person but he was also an astute judge of character. I have never known anyone who can tell someone's weaknesses so readily from a single glance. He had worked out that I was an engineer like him, and therefore someone worth talking to. When someone who was deeply hostile to the world and everybody in it takes a liking to you, it is kind of flattering.

"How do you know I'm not a corporate tart? I could be here for my gin and tonic fix?"

This provoked a wry laugh from the pair of them and Jeff smiled at me.

"Nah, you're a techie like us, one of the workers that makes all this stuff possible. So come on them, what you doing here?"

"We have a new range of test equipment that we're trying to launch into the cellular market. We came here to try and make some contacts."

"Oh right," replied Jeff. "This probably isn't the right place for that. This is more about the big deals between companies, those sort of decisions are made at a lower level. What exactly are you selling?"

I unzipped my trusty, leatherette folder, which I had placed on the bar, and took out the glossies we had made for the new product range. Jeff took them and showed them to his skinny friend, making approving noises.

"Good work. We could definitely do with some of these! Hang on a moment, this is something we can help with."

He took out a pen and his mobile phone — a sturdy Nokia that would find its place in a museum these days. He cycled through his contact list and begins writing names, email addresses and phone numbers from his contacts. In all, he produced twelve key contacts.

"OK, email these guys with an electronic version of the datasheet and put some covering notes into the email text. I can guarantee that'll you get some interest," he said before noticing the eventual reappearance of the barmaid. "Oh at last! We can finally get a drink!"

"Don't worry lads, it's my shout," boomed a voice behind us.

Ken looked exhausted but his persona had kicked in and he was all smile and charm. I watched as Jeff appraised him, and I knew exactly what he was thinking.

I hated myself for feeling embarrassed by Ken, his old style clothes looked ridiculous and he just did not belong in that environment. Jeff did not smile back but replied in a dead pan voice.

"We're drinking Carlsberg."

Ken's smile wavered. We drank only ale at Hamiltons. Lager was for underage drinkers, wife beaters and football hooligans. I realised that this could become an issue quickly.

"We're drinking Carlsberg, Ken," I repeated emphatically. Although had you asked me the day before, I would have replied that I would rather have drunk a pint of warm piss.

"Right you are," replied Ken, bouncing back. "Four pints of Carlsberg, please!"

We got so drunk that we had to abandon the car and take a taxi back to the hotel. It was a strange meeting that was a real turning point in my life for the immediate survival of Hamiltons, its longer term prospects, and for me personally. Jeff and I exchanged numbers and we became close friends, one of the few outside of the Hamiltons community. Looking back, he was a terrible influence on my life at a critical time. Ken never did email those companies, he simply didn't know how to. Instead, he rang them all the next day and got a meeting setup with each and every one. Our tour was set to continue for another week and the sense of failure evaporated for the moment.

***

"Okay everyone, if you could just gather round for a minute," says Martin.

He does not have a lot of presence at the best of times but the poor guy looks drained and ill. He is holding a sheaf of handwritten notes and I know that he has just got off the management briefing announcing our imminent demise. I never really rated Martin as a manager, thinking of him as an over-promoted lapdog, but today I do feel for him. He is shaking slightly and sweat patches show through the cotton of his cheap shirt near the armpits. The air of concern is palpable and people move quickly to form an anxious ring around him. I scan my colleagues with their folded arms and wide eyes. Nearly the entire office is here and it sinks in then how much we have shrunk over the years. Ben and Denise are sat together on a desk. Denise is practically shaking. Alison is stood next to them. Kevin and Mark, representing two-thirds of the sale function, sit apart from their manager Giles. There had been twenty people when I started and a full time receptionist. There is no hiding that this is the inevitable outcome of the last few years. I have seen this happen a number of times now and know I will survive.

"I have just got off the phone and I have an announcement to relay to you," he says, gulping heavily. "The drop in European sales and the generally bleak outlook in this market have compelled the central office to look seriously at our cost base. They have analysed a number of ways to stem the decline and have spent considerable time modelling a number of go-forward scenarios. It is with extreme regret that there is no other option than to close the European office and relocate support services back to the central office."

Martin breaks off here as there is a despondent groan from the room. I think he is going to give up entirely for a moment, but as a veteran of many a management seminar, he soldiers on to the finish.

"We will enter a period of consultation as all UK roles are now at risk. Everyone will have at least three interviews to discuss relocation options. It is planned that the office will close in three months."

There is a barrage of questions thrown at him and he wilts under the onslaught, but the voices of the sales team are loudest in the cacophony.

"How long have you known about this?" screams Kevin.

"You better still pay me my full bonus!" shouts Mark.

I nearly laugh. Mark has never come close to his bonus in the years that he has been here. Martin is looking at the floor but his palms are outstretched as he tries to make calming motions. He is lucky that there is no longer a full complement of people here. Anyway, three months is fine. Plenty of time to find a new job and walk out with a nice payout. I am already spending the money as I go to leave, but Denise grabs my arm as I turn.

"Johnny! What am I going to do? The operation is next week and now I won't have a job to come back to!"

Her voice is desperate and pleading but I have no advice to give. I stare into her eyes and give a sad shake of the head. She releases my arm and I make for the door. There will be no more work today and I have a hot date to prepare for.

## Chapter 13 – The Summer of Love

I have grown addicted to the small excitements of life: the buzz of a text, the ping of an email, the notification of messages, winks and flirts on my dating apps, but most importantly the preparation for a hot date. It is these things that have kept me going through a stagnant professional life and the lack of any domestic stability, and even when I have those moments when my life choices seem bleak, I am never far from fleeting distraction to push the demons away. I have established a routine for preparing for an evening out, starting with a frantic burst of activity at the gym, a long shower employing plenty of hair and body product, a close shave in a steam filled bathroom, hair plucking (nose and ears mostly but the occasional rogue eyebrows), a trim downstairs to make everything presentable, an 'all over' moisturise, and then deodorant and aftershave. I have heard women complain about the expectations of society in terms of appearance, but I think that things have evened out over the years.

Finally, when I am dressed, I look in the full-length mirror in the hall and admire myself. I look good, and not just for my age. It is one of the reasons that I do so well on the dating scene: I am presentable. I am also articulate and have no baggage, which helps a lot. The dating field has narrowed considerably at my age so there is less choice for me than there used to be, hence it is important that I come across well. However, my mind is now on this evening. Emma has gone on radio silence this afternoon and it is only the excitement at going out that is keeping my mind off her. I tell myself that it's no more than a drink with a friend. We've been messaging for a while now and the least that I can do is to let her down easily with a decent explanation that I have met someone. I tell myself this but in my head I can imagine Ben tutting and rolling his eyes, in the way that he does when he thinks that I am being sexually promiscuous. I dismiss the doubts quickly as I see the taxi pull up outside.

The best nights out in my life have been almost entirely spontaneous. Planning kills fun. I have adapted this to my entire dating philosophy: keep the options open. Take a taxi so you can drink, don't make dinner plans, meet somewhere central so there are lots of place to go easily and have lots of cash because there are some things that plastic is still no good for. I practically bound out of the house and leap into the taxi. The driver is an old guy who looks at me with a hint of disdain. I suppose to him I am old enough to be at home with the family on a Friday night, and not gallivanting around on the town like a young man.

"Good evening!" I say pleasantly. "The King's Head, please."

The driver does not reply but gives a slow nod as he throws the car into gear. I am too charged with energy to sit quietly and instead try and engage him in conversation.

"So, have you had a busy evening?"

He gives me a glance in the rearview mirror and I can tell that he wants nothing more than for me to sit quietly. I have put on a heavy layer of aftershave, which I am finding a bit much in this enclosed space, and it must be eye watering for him.

"Just started," he mumbles gruffly.

I sit back in my chair. My phone gives a happy buzz in my pocket and I can't resist taking it out. Every message is like a small Christmas present to a child. It is from Abigail.

**'I am here early. I got you a beer. x'**

Part of me was hoping that the message was from Emma, who I am thinking about even if I am meeting Abigail. Another technique I have is to get there first and be the one who orders the drinks. I can then ensure that I am drinking the same as my date, it's one of my methods to make it feel like we have something in common. I bash a quick reply out.

**'Great, thanks. In taxi. Will be 15mins.'**

Fifteen minutes may be slightly optimistic given the fact that we are in evening commuter traffic. I try and stem the agitation as we slow down, every junction packed and each light against us.

**I am sat on a bench on the left hand side.**

Time starts to drag as we crawl towards the destination. I look at my phone every minute to check the passage of time, fighting the agitation and knowing that she is sat there alone. It takes closer to twenty-five minutes before we draw up outside, and I practically throw the money at the driver and charge inside. I see her immediately, sat on her own, staring at her phone, and all hunched up and closed off from the world. I am old enough to remember when people had the luxury of boredom when they were waiting, or maybe had to take solace in a book, rather than having the glowing distraction of the internet ever present.

Abigail looks good though, I can tell that I am not the only one who has made an effort for the evening. She is wearing what looks like an off the shoulder, thigh length, grey woollen dress. It shows off her bra strap on one side. She has these strange boots which extend just above the knee, which look a bit like something a pantomime pirate may wear, but kind of work for me. All in all, she does look adorable and I am happy to see her.

"Hey you," I say and she looks up.

"Hi," replies Abigail.

She is unsure whether to stand up or not and as she hesitates, I lean down and kiss her on the cheek. I smell her shampoo and perfume and I let it fill my lungs. She rewards me with a shy smile. I notice that she has bought herself a glass of sparkling wine.

"How have you been?" I ask.

I sit down and pick up the drink she has bought for me. I give a happy smile and we chink glasses as she considers her reply.

"I am ok," she says at length.

"You look nice."

"Thanks."

The conversation is in danger of running flat. This is not the funny, sharp-witted girl I remember. It is not the first time that this has happened to me on a date, and I have learned to keep things going even if it feels uphill. Normally, I will bail on a date after one drink if it is not going well but usually I have a list of alternatives to call through and see if I can meet up with a better option so as not to waste the evening.

"I was a bit surprised to hear from you to be honest," I confess. "Normally walking out on the second date is a good way to end things."

"I know why you did that," she says. "And I wanted to walk out with you, or at least message you straight after and make sure that everything was okay."

"So why didn't you?"

"I don't know," she says, clearly uncomfortable. "Well, I suppose I do. My friends can be a bit funny when I have a boyfriend, and they had made such a thing of you being a bit older. When you walked out, I didn't know what to do and just froze."

"I see. And what did your friends say?"

"Not much. A few sarcastic comments with the hint of 'I told you so'."

"Nice friends you have," I snap.

I am genuinely angry and struggling to hide it. I understand the age gap, or at least I convince myself I do, but they were just nasty people and I don't understand why Abigail wants to be friends with them.

"Yeah, I know, but we've been friends for a while."

"The reason that they act funny when you have a boyfriend is simple jealously. They do not want you to be happy."

I expect her to attack that statement. It is enough to provoke most people but she looks really sad and I worry that she is going to cry.

"I know that too. And that's why we're here, because I thought about it and I chose you."

I am completely blindsided by her words. I had come here for a couple of drinks and to explain about Emma, but this is one of the nicest, sweetest things that anyone has ever said to me. For all my practise at dating and experience of relationships, I am left floundering and it has been a long time since that has happened.

"Wow," is all I can manage.

Abigail laughs a loud, flirty bellow of amusement. She raises her drink, makes a toast in the air and then downs it.

"I never thought that Mr Silver Tongue would be lost for words," she grins.

"I think you'll find that it's my hair not my tongue that is silver," I reply as my brain kicks back into gear.

"I'll let you know when I've had the chance for a closer examination later," she fires back, raising her eyebrows and giving me a sideways smile.

Whatever my intentions were this evening, I feel a powerful surge of attraction and suddenly Emma is gone completely from my thoughts.

"So what have you been up to this week?" I ask, lost for something better to say.

"Oh you know, the usual. Worked, went shopping, couldn't get this guy out of my head."

"Did you buy anything nice?"

"I'll show you," she replied.

Abigail pats the bench beside her and I move around from the chair to join her. She unlocks her phone and then shuffles up next to me, so that our bums are pressed together. It is incredibly erotic. There is nowhere for my arm to go, so I end up putting it around her. It slips down her side, and then over her hip and comes to rest on her bottom. She doesn't say anything but smiles as she sorts through her phone. I give it a gentle caress and she rests her head on my shoulder.

"Here, we are," she says and begins to flick through a range of photos of different outfits she has taken in the changing room. "Guess which ones I bought? Oh whoops!"

There is a photo of her just in her underwear, a nice lacy thong and a matching bra. She knew the photo was there, of course. I get the message. The game is on.

***

I called it The Summer of Love, and it was nothing to do with the Woodstock festival but rather my final months at Hamiltons as the purchase orders started to roll in. Success seemed to breed success and the initial flood of orders appeared to swell as news got out there about our products. The company was simply unprepared for it, and the production floor, which had been fine crafted to be as busy as possible to do the minimum acceptable, suddenly did not know what to do. I had designed the product to snap together like a kit, but it was so different from anything the technicians had seen before that they just failed to cope. I left my office and with the two other engineers we became a permanent feature on the shop floor, training, helping and encouraging. Anna left Edith to her own devices and joined us on the line, writing the batch cards and keeping the records in order. There was a sense of camaraderie and fun that I have never felt anywhere, and every morning we would stop for coffee and cake. Then, in the afternoon we would break from work for half an hour, walk down the road to an ice cream van and sit on the wall and enjoy the summer sun. We called it 'cake o'clock' and 'ice cream o'clock' respectively and somehow no one minded the long hours and repetitive work.

Anna and I had become a thing even at work. It was more relaxed back then and it seemed like some fairytale romance, and there were no objections to us hugging (and occasionally kissing) in the office. We both were living in shared houses, which made privacy difficult, and we had begun seriously discussing getting a place together based on our joint income. She was so lovely to be with, so undemanding, so passionate and giving of herself. I do worry that my brain could not accept on some level this happiness and that someone loved me with the intensity that she did. Every Thursday, we would go out with our colleagues and then back to her place (since she had a double bed) but Friday and the weekend were ours. I wanted to know every detail of her life and occasionally I had a sickening feeling of having missed out on not having met her earlier. We were happy, we were in love, and we were part of a community that cared about us. I knew even back then that it was not going to last.

The first hint with retrospect was when I was summoned to one of the directors' meetings, which had happened without fail every Wednesday afternoon since the company was founded. They took place in the boardroom, with printed reports laid out for each director and a secretary to take the minutes and record the actions. There was fresh coffee laid on in china cups. It was so wonderfully old-fashioned. Ken had submitted his sales report, which had caused quite a stir because he had repeated verbatim that for the growth to continue we needed to further develop new products and refresh what we had. The Old Man knew exactly where that had come, and not for the first time, I was summoned to see him. It was different this time. Success had made me a bit arrogant and slightly entitled, and I strode into the room ready for confrontation.

"Come in, Johnny, sit down," commanded the Old Man, giving a wave to an empty chair. "Sandra, please get him some coffee."

Sandra leapt to her feet and scurried over to the coffee as fast as one could in heels. There was a secretary for every director, as well as the Old Man. They were all cut from the same cloth, looking like Stepford Wives grown old, still dressing in a polished, traditionally feminine manner and cheerfully obedient. She brought me coffee, a small jug of fresh cream and the sugar bowl. I waited for the Old Man to speak and took in my surroundings, while the directors regarded me impassively. There were a couple of things that stuck out. The first was the Old Man looking grey and haggard. It had been a couple of months since I had seen him properly and in that time he had lost weight and his once thick mane of hair had thinned. I dismissed it as stress from the continued responsibility piled onto the patriarch of the organisation. There was also a new face, younger than the directors and snappily dressed in well-cut clothes. He had perfect teeth and immaculate hair, and he met my gaze with a cheerfulness so at odds with the dour expressions of the directors.

"Well, here he is!" boomed the man in a soft, Californian drawl. "The man I have heard so much about."

"Johnny, this is Charles," explained the Old Man. "I have brought him in to help out with things. We were just going through the sales reports and were interested in some of the commentary."

I gave Charles a nod and he returned a wave. I took a liking to him and made the mistake of letting my guard down.

"It says here that there is a lot more to do on the product lines if the sales are to be kept up," said the Old Man, peering at the report in front of him.

His eyesight was not what it once was but he was too proud to wear glasses. I admired his stubbornness.

The directors continued their silent vigil and I resented their irrelevance to everything we were doing.

"That is one of the things, yes," I replied defensively.

"One of the things?" picked up Charles. "Could you shed a little more light on that?"

I cast a lingering glance at the directors to show my displeasure at their silence, before giving a dramatic sigh and starting to unload.

"We are in a fast moving market now, and our products need to keep pace with the things they are testing. This equates to a new product drop every couple of months, which isn't happening."

"Why not?" pushed Charles.

It was exceptional for someone other than the Old Man to lead the conversation. I looked to him before answering, and he gave me a nod. I noticed for the first time how fatigued he looked. It did not make me consider my answer better before it came out.

"It won't happen because what engineers we do have are downstairs in production, supporting getting the stuff off the line. We have technicians who have not had to deal with anything new in a decade and need a lot of hand holding."

"Okay, so we have some training needs there, I guess," said Charles and made a note. "Do we have enough resources to process this capacity?"

I gave a snide laugh and then turn my attention fully on him.

"We have more than enough people to double the production rate, we just have them doing the wrong things. We seem to have a load of people making themselves busy in jobs that would not be noticed if they disappeared tomorrow. This company has an unbelievable case of overmanning, and the reason that there is so much resistance to change is that they don't want to have to lose their comfortable lives by actually needing to work for a living!"

Finally, this provoked a roar of contradiction from the directors, who leapt to the defence of their departments lest they look remiss as leaders. Charles raised an eyebrow, continued to write what I had said, before giving an appreciative nod.

"I appreciate your candour, Johnny," he replied and the directors fell silent. "And I must echo your sentiments from my own observations within the company."

I realised then how much authority this individual carried and I wished that I had better controlled my response. Charles made a point of putting the lid on his pen and placing it down, a subtle signal that the meeting had ended. My mind raced to work out who he was. Charles turned back to me.

"Thank you, Johnny," he said calmly. "We shall now work on a plan to get your engineers the headspace they need to design, while looking to optimise the other aspects of this business."

It all felt wrong, this strange American speaking and the Old Man silent. I knew that I had been dismissed and left my coffee untouched as I made my way back downstairs. I told Anna that evening about it after we had made love in her room. She shared a house with other girls, which was to say that it was cleaner and more homely than mine. Her room was cramped with most of the floor space occupied by a compact double bed, which meant we had to sleep cuddled tight. It was still infinitely better than my place though. I was lying on my back, with her head on my shoulder and I explained what had happened. She loved to know every detail, and would question specifics to ensure she understood everything exactly, while her fingers caressed and stroked me. She took a more positive message from it: that our recent success was attracting more attention. I suppose in a way she was right. I had forgotten about it the next morning when we were back into the fray with targets to meet, but a few days later Charles sought me out and took me for lunch at the Nag's Head. We were sat seemingly enjoying a lunch time pint, as I waited for him to get to the point but instead he seemed self-reflective.

"You know, Johnny, you have no idea how lucky you are," he said as he stared off in a reverie.

"What do you mean? All these long hours and no overtime?" I pushed back.

Charles put his pint down and laughed out loud. It took him a few minutes to recover himself before he turned to explain. He looked a lot older with his guard down, like some grizzled veteran carrying the scars of his experience. I was impressed by his quiet gravitas and instinctively liked him, but I felt very narrow and immature in comparison to his sophistication.

"You are lucky for so many reasons. I know you don't mind the long hours because you are doing what you are good at, and it's a success. You are lucky because you are seeing a beautiful woman who clearly adores you. You are lucky that you can drink beer at lunch time — something that would get me fired back home —and no one blinks an eye! But most of all you are lucky because you can speak the truth in meetings without fear of the consequences," he replied.

"And are you telling me you can't?" I asked.

"Well, of course I could," he said with a lopsided smile. "But I would be able to do it only once."

"Sounds like you need a new employer," I dismissed.

"I am afraid that the era of not being on message is over, no matter where I choose to work."

"You what?"

"Ah, I am not sure that expression has entered the corporate vocabulary over here yet but I am certain that it will. Let me try and speak more colloquially: if I do not toe the line, then I shall be fired," he said. "Unless, of course, I elect to move into some small 'mom and pop shop' like Hamiltons, but that would not offer me the breadth of options that I am after."

"So basically, you're too ambitious to work for a small company so you need to be politically attuned to survive in a large corporation?"

"Exactly."

"So what are you doing here exactly?"

"Advising mostly."

"I don't think that the Old Man needs your advice. He has been running this company for long enough."

"I did not say that it was Arthur Hamilton who I was advising."

"What?"

Charles never answered the question but batted it away with a wave of the hand. His moment of reflection was over and he had an agenda to get through.

"The company has turned a corner recently," he mused. "Six months ago it was not worth a second look. Another company that has failed to adapt to the world."

"I suppose."

"And then there's the reason behind what has caused this sudden shift at a time when there has been no change in the senior management team."

I give an angry snort because I know where this is going and I am uncomfortable with it.

"Hamiltons recruits a single engineer and suddenly we see new products emerging in the right markets. Six products in six months. That's an impressive achievement."

"We were lucky."

Charles gives a short laugh and I see his controlled expression slip and be replaced with genuine pain.

"I have got to the age that I no longer believe in luck, but what I do know is that one cannot base a company on a single individual."

"What do you mean?" I asked.

I knew then the subtext of the meeting. I was unsure whether to be flattered or concerned. I studied Charles's face but I could read nothing. He really could have been anywhere between thirty-five and fifty-five, I suspect now the latter but he had maintained himself carefully over the years.

"How long do you plan to remain at Hamiltons?" he asked directly.

His gaze was disturbing in its intensity and I saw for the first time the steel beneath the charm. He was watching my body language rather than listening to my words.

"I don't know really. I have no plans to leave."

"And Anna? What are her aspirations?"

I gave a shrug. I really could not answer for her. It was not like we had not discussed the future or her dreams, because we had at length. Her dreams were so modest: a small house with a nice garden, to travel a bit, and a loving family around her. I knew that she loved Hamiltons, despite the fact it was so frustrating and impossible to get anything done, but she had been adopted into a surrogate family and I could never imagine her leaving. Sometimes, I worried about her returning home but she seemed happy in the UK.

"She loves this company," was all I could think of.

Charles was still staring at me. He processed my response for a few seconds before his perfect smile exploded across his face, and all seriousness vanished. He leaned back in his chair and pretended to relax.

"Well anyway, that's enough talk about work for one day. This soft, summer sun is too nice for serious conversations. Let's talk about your next vacation."

The lunch left me more confused than the management meeting. I had no idea who this shadowy figure was or what he was really after. However, Charles was not the only influence in my life at that time. I may have been surrounded by the Hamiltons community socially, as well as at work, but I had become friends with Jeff and we had started hanging out every week. I enjoyed his nasty streak of humour, largely because it was never aimed at me, and I enjoyed relaxing at his flat. While I was living in a shared house that was noisy and damp, Jeff had a modern flat in Slough which was decked out with large, leather sofas and a television so enormous that I joked it was like being at the cinema. He also had a huge fridge that was packed with imported beer and cupboards that were filled with snacks. His disposable income impressed me and I admired his standard of living. He seemed to have worked in every company in the south-east, and it gave him experience that made me feel naïve. I suppose it was similar to how I had felt with Charles, like I was the junior in the relationship, and my time at Hamiltons had made me a big fish in a very small pond.

I would buy chocolate, popcorn and fizzy drinks and we would settle in to watch some film, usually a horror film or something violent. Jeff had a collection of rare overseas films, many of which had subtitles, which I am sure were so graphic that they had not made it past a film censor. We would stuff ourselves stupid, drink fizzy drinks by the gallon, and see who had to give in first and go to the toilet. We both strived to outdo the other in providing the most humorous commentary to the disturbing violence of whatever we were watching, and afterwards we just used to chat. I miss having uncomplicated friendships like that. I was never the butt of Jeff's humour but Hamiltons didn't enjoy the same protection, and after a while it began to change my perception of the job.

"So, how is life at the Funny Farm?"

Funny Farm was his name for Hamiltons. This was mostly due to the stories I told of the place, with its collection of oddballs, misfits and the terminally lazy.

"Yeah, alright," I replied. "Another busy week but it's good to see things coming together."

"Is that your way of saying that you worked a load of unpaid overtime for someone else's benefit?"

"Something like that."

"Well, at least you should get a juicy bonus for all your efforts."

"That would be nice but I told you before, we don't get those. The place is old-fashioned like that."

"What about stock options?"

"Nope."

"I'll tell you what is old-fashioned: slavery," snapped Jeff, aggrieved on my behalf. "You're carrying that company and they're giving you nothing back!"

Looking back, perhaps I should have contradicted him. Told him how much I liked the people, enjoyed my status in a tight-knit community, and loved the way that Anna looked at me for all I had achieved. At the time, I enjoyed his attention too. It made me feel more heroic and underappreciated.

"Yeah, I know."

"I mean, they should fire half of those directors! They have done nothing and I bet that they earn five times what you do!"

I suspected that this wasn't true. The deal at Hamiltons was that although the pay was low and the wider package was non-existent, people never got fired and to be fair, didn't have to achieve that much either.

"I don't think that's ever going to happen."

"Mate, you need to get a grip. You've crossed thirty and live in some shitty shared house! You drive a battered second-hand car and you struggle to afford a holiday! You've got to stop people taking advantage of you. You know, I could help set you up as a contractor and you could start living properly!"

He was right as well. My life was modest and even the recent success had left me with little to show for it. My parents had started to ask pointed questions about my future, a situation which had got much worse when they had met Anna and decided that it was time for me to grow up. However, for all his material advantages, there was one area where Jeff could not compete. We had met for a drink after work, and Anna had agreed to pick me up so I could have a few beers. She swept into the bar, dived into my arms and kissed me with a passion that made me dizzy, and when I finally surfaced for air, I caught Jeff's expression which was green with envy. The old cliché was right: there are some things that money cannot buy.

***

I am starting to flag and I know that if I don't get Abigail home soon then I will be too tired. I have got to that age where the prospect of sleep can be more enticing than hot sex with a younger woman. We have drunk a lot, and are full of second-rate food, and I can sense that she is beginning to tire as well. I have half a pint of beer, which my stomach is too full to absorb and from a thousand accidental touches and those lingering looks, she is waiting for me to ask.

"So you want to get out of here?" I enquire.

She puts her drink down quickly, gives a brief nod and grabs her handbag. I smile inwardly and take her hand as we head out of the crowded pub. I am glad to be out of there. It was so loud that I had to concentrate hard to make out what she was saying, and I had to keep asking her to repeat herself even though our faces were pressed close together. We head to find a taxi and I do my usual trick of walking a hundred yards, using her hand to flick her around to face me, and then going for the kiss. It is a well-practised move, and I cannot remember the last time it failed. Of course, I wait until I am sure that it is welcome, I do not want a pass to be rebuffed. That would be seriously humiliating.

Abigail leans back to accept the kiss. I think she is pulling away for a second and panic, but she receives me and we kiss. I start gently with my lips on hers, before turning my head and pushing my tongue in. Once more I am left uncertain, she opens her mouth a modest amount to accommodate me but it does not feel like she is kissing me back. This is not good. I don't like it. I break off.

"Are you okay?" I question.

"Yes, fine. Why did you stop?"

"Oh sorry, I thought that you weren't that into it."

"No, it was nice."

I get a whiff of her breath. It is not good. I mean, not as bad as I remember and certainly not that 'something has just died in my mouth', rancid, stomach turning stench. But not that great either. I go in for a second kiss with exactly the same result before. Either Abigail really isn't into this or she is an awful kisser. Maybe both. This time she pulls away.

"Why don't you take me home? It's freezing out here," she asks.

I do not wait to be asked twice but I can feel my passion waning. I should really call her a taxi and send her home, but there is a stubborn part of me that refuses to accept that this is going to be a car crash. We get in a taxi and hold hands on the way back to mine. I fumble to open the door and worry that it makes me look nervous. We start the kissing again in the hall. I am really starting to notice her breath.

"Would you like some water?" I ask.

I am not being considerate but rather hope that the halitosis is exacerbated by alcohol and dehydration.

"No, I'm good. Just get me upstairs."

I take her upstairs to a bed that was only exited by Emma this morning. I worry for a moment that she will smell the scent of another woman on the sheets but then reason that there is no way that she can smell anything. We kiss and I start to pull at her clothes. My hands slip under her armpits as I struggle to remove her dress. They are soaked with sweat, which has a bitter reek. We are clumsy together and uncertain, neither that aroused but both determined to see it to the bitter end. I respond to her downstairs but it is more instinct than passion, and the sex is quick and unsatisfactory for both of us. I try to take her in my arms afterwards but she shakes me off.

"Look, I need to head home."

She stares at the floor as she struggles back into her clothes. She is a pretty girl but the chemistry just isn't there. It's a shame: we get on so well intellectually, but just don't click physically. I should persuade her to stay but the truth is that I am relieved. She calls a taxi as I put on my dressing gown. There is an awkward ten minutes as we sit in silence until it arrives, and I walk her to the front door. Only there, does she finally turn to me and say something.

"I'll call you tomorrow, ok?" she says.

"OK," I reply.

We both know this is a lie.

***

The final act at Hamiltons was as quick as it was brutal. Anna and I had saved up for a one-week holiday in

Majorca in late September. We had hired a villa just out of season when the schools had gone back and the prices were affordable. It was just the two of us, exploring the island, and barbequing every evening. I have never enjoyed a holiday more and when we drove back to the airport on the final day, I felt a deep wave of uncontrollable depression sink into me; even the warmth of her arms could not dispel it. The villa had a colossal double bed, and I had loved waking up in her arms, feeling her nuzzle into my neck and telling me she loved me, still half-asleep. The few photos that I have of us are from that holiday. I wish now that I could have recorded every moment but there were no phones with camera and no social media. We had discussed her taking me back to the Czech Republic over Christmas to meet her family, and even spending a few days in Prague. It all felt so perfect. My parents had always warned me that all good things must come to an end, and how true they were about to be proved.

I got into work early on Monday morning. Anna and I had spent the night apart and there was something deeply wrong with my mood and to this day, I do not know what it was. Jeff would always claim that it was premonition but this was nothing of the sort. I should have come back from the holiday refreshed but instead my state of my mind was volatile. I headed for the canteen, largely because it was where my team gathered first thing and I had missed them, but when I got there only Ken was in attendance and I saw he looked like he was about to cry.

"Johnny, Johnny," he shouted and waved me over.

Curiosity compelled me to do what he said. He had a cup of tea in a chipped, canteen mug and a copy of the Daily Mail but there was no sign of his beloved bacon and egg.

"You alright, Ken?" I asked.

"No, Johnny. It's all gone wrong. The Old Man has been diagnosed with cancer and the company is going to be sold to the Americans," he wailed.

I cursed my naivety and suddenly the role of Charles was shockingly clear. Ken was staring at me like a lost child, and I found myself angry at his dependency. He was a grown man looking to me to fix the problem, but all I felt was anger.

"He sold us out," I snapped. "After all we did. We made his stupid company worth something again and he took it to the bank and left us to face the sharks."

"No, Johnny, he would never do that," wailed Ken.

It was clear from his face that his words did not agree with his thoughts. I turned on my heel and walked straight back out of the building and went home. I had a choice of who to turn to: Anna the angel or Jeff the devil. I went with Jeff. We met up in the evening and I saw a side of him that I only ever saw once: a supportive friend who wanted the best for me. We talked until late over Chinese take-away and bottled lagers. I had switched my phone off so that Anna could not call me, and I wrote out my resignation letter on his computer. I stormed into Hamiltons in the morning, refusing a summons to see the Old Man, and handed the letter to Steve. I took the opportunity to tell him what I thought of him as a technical director, just to make sure that my bridges were well and truly burned. Then I stormed out for a second time. A small part of me quite enjoyed it.

I avoided Anna until the end of the week but she came round to my house after work and we argued. I have never fought like that since. She cursed me for being a coward and leaving when people needed me the most. I responded by dumping her. She broke down completely, screamed like a wounded animal, her pretty face covered in snot and tears, and for the first time her English failed her. She beat at my chest, shouting how much she loved me and that she would have married me. I suppose that I was so hurt that I wanted her to feel some of my pain as well, like a selfish urge to project some of it onto someone else. When she left after two hours, I assumed that she would come crawling back at some point, and I was resolved that it would not be me who gave in first. I underestimated her stubbornness, or maybe she finally saw me for what I really was. It was the last time we ever spoke. It is this incident in my life, the turning point, that I have revisited the most.

I later found out from one of the technicians that Charles had assumed control of the company on Monday. The first round of redundancies was announced two weeks later. The Old Man passed nine months after that, losing his fight to cancer, and to my shame, I refused to take Ken's calls and avoided the funeral. Sometimes, when I reflect on how my life is a mess, I feel that I deserve it.

## Chapter 14 – Contractor

I can't face getting out of bed on Saturday morning. I love weekends normally and I am usually up sharp and early, not wanting to waste the day. As a teenager, I used to love staying in bed most of the weekend, but as I have gotten older, time has become more precious and the idea of idling it away seems more and more abhorrent. But this morning I feel only apathy, laying in sheets that smell of two different women's scents. I need to get up, wash the bedding and do something with my day, but I am unable to move. Every now and then, I pick up my phone and check for messages but there is nothing, and this makes me feel even worse. I am not sure that a smartphone has made me any happier. I love the feeling of being connected, but I have developed a dependency that cannot be healthy. I check it again just to be sure. Still nothing. Great.

The landline rings at eleven o'clock on the dot. There are only two types of call I receive on the landline: my parents and wrong numbers. I struggle out of bed, which is good as my back is starting to ache from lying down too long, and walk downstairs to the handset, which lies unloved on a table by the front door.

"Hello," I say.

My voice comes out gruff and it sounds like I've been drinking whiskey and smoking cigars. I wish.

"Hello, dear. It's your mother."

The clipped tones of my mother sound like a BBC presenter in the time of Received Pronunciation before it was admitted that regional accents existed. There is a formality to her voice on the telephone, even when she is speaking with family members. She is nearly eighty and her manners and quiet consideration seem like throw backs to some bygone era. I worry how she copes with the busyness and inconsiderate nature of the modern world.

"Hi mum, how are you?"

"Your father and I were wondering if you would care to have Sunday lunch with us tomorrow?" she replies.

I know that mum has already scripted this conversation in her head and any of my off-topic questions will be ignored. I used to try and derail the conversation with the most bizarre themes I could, while my mother steadfastly worked through what she wanted to say. I never could win so I gave up eventually.

"Yes, that would be lovely," I find myself saying.

My voice has mirrored her polite tones, like she was some distant relative who I saw rarely and required best behaviour. I schedule into my mind that this means needing to leave the house today for the florist. Flowers are such a simple thing that makes her happy, so she can show her friends that her children think about her. It's a bit like sending postcards from holidays for her to put on the mantelpiece until they turn yellow, another sign that they have not been forgotten by their family. I used to rail at my parents' values — the stoicism, the making do and the keeping up appearances —but as time has passed, I have started to admire them. I know that I must be a disappointment to them, with one failed marriage and no children, but they have never shown it.

"We shall see you tomorrow then," she rings off in a distracted voice without saying goodbye.

I hang up the receiver and return to the bedroom, where I stand in front of the mirror. I stare at my reflection critically, as I have come to do so regularly. When I am coursing with adrenalin and dolled up for a night out, I convince myself that I am not only in great condition for my age, but that I am still just as toned as when I was a young man. The cold morning light shows a different picture: my skin is starting to look grey and wane, my stomach is saggy, there are panniers at the sides, and my face looks so wrinkled and old. I suddenly feel tired. I should have children, a garage and maybe a shed to hide in, not a house that looks like a building site. And I should not still be hunting for something, I should be settled.

I pull on a dressing gown and start pulling off the sheets from the bed. The action distracts from the utter feelings of emptiness. I glance at my phone: still nothing from Emma. Even a message from Abigail would be something. I look to the laptop and know that a dozen dating sites are waiting for my attention, but I also know that this lies at the heart of what has been making me miserable for years. I need more than a dead-end job and endless, disappointing dates. I have an opportunity for a new job and a new life with Emma. I screw the bedding up furiously into a tight ball and stamp downstairs to the washing machine. I know I should get out of the house, maybe go find somewhere for breakfast but I also feel paralysed. I have taken so many dates to the places that I like that it feels awkward for me to go there alone. I cannot bear either contempt or pity at the moment.

***

Jeff may seem like the villain of my story but there is no way that I can pretend he wasn't a positive influence on my life. Without him, there is no doubt that I would have stuck with Hamiltons for what was obviously going to have been a difficult transition. Maybe I could have protected that eclectic mix of eccentrics and helped them find their place in the modern world. Maybe I would have been another casualty of the lay-offs. There is no doubt that I would have married Anna and my life would have settled in the pleasing routine of middle class boredom that I have come to admire. But Jeff was true to his word. He helped me to form my own company and to find my first contract assignment at a bland, forgettable organisation called SCHEMA. It was a something and nothing company that has long since disappeared, and seemed to pick up contracts that it had no chance of delivering. The transition to Slough was easy enough. I took a gamble on my future earnings and rented a flat, which was best described as compact but at least it had its own parking space and all the appliances were modern.

My parents were my only constant at the time, I cut everything else off and it felt cathartic. I showed up for my first day at SCHEMA and marvelled at a company that had no character whatsoever compared to the places I had worked, and which had managed to attract a mixed bag of permanent and temporary staff, who seemed to have no interest in ever doing any work. It was all held together by a handful of rather diligent managers, who carried the place on their shoulders and spent every day chasing progress from people who seemed to prefer to spend more of their time excusing why work had not been done than it would have taken to have done it. Jeff was in his absolute element, even driving me there on my first day, before abandoning me in reception with a wink when he headed off to one of the kitchen areas where he would spend his days drinking free coffee from the dispensing machine while pretending to write code. I sat and waited for my new line manager to run through the induction and then set me up with whatever they were going to pay me contract rates to do.

I was secretly terrified. I had never actually worked anywhere professional before and most of what I was good at was self-learned. The contract rates I was now commanding were a step up from what I had earned at Hamiltons, and I was worried that I was just not worth them. The only source of comfort to me was that I had met a number of Jeff's contractor mates and they were all thick and lazy. I'm sure most had chosen the contractor route to avoid annual staff assessments and so they could move on every six months when it was clear they were rubbish without it looking strange on their CV. I sat in a soulless reception for ten minutes before my line manager arrived. Her name was Claire and she looked absolutely exhausted first thing on that Monday morning, which did not bode well, and as we introduced ourselves and shook hands I studied her closely. I normally make an instant decision about whether I find someone attractive or not but with Claire I never resolved it one way or another. She was tall with a pretty enough if bland face, she was skinny (which I like) but flat chested (which I don't), and she had mid-length black hair streaked with enough white to be noticeable. Her flat shoes and baggy work clothes suggested someone who was not too fussed about her appearance. I checked her hands: no wedding ring.

"Hello, you must be Jonathan," she said in a flat voice. "Welcome to the team."

She was studying with me an intensity that was unnerving. I was to come to understand Claire and why she acted the way she did a lot over the coming months, but my first impression of her was that she had taken a deep dislike to me.

"Oh, hello, great to be here," I said.

Her handshake was limp but I felt that was more from the fact that it was only manners making her shake hands at all rather than some perceived weakness. She was carrying a huge, ring binder which she hefted from her left arm to her right as soon as the shake was done.

"I have a meeting room booked to run through the induction pack. We can grab a coffee on the way."

She turned to walk off without waiting any response.

"Hey, don't I need a pass or something?"

"We will pick it up later. They are never ready first thing."

She buzzed through a door, led us upstairs and then through an open-plan office. I had always had an office either to myself or shared with a couple of others, and the open-plan arrangement horrified me. The cubicles looked like animal pens and I had the sudden image of a battery farm. There was less noise than I expected but then again, half the desks were empty and no one seemed to be talking or using a phone. We stopped at the kitchen area to get some coffee and there was Jeff and three other guys lounging around and laughing. It was clearly not about work. I sensed Claire bristle and the four of them fell silent and all looked off into the distance.

"How is that code coming along, Jeff?" said Claire.

Her voice was cold with a whiff of restrained anger. I recalled now a number of times how Jeff had told stories of a nightmare manager who was always on his back, and how he ran rings around her in the office. The stories had sounded funny over a beer but here in real life, it was very awkward. Jeff looked up at Claire and opened his arms to give a shrug of helplessness.

"What can I say, Claire? There are still a lot of issues," he said with a smile that did not reassure.

"I am hoping that you can say more than that. The project reviews start at ten and I need to report to the seniors about why we are late with no commitment to a date."

"A date?" said Jeff with mock surprise. "Hard to commit to anything with things the way they are."

"That has been the same story for three months and the patience has run out."

"Hey, we're working it as hard as we can."

"You don't seem to be working it at all at the moment," snapped Claire.

She was not far from exploding and then she turned away and punched out the code for a coffee on the machine. Jeff did an exaggerated eye roll behind her back and his companions suppressed their sniggers. I stepped up and selected a white coffee and then followed the silently fuming manager to the meeting room.

"I am sorry about that," she said. "I cannot believe he just doesn't give a shit and I am going to be torn apart at ten o'clock for something I can do nothing about."

She was close to tears and I really felt for her.

"Yeah, Jeff can be a bit of a handful," I agreed.

"What? You know him?" she said.

"Well, socially. We've never worked together before."

That was enough. Claire's defences were back up and she ran through the induction back with an apathy which bordered on rudeness. We rushed through it in ten minutes and I guessed that her mind was already on her ten o'clock review and my induction was another chore in the way of getting ready. She finished and closed the pack.

"Any questions?" she asked.

"No, I think I got all that."

"I doubt that," she dismissed. "I will show you to your desk. You will be picking up one of Roger's designs."

"Roger?"

"The last idiot who spent six months achieving nothing," she snapped. "Between Roger and Jeff, an easy project has become our worst loss maker. And every Monday, a bunch of arrogant seniors love to spend thirty minutes rubbing my nose in it."

"Oh right," I replied. It was all I could think of.

Claire dumped me with the team and stalked off. They were a friendly enough bunch who showed me how to log on and where to find the files. Roger had left a right mess but what bothered me was how easy his design task had been. I trailed through his schematics and they were riddled with basic errors. I checked the specification, confirmed that it really was as easy as it looked, and then started to work my way through the designs. There was a heap of datasheets, which all came with recommended designs, and it was not exactly hard to string them together. Claire caught up with me at lunchtime and I could see that she had been crying. The seniors had clearly given her a rough time.

"How you getting on?" she asked as she dropped my pass on the desk.

"Yeah, I think I've finished. I just ran it through the checker to get rid of the errors and it now seems to pass. I was going to get one of the others to check it but I think it's okay. There's not much to it."

"What? You've finished? In two hours?" she said.

She leant over me to look at my screen, reading the "no errors found" report. She was right in my personal space and I smelt her shampoo. It was strangely arousing.

"Well, that's amazing," she said and looked at me for the first time like I wasn't something unpleasant. "It's a shame there's a backlog in board layout. There will be two weeks before it gets picked up."

"Well, I can do that too and you can get one of them to check it. A lot quicker that way."

"You can do that?"

"Yeah sure, the tools are already installed on this machine and I found another example to copy. It already has the footprints and the lay-up, so it's quite straight forward."

"Did you generate a Bill of Materials?"

"I have, yes."

"Good. Print it out and attach to a purchase order for me to sign. We can get stuff on order."

"Will do."

"Thank you, Jonathan," she said and this time her look was softer.

I suffer from "white knight" syndrome and her appreciative gaze gave me a tingle. Claire was essentially a good person and a highly organised manager who was just not in the position to choose the people who worked for her. Her team really didn't care and were happy for her to be thrown to the wolves every week. It tore her apart. Her husband had left her, and she was trying to hold down a particularly difficult job and manage raising two children. It was no wonder that it had left her with white hairs and I marvel to this day how she managed to remain so professional. We came to like each other, but never romantically, and I became her right hand, following her projects around and clearing up for her. The work was not exactly hard and I was keen to do a good job, working late if necessary to sort things out and writing everything up diligently and, after a while, enough other people started following my example since most people do come to work to do a good job. I even started writing her slides for the Monday morning meeting which charted progress and included lots of impressive looking pictures from the design tools, suggesting that lots of headway was being made.

I don't know what happened but everything was fine for the first six months and then one morning I woke up with an aching sense of loss. The novelty of my new life was over and I realised how much I missed Anna. I had been on a few dates with women I had picked up at pubs and clubs but the feelings I had for Anna were still overwhelming. I was sick in the toilet after I woke up and I arrived at the office late. Things were even stranger when I got into work, the place was like a morgue and I noticed that all the contract staff had gone and the permies were giving me strange looks. There was a note on my desk from Claire asking me to come to meeting room seven when I got in. I arrived in a daze.

"Are you alright, Johnny?" she asked with genuine concern.

"Yeah, sure. Where is everyone?"

The look of concern did not leave her face. I was clearly upset or ill, or even both. I noticed she looked different today in a well cut black suit and a dash of lipstick. I knew then she had been asked to do something difficult — the more she was struggling, the more she dressed like a corporate drone.

"Why don't you sit down?"

We both sat. She had been stood by the window, gazing across the half-empty car park as the rain lashed down. It felt like the scene from a film.

"I am afraid that despite the recent improved performance on our projects, we have made a loss this year and the late runs have made it difficult to win new work. The seniors have decreed that we need to release all contractors immediately as a cost saving measure," she stated and her voice was kind and soft.

"I am being fired?" I asked.

"No, not at all! This is nothing personal! We just need to re-balance the books. You have done amazing things here and we are all so grateful for your efforts. We shall of course pay you to the end of the week."

It was just another thing and I stood up to leave. This was the last time I would ever see Claire but just walking out seemed to have become part of my life. In my defence, I was in no position to act in a rational manner, and I struggled to say anything.

"I'll get my things," I mumbled.

"Johnny, are you okay? Has something else happened? This is just part of the life of a contractor."

She reached over to touch my arm but I moved away repulsed. Claire had a high pressure job and a family to look after, but she still had the compassion to try and hold me up as well. My response was to walk out of the room and not look back. As the door closed, I heard her one last time.

"They were all planning to meet up at the Queen's Head later for a drink if you want to meet them."

I drove my car home and dumped it, before catching a bus back into the town centre. It was half twelve when I arrived and I have no idea how it took so long. Jeff and a few others were smoking outside as I approached and seemed genuinely pleased to see me.

"There he is!" shouted Jeff unnecessarily and waved me over. "Come on mate, fuck them and let's get shit faced."

"Hey, it'll be alright," said John looking at my sullen face. "We're being paid to the end of the week and there will be another gig soon enough."

A gig. Like we were rockstars and not some pathetic bunch of losers whose laziness had lost us our own contracts. John was called "Alchie John" because he was a high functioning alcoholic. He was as thin as a post with a shock of curly hair, which made him resemble a microphone. He used to hang out a lot with us, in fact, he was a stalwart of any event that could involve booze.

"That's right, mate," said Jeff and he reached up to put an arm around me (a comic sight as I was a foot taller than him). "I always have a few irons in the fire. I'll have us sorted out by Wednesday."

We went on a bender, which, had we stayed friends, we would still be reminiscing about. We went from pub-to-pub on a lager binge before back to Jeff's for shots. I passed out in his toilet while vomiting in the early hours of the morning — a fact that saved me from a colossal hangover — and to be fair, the others dragged me back to the sofa and made me drink lots of water. I woke up in the morning with a stiff neck and smelling revolting, but we hung out at Jeff's place and he cooked us all breakfast. I had exchanged the tight knit community at Hamiltons for another group of friends, and it felt okay. Jeff was as good as his word and sorted us both jobs out for the following Monday, so it was nice to have a few paid days off, even if we did waste them watching violent Japanese horror films and eating junk food.

I fell into the contracting role easily after that. I got a new mobile phone — a Nokia that looked like a brick — and learned the pleasure of texting. The placements lasted from six months to a maximum of two years, and the longest was only brought to an end because I slept with one of the HR women and leaving seemed the easiest way to avoid her. I dated a few girls although only one was serious. Her name was Alice and despite being a self-proclaimed feminist, she was incredibly attentive and sweet. She used to love to cook, as well as dress up for me. She was the first (but not the last) woman to indulge my fantasy for fishnets and corsets. When I spoke of taking a career break and going to Australia for year, she even started planning a sabbatical so she could come with me. She was keen and I suppose we could have ended up together properly had I not still been in love with someone else. I remember the climax (literally) of our relationship, where I was taking her from behind over the kitchen table.

"Harder," she kept screaming.

I closed my eyes and went for it but the combination of alcohol and unresolved feelings came to the fore unexpectedly.

"Anna!" I shouted as I ejaculated.

"Who the fuck is Anna?" said Alice.

She stormed out of my flat, slamming the door so hard that the neighbours complained in the morning. I was strangely unmoved when I recounted what had happened to Jeff, who found the whole thing hilarious.

"Oh man! You got to play rodeo!" he laughed.

"I did what?"

"Got her name wrong and then saw how long you can ride the bucking bronco!" he gasped, through tears and howls of laughter. "Man, you are a hero!"

"It wasn't deliberate," I said.

"Man, you are cold. There goes another one! And you just don't care," he said with a shake of the head.

"Well, I still care about my ex apparently," I said.

I missed Anna. I still ached for her after two years. Time was supposed to heal all wounds but this was still a gaping sore in my heart. I still thought about her every day. I used to have imaginary conversations with her. When I went to new places, I wanted to share them with her. I had even started to go back to the old Hamiltons haunts on Thursday evenings to see if I could bump into her, but there was no sign of my old colleagues. I wanted to have a serious conversation with someone and Jeff was the closest, or at least the person I spent the most time with, but that was never going to happen. For all his bluster and pseudo-confidence, he could barely bring himself to speak to a woman that he had not paid for. He had seemed so sophisticated when we first met but his lifestyle was shallow and unsatisfying.

"I don't know how to find her," I said.

"Move on, man, there's always another one."

I tried to take his advice but I wonder now if I had returned, either to her old address or to Hamiltons reception and asked to see her, how different my life would be but shame held me back. You know you're in trouble when even a boring life with someone is infinitely preferable to the most exciting times without them. It was actually Alchie John I turned to one night to ask his advice. We had fallen behind in a pub crawl around Slough and were sipping whiskey at the bar. It didn't seem to faze him that I suddenly opened up to him and he listened to me gush about lost love for thirty minutes. He was normally a taciturn guy but he called for two more drinks and finally replied.

"Look man, it is clear you have been in pain for a while. Ever since I have known you, you have carried this around with you," he slurred.

"I don't know what to do," I lamented.

"You got to choose man," he replied with a swish of hand down the bar. "Look, when we were children we used to go to the Fun Fair at Barry Island. We would save up our pocket money for weeks but at the end of the day, you could only buy so many tickets. There were big rides, the ones actually worth going on, which cost quite a few tickets and then there were the little rides, which only cost a couple. So you had to choose: just go on a couple of the bigger rides, or lots of the little rides or maybe a combination of one or two big ones and the rest little."

"Yeah, okay. Not sure that this is really relevant."

"It is a metaphor, man. Those tickets are the days of your life and you need to choose what you are doing, and it is doesn't matter if it's big or little stuff, but you are doing nothing. You are wasting them man, and they are never coming back. That chapter of your life is closed and no amount of nostalgia will re-open it."

I don't know where he had heard this before but in my drunken state, it was one of the most profound things that anyone had ever said to me. I decided then to bury the past and only move forward, and it is only the proximity of the 'big five-oh' that has made it all come flooding back. I have used over half my tickets now, and I don't feel I have used them well.

***

Saturday was a waste. I go to the florist and choose the lilies which my mother likes and then go to Waitrose where I waste an hour choosing two bottles of wine, one white and one red. I drive out into the country to find a pub. The food is okay, home cooked but no better than I could cook for myself, and the service is reluctant. It is quiet and most importantly, there is no one I know. I take my time getting home, driving at random through the country lanes and pretending that I am seeking out new cycling routes. I get home at six and feel empty and guilty for squandering a day. There are still no messages from Emma and it is starting to bother me. I can convince myself that there is no service where she is, but I know full well that if she really wanted to message me then she would find a way. I am starting to feel resentful (which is not good).

I look at my laptop but fight the temptation to have a quick check of the sites. I have wasted so many Saturday evenings over the years chasing women who I have no real interest in, and never understanding what compels me to keep doing it. I have spent years honing my profiles, paid a professional to do the photos, but even with all of this I have to chase ten women to get any response, and then again only a few of the responses go anywhere. It requires a huge amount of effort, like a second job, and to be blunt, the results have never really done anything but disappoint. I wonder what I could have done with that time had I employed it for something constructive.

I turn away from the laptop, go downstairs and switch on the television. There is more than one way to waste a life.

## Chapter 15 – Suburbia

I have got to that age where I worry about my parents. It has got worse and worse over the last few years as I have watched them become frailer and fret about even the simple things. The world has got faster and much less forgiving, with no consideration for the elderly, whose manners and politeness do them no favours against the sharp elbowed and pushy. I worry about them having a fall. I worry about them driving. And I worry about that call that one of them has been taken to hospital and please could I come. I visit at least once a month, mow the lawns, lift anything heavy, and perform more DIY for them than I do at my own house. My mum rewards me with home cooked meals, and my father with his gentle conversation. My sister has produced three grandchildren for them in a marriage that is notable for its lack of drama. I am still a concern to them, unmarried and with a job that I clearly hate. I worry that I should do something about this. I worry that I have not. And I worry that time is not on my side.

I pack my lawnmower, some gardening equipment, my toolbox and old clothes into the car, in case there is something practical that needs doing. I dress smartly in a shirt and jacket, load up the flowers and wine and make sure that I arrive at twelve on the dot. The drive takes less than an hour, with the last few miles of gentle suburbia taking a third of the time. My parents aspired to the house they bought, a four bedroomed semi-detached home made from handsome red brick and with its own garage. It is located on a street of identical houses, which can only be told apart by the detail of the gardens or the colours of the front doors. It was a gentle place to grow up, where I could walk to school and the local shop sold a dazzling array of sweets for hungry children. I know that they would never move, the house is a shrine to the memories of their life together and one can trace the story through the cluttered photos, starting with them as a young married couple in black and white, through to my sister and I growing up, and onto the grandchildren now. It breaks my heart every time I see it, and so does the sense of loss that I should have followed this path.

The street looks different now. Extensions have given the houses a crude individuality, the gardens have been paved over for ugly, over sized cars and children no longer play out in the street. I pull up outside at twelve o'clock and see my mother in the bay window looking out for me. She smiles and waves. I gather up the wine and flowers and walk to the front door. Mum opens it before I get there, and accepts a kiss on the cheeks, and takes the presents from me.

"Oh, you shouldn't have," she smiles. "Lilies. My favourite."

But I should have. I know how much this means to her and how happy these simple things make her. Family means everything to her and in a few years, my parents will be gone and my life will be emptier than ever.

"You okay, mum?"

"Yes, dear, come in. Your father is dozing in the garden. Why don't you pop out and keep him company while I do the vegetables?"

"Do you need any help?"

She gives me a look of bemused disdain. She runs her roast meals to a finely tuned plan and I will only get in the way and slow things down.

"I'll bring you both a sherry out when I have a moment."

I walk through the hallway where the photo shrine begins, before extending up the stairs and onto the landing. The order is largely random as they have been added to over so many years but never rearranged, each fresh set filling in whatever gaps that were left. You can see my parents on their wedding day, grinning away so full of hope and happiness, see my sister and I as newborns, chart our progress through school and university, to the arrival of my sister's own children. They have even kept a picture of me and Karen from our wedding day, although the divorce was over a decade ago. I glance at the photo every time I visit and I see the doubt in my eyes, the false smile and a shirt collar so tight that it was digging into my neck.

I enter the kitchen and my mum follows. The air is heavy with the smell of roasting chicken and potatoes. There are pans starting to simmer for the vegetables, which are chopped ready on the side. The door to the garden is ajar, and I squeeze through it. Mum has it opened just the right amount to stop the window from steaming up but not enough to let the room get cold. She always felt the cold easily but as she has become older, she lives in terror of getting a chill. I don't know if that's because she's afraid of not being able to look after my dad.

Dad is sat outside on a bench they bought years ago and placed in the suntrap in the garden. He is covered in blankets, which are a little unnecessary in early summer, and he is dozing with the unread Sunday papers in a pile next to him. I walk over quietly and sit beside him on the bench. The garden looks immaculate, with no blade of grass out of place. There are no weeds in the flower beds and the shed still glistens from the layers of wood preservative which I painted in the spring. I wish that I could enjoy my garden like this but apart from cutting the lawn every couple of weeks, I have done nothing with it since I moved in. It is another job on the list, another thing that I have never gotten around to. My dad gives a slight snore and then wakes up.

"Hello there, son. I didn't hear you," he says with a tired smile.

"Hi dad, thought I would let you doze," I reply.

"You shouldn't have done that," he replies but he is not really chiding me. This is a fairly typical routine for us. "How has your week been?"

Normally there is absolutely nothing for me to say. My parents have never criticised my dating habits but they are experts at quiet disapproval. This leaves us with little to talk about since apart from grocery shopping, my sister and the neighbours, there is little in their lives either.

"Chimera is closing down, dad," I say.

It takes him a minute to process this. He struggles to remember the names of places I have worked beyond my first job at the Agency. He frowns as he makes sense of it.

"You're losing your job?" he asks.

"Well, I am being made redundant so there will be a pay-off but essentially yes," I reply.

"What about your mortgage?" he asks.

I can hear the concern in his voice and see the panic in his face. He worked hard to pay for his house, I still remember the day when he paid it off and how proud he was, and he always lived in secret terror of losing his one big investment.

"It'll be okay, dad, I have a couple of interviews next week. I will get another job," I say. "In some ways, it's an opportunity. I haven't been happy there in a while and it is time that I do something better."

There are so many things I want to say to him in order to convince him that this is a good thing, but his expression has fixed off into the distance. I know that means he is worried and also that he has stopped listening. I fall silent and allow the gentle sunshine to warm by face. I can feel my phone in my pocket and I want to check for messages from Emma, but I also know that my parents find it rude when I look at it in front of them. We sit there in silence until mum comes out carrying a small tray with two glasses of sherry.

"Here you go, boys," says mum and lays the tray down on a stone table near us.

Her voice is high pitch and girly and I notice that this is how she has started speaking to my father. I find it annoying but worse than that, I worry why she needs to speak to my father like he is a child. His hearing is not what it was but his mind is still fine.

"Thanks, mum," I say.

I pick up both glasses and hand one to my father, who accepts it but continues to stare off into space.

"So, what are you talking about?" she coos at us.

"I was telling dad that I am looking for a new job," I say.

Mum looks at dad in fear. He has put his sherry glass down without even a sip and has folded his arms.

"It is okay, mum, I needed to get a new job anyway. I have been stuck at Chimera and it is no shame that it is closing down."

"It's closing then? You haven't been fired?" she gasps in terror.

"No, of course not!" I gasp in disbelief. I want to get angry but there is nothing surprising in this complete lack of faith in their son.

"How long have you got?" she asks, like it is a terminal illness.

"Three months, so plenty of time. And like I said, I have some interviews already."

I am a grown man and yet my voice has developed a distinct whine, once more the foolish child trying to get out of trouble. I look from one to the other but they both have that far away stare. Mum finally wipes her hands on her apron.

"Lunch will be ready. You'd both best come in," she says.

The sherries are left on the garden table.

***

The meal is perfect. The same as it always is. I have learned to leave room for pudding, since mum is a fan of apple crumble. We eat in near silence but my news has left little desire to talk or reminisce about the past or how my sister and her children are doing. I help mum clear away and then do the washing up as she dries. She finally breaks the reverie.

"Nearly your fiftieth birthday, Johnny. Do you have any plans?"

"Not really, mum."

"Well, perhaps we can do something as a family."

My heart falls. Half a century of my life and the best part over, and this is the best offer I have. The loss of Chimera didn't really move me, but the fact that I have no one else in my life apart from my elderly parents crushes me.

"That'll be nice, mum," I reply with a forced smile.

It has been a long time since I felt this low.

***

I met Karen at a party. It was wedding anniversary of someone from work and even though I was still contracting, I was invited. Jeff and I were working in different places back then but he wouldn't have gone anyway. He didn't like groups of people, and he hated people who he thought were cooler than him, which meant he went to great lengths to avoid any situation where he could be looked down on or patronised. It was a pretty lame party to be honest, with a rubbish stereo playing a compilation of bad taste in the living room and most people hiding in the kitchen. I had not met anybody in a while after the Alice episode and the people at the firms where I worked were overwhelmingly middle aged men, and the few eligible females were rarely single.

I could hear Karen across the room and noticed how much she was laughing and having fun. She was loud but everyone around her seemed to be enjoying themselves, whereas the rest of the party seemed to be a bit pathetic. In what has become to be known as "fear of missing out" since, I knocked back a few drinks and headed over to join her circle. I don't recall the details much but we drank a lot, laughed more and ended up snogging like teenagers in the back garden. We exchanged phone numbers at the end of the night, which was really the early hours of the morning, and I staggered home convinced that I had met someone amazing. However, little in life is as it first appears.

We started dating but we never recaptured that wild abandon of the first evening. Karen was a single mother with a twelve-year-old son and she very rarely got to go out, so on the few times that she did, she went at it hard. Her parents, who I will explain more about later, did not approve of babysitting for their daughter to go out and drink. This made dating difficult as we were usually on the clock for her to be home at a certain time.

I understand that this is just reality for parents, but back then I lived in a world when I only had myself to think about. I suppose that hasn't changed much either. I liked Karen though. She was fun and thoughtful and loved to laugh, and somehow I became drawn into her world. I was also not in great place. I had no roots anywhere. My work was transitory and I was never in one place long enough to make real friends. I was renting a flat, but it was not mine. I had no one to go on holiday with. My parents were constantly telling me that someone else from my school had got married or started a family. I had passed my thirty-fifth birthday and I was ready for things to change.

We never really clicked that well in bed but Karen was always really keen. I think part of it was that she just wanted someone too, and on paper I was a good enough match for it not to need to be perfect. We went out for a few months before I was introduced to her son, Martin, (not to be confused with my current boss!), who was a quiet, introverted lad with a love of computer games and fantasy books. Karen was worried about him and thought that he needed a male role model in his life. We got on well. I started taking him to the cinema and we went out hiking together, and in many ways I preferred his company to his mother's, who it was increasingly clear I had little in common with apart from we both liked eating out and drinking wine. The whole situation became worse when I finally met her parents. Karen had always portrayed them as austere and cold people, and it had left me feeling rather intimidated of meeting them. Once again, things were never as they seemed.

Her parents were odd. Traditional. Xenophobic. Opinionated. It's hard to describe really. They were generally unhappy with the state of the world and every piece of bad news in the media somehow reinforced their negative views. They had a nice house out in the country but they lived in terror of being burgled. They had two burglar alarms and half a dozen locks on the front door. There were CCTV cameras all around the property and the downstairs study had been converted into a makeshift control room where her father Malcolm could survey his property in grainy black and white footage for any hint of burglars or immigrants. They lived off roast dinners every Sunday, and the same rota of meals every week. Monday was Shepherd's Pie, Tuesday was steak, and, well, you get the drift. The idea of foreign food was an anathema, and their local pub was the only place they would consider eating out at. I still remember the landlord well: the friendliest bigot I have every encountered. Her parents loved him.

I was introduced over Sunday lunch. I had dressed up in a suit, which sounds crazy now, but Karen was pathetically grateful. I bought flowers for her mother Sally and a bottle of French, red wine for her father. We were met at the front door and I was expecting some level of hostility and perhaps even some questions on my intentions towards his daughter, but the reception was quite the opposite. They were clearly delighted to see me. Malcolm (her father) commented on how well dressed I was. After the formal handshakes and thanks for the wine, I was taken through to the conservatory for a sherry. We sat inside on expensive garden furniture, sipping our drinks and admiring their immaculate garden. Malcolm spoke about his family at great length, as the smell of roast beef slowly filled the room, and in particular his two daughters. Karen was the eldest and clearly his favourite, although she had been taken advantage of and then cruelly dumped by the father of her son. Malcolm was so bitter about it that he could barely bring himself to say the father's name, and seemed more angry about his grandson's illegitimacy than he was about the boy's wellbeing. His younger daughter, Sophie, was the outcast of the family, a lecturer of psychology at a local college and who had dated non-white people, and even worse, was an advocate of the Labour Party.

Lunch was more of the same. The five of us sat in silence (in fact, I cannot remember Martin ever speaking) while Malcolm held forth about the state of the world and its ills. Our agreement was taken as read. Looking back, I sometimes think that I should have challenged him more but there was a narrative emerging. He was so friendly to me because I was clearly a white knight who had come to save his daughter from being a single mother (of which he strongly disapproved) and his grandson from growing up without a father figure. It must have been mortifying for both Karen and Martin to be spoken about like that as they tried to choke down their lunch, but I had been in a vacuum for a while and suddenly I had a noble sense of purpose. I didn't really like Malcolm, and Sally was little more than an insipid drudge, whose character had long since been crushed out of her, but somehow I enjoyed his approval. He tried forcing more wine on me and I kept refusing as I needed to drive us home, and I saw his frustration that silly things like drink-driving laws should somehow apply to respectable people like us.

The next year passed with Sunday lunch once a month and even our parents meeting around the six-month mark. Malcolm approved of my parents but although mine were always polite in return, my mother thought he was a domineering prat and dismissed him as a Daily Mail reader. However, now that Karen was in a proper relationship, babysitting was gratefully offered, even if Martin preferred to stay home and play computer games. I moved out of the flat after nine months and in with Karen, which seemed to go easily enough but it was then I began to realise how little we had in common. Dates stopped being something special. Karen put on weight and stopped making any effort with her appearance. I realised how much television she watched, and how all she seemed to really want was someone to watch it with and then share the chores. My friendships with Jeff and the other lads withered with surprising speed, and in fact it was Martin that seemed to replace them. We started playing console games together a lot, and we were talking to each other more than I spoke with his mother.

I never proposed, as such, but after exactly twelve months, we had a strange discussion about our future.

We had gone out for dinner in a local bistro, which was an amazing place, and Karen had obviously spent weeks rehearsing it. She started talking about how everyone our age was married, and then about her parents giving her a hard time about it, and then how Martin needed a real father figure. I still cannot quite recall how on some random Friday night we agreed to tie the knot over a nice bottle of red wine and a rack of lamb. The next day we got up and chose the ring together (she had already decided which one she wanted and led me straight to it), all ready for Sunday lunch with her parents the following day. Karen was bouncing with excitement when we drove over, and constantly examining the ring on her finger. I had intended to ask Malcolm's permission, since he was old-fashioned and patriarchal like that, but I never got the chance. As soon as Sally opened the door, Karen was showing her the ring and practically squealing with joy. Sally was delighted to the point of being reduced to tears, well I assume that it was delight but her own marriage had been so awful perhaps it was despair. Malcolm led me into his study, gave me a long handshake, and told me how proud he was of me and how good this was for our (!) family.

I sat in silence at lunch while Karen and Sally began to plan every detail of the wedding. I had become a mere actor in my own life, a character in a scene who would be told what to wear and what to say. Malcolm was beaming with pride but for once was happy not to lead the conversation, although he gave me the occasional wink. I knew then that he had manipulated this. He wanted his daughter married and I was far from perfect, but I was good enough. They would no longer give him pitiful glances behind his back at the golf club, or have to avoid the topic of single mothers at the pub. My brain just switched off from the conversation as I mechanically chewed my food and my attention turned to Malcolm. I never really came to understand him, how a man with a comfortable background and such an unchallenging, safe life was so full anger and hatred. I could never fathom why he saw himself as such a victim in life, fuelled by disgust at trade unions, immigrants, and those who did not conform to his standards. I have to come realise since how many people there are like him in the world, and it scares me.

Her family was mad. They were entertaining for sure but looking back, it was never going to work. I liked Martin but I assume that he got most of his genetic stock from his absent father (who clearly had the sense to run rather than stick around out of some morbid sense of curiosity). However, the person that kept me going through all the atrocious family events which were to follow was Karen's sister Sophie. The wedding planning consumed our lives for over a year, and I used to think that if Karen had applied the same passion to other parts of her life, what an accomplished person she could have been. The task was made so onerous by the level of thought that went into every small decision about each detail, but it did seem to amuse Sally and Karen. I was informed of choices, occasionally there was a pretence of soliciting my opinion, but in the end there was only choice that was really mine: a honeymoon tour of North America, including a brief stop at the Grand Canyon.

***

I am not really sure how much help Mum needs with her chores or whether she just stores them up to make sure that I come over. There are heavy boxes that are needed to be lifted in and out of attic, two cars to wash (but so regularly that there is never much dirt on them), a lawn so short that there is no point pushing a mower over it, and furniture to rearrange. I am done by four and ready to go home but there is something that I always find myself doing before I leave. My old bedroom was converted into a study over twenty years ago, which I resented bitterly in silence rather than them keeping it as a mausoleum to my childhood. Every time I visit, I take five minutes to visit and stare out of the window as I did so many times when I was growing up. After all these years, I expect to see the same children outside playing and laughing. Children do not play outside so much anymore since the road is too busy for football, and these children have long grown up and I see them occasionally with kids of their own now. Somehow, I cannot accept this, as if time only passes when I am there to witness it. My parents' house may be a mausoleum to the past but the world outside has moved on.

The comparison with my own life is not lost on me, and that was in part why I went along with marriage. I remembered how happy my parents were growing up and how much the family meant to them. It sounds ridiculous that in my mid-thirties I felt that I was getting old as life passed me by. Karen seemed like the last chance to create something of my own, to be happy when the autumn years arrived. Karen and I had discussed having a child to the point that it was part of our plans. It never happened and we never pushed it, once it was clear that there was no real affection there, then having a child together would have brought cruelty to the poor kid. My parents were always nice to Martin but they never doted on him the way they would have done on their own actual grandchild, like the way they act around my nieces and nephews. I don't resent it. At least my sister managed to keep the family going.

It is time to go. I feel the crushing weight of depression that I always feel when I am here. The memories make it worse. The big five-oh is coming and I have missed my chance for all of this. Dating will never fill this void in my life. Neither will exercise. Nor books. Nor any other distraction that I can think of. The best years of my life are gone. I need to sort myself out before I continue to allow the remainder to slip away.

***

It takes a lot of willpower to avoid checking my phone until I get home in the late afternoon. I cannot hide from myself how much I am missing Emma, nor the sickening feeling in my stomach when I see there is nothing from her. There are a few messages from other people, but in my current state, I can't even be bothered to open them. I keep looking at my laptop, the perennial source of distraction, but I am resolved to delete my accounts. I have a chance with Emma. I had wanted to tell my mum about her, mostly to give her some hope that I was not a complete lost cause, but I could not have told her Emma's age. She would have pulled the same face she had when I said that I was at risk at work, only worse because she would have found the gap in our ages disgusting. But Emma is the path to redemption. I messed up with Anna and I have come to hate myself for that in my darker moments, knowing that she was the one who would have made my life complete. I have a second chance with Emma. I will not make the same mistake twice. I practically stand up when my phone gives a buzz.

**'Hi! Just got your messages. Sorry the reception has been so bad. Hope you had a good weekend x'**

I am smiling to myself in sudden happiness, and frantically type a message.

**'Do you want to come over?'**

It takes a full fifteen minutes for the reply to come. I am pacing the room awaiting its arrival.

**'Sorry, I am super tired. It has been a long few days.'**

I had expected this response but it still comes as a disappointment nevertheless. It feels too long since we have seen each other and I am lonely. Weekends are always the worst. I don't want to give up.

**'Dinner tomorrow?'**

The response is a lot quicker this time. Good news usually is.

**'Sure. Text me tomorrow with the details x'**

It is not the same but it is something. I have an interview on Tuesday which means that I have Monday to prepare and then dinner with Emma. The perfect end to the day really. It is too early for bed but there is nothing I really want to do. I return to my bedroom mirror. I brought it with me from my bedroom in my parent's house. It is the same mirror I have looked into every day since I can remember. It has seen my reflection change from a child, to an adolescent, to an adult, through middle age and now to the beginnings of being an old man.

I make a note to buy a new one from IKEA. I have enough sources of painful nostalgia in my life, and it is time to move on and get my life in order.

# Chapter 16 – New Beginnings

I hit snooze on my alarm without even waking up and end up oversleeping. I skip most of my morning routine and head into work late. This puts me automatically in a bad mood because the traffic is worse and I may lose my car parking space. And yes, it is mine on weekdays as it's the one I want to park in. I skipped breakfast and my stomach angrily awakes when I am half way to work. I could stop for something but that would make me even later, and somehow I am hardwired to have to get there as early as possible. This is something I will need to wean myself off at my new job. Arriving early impresses most bosses but all it means is that I will spend the first hour pottering around, drinking coffee and pretending to read my emails. I won't actually start doing anything productive until most of the office has arrived. It's not like I get paid overtime or anything.

My space is still there and so the negative mood evaporates instantly. I park up and then walk half a mile to the local supermarket where I buy some croissants in plastic packaging (that I know will taste stale), a small pot of jam, some paper plates and some plastic knives. I hesitate about buying some orange juice as well, that would seem like taking the mick. I make my way back in a leisurely fashion, feeling relaxed that whatever I do no longer really matters. I have three months to sort myself out and I know from my contracting days that I can do it in a few weeks. I have survived a lot of stuff over the years with the result that I no longer care that much about life's little downturns. I am in a happy mood and step aside on the pavement to let some young woman past. I think that I am being chivalrous with a happy wave and letting her go for first, but she looks back at me with such hostility that I am shocked. It is not enough to take the edge off my morning though and I bounce onwards to work.

I punch the security code for the office and enter a room that is nearly empty. Ben looks up from his desk and gives me a friendly wave and I wave back. I look upon the office with fresh eyes and notice how small and shabby everything is. It needs gutting and completely rejuvenating. The nylon carpet has worn paths trodden into it and patched discolouration from hundreds of spilled drinks. Parts of it are held down by tape. The desks are chipped and battered, and most of the chairs don't match. It all needs a proper clean as well. The lack of investment is pitiful and a classic symptom of an organisation in decline. I stride over to the kitchen and pass Ben's desk.

"Morning, mate," I say. "You want a croissant? I bought a packet of four and I can't eat them all. I even have some jam!"

He looks at me in confusion before finally catching on.

"Yeah, sure. That would be nice."

I put the kettle and root around in the cupboards for plates and mugs. It takes five minutes before I drop him off two croissants and a steaming mug of coffee.

"I could get used to this," he laughs.

"It's a one-time only I am afraid! I didn't manage to sort myself out this weekend so had to skip breakfast at home."

"Oh really?" he asks, sitting up ready for the soap opera.

I return with mine a few minutes later and sit down at my desk. I turn on my computer but I know that Ben wants to chat so I turn around while it fires up. His curiosity does not hide his apprehension of redundancy from his voice.

"So, you had a good weekend?" he asks.

I can tell that he worried. He had to break the news of his redundancy to his family over the weekend and they have a mortgage to pay. I am not sure whether he really wants to talk about what he got up to or whether he just wants the distraction.

"Yeah, not bad. The usual," I reply between mouthfuls of rather stiff croissant. "What about you?"

"I had to tell Mary about the closure. It did not go down well," he replies.

He is expecting some sympathy for this, but I would be doing him no favours to indulge this. I dismiss it with a shake of the head.

"You'll get a new job quickly enough. This place is a bit crap to be honest, and it closing down will probably do us all a favour in the long run."

"Do you think so?" he asks.

"I really do."

"Have you started looking for something else yet?"

"Yeah, I have my first interview," I add carelessly.

"Wow, so quickly? I haven't even started to pull my CV back together," he says.

I notice that he looks crestfallen. I should have realised that the one drop of comfort was that we were all in this together, and now that I am out of the blocks with the potential of a job offer, he is left alone.

"Hey, believe me, once you get your CV out there, the offers will come flooding in," I reply.

He looks at me with pathetic gratitude and I curse myself for not having been more thoughtful. Janice had done me a favour in warning me before the hammer fell but the problem about living alone, is that you just don't think about other people so much. I glance at Denise's empty desk and Ben follows my gaze.

"I haven't heard a peep out of her. I did message her a couple of times over the weekend," says Ben.

I give a thoughtful nod to hide the fact that I had not shown the same level of consideration. On some selfish level, I am glad that she is not here. I just don't have the energy to give her the emotional support that I know she will need.

***

Martin comes in after nine and he looks terrified. He addresses us all and says that we need to have a staff meeting at ten o'clock. We are the only ones in so it slips back until lunch time when the office is half full. There are so few of us that we all easily fit in the larger meeting room. Martin is holding a clutch of hand written notes when he stands up to address us. His shirt is unironed and he clearly hasn't shaved. I understand his worry but this is no time to look like you have given up.

"Okay team," he begins and then stops. He clears his throat and starts again. "I know the news was a bit of a shock on Friday, but it's important that we keep going and don't let our standards drop."

"Why?" I ask.

I am not being bolshie but the company has just cut us off. I have no idea why they think that we should continue to fight and act in their best interest.

"Well, it's important," he begins and then falters.

"Look, this has happened to me a few times," I reply. "Chimera has just cut us all off with the statutory minimum, which is fine because that is what companies do when the money runs out, but they cannot expect us to keep going like nothing has happened. I am afraid that this is a time to be selfish, people need to be looking for new jobs. They have mortgages to pay and families to look after."

Martin could have called me out as having no one to look after but myself, but he just stares at me weakly. The mention of family has hit a nerve and I can tell that this is all he really cares about as well.

"Unless you are telling me that Chimera is offering some incentivisation to stay on and keep going?" I push.

I don't know what has got into me. I am not one of those barrack-room lawyer types who pretends to be speaking for the team while looking out for his own interests. Martin is the wrong person to be taking this out on but I need to be clear that I will be making zero effort from now on.

"Well, I think they are hoping that we will continue to give it our best," he says at length.

There is an exasperated snort from the room. Martin never was very good at this and there is a danger that the whole room will turn on him. I suppose there was no management seminar on laying people off.

"Right," I say.

I have had enough. I want to be preparing for my interview and even more, I want to be checking my phone for messages from Emma. I get up to leave and Martin says nothing, so the others get up and follow me out. I head back to my desk, duck down behind the monitor and pull my phone out. The initial excitement on seeing that there are unread messages soon fades as I realise that one is billing information and the other is from my mother. I feel a wave of annoyance but decide it is better not to wait and type out a quick message.

**'Hey, you're quiet. You still want dinner later?'**

I pull up my CV on the monitor and read through it. It is important to know it well because the interviewers will base their questions on it. I read it over and over, picturing myself in the interview and running through the obvious questions that they will ask. I rehearse the answers mentally over and over, so that they seem both considered and thorough. I know that the secret is to turn the conversation back to myself and take control to make sure we talk about my strengths. I have not felt like this since my finals at university and I must confess to enjoying the feeling. I am completely switched off from work but I steal a glance at my phone occasionally, hoping to see the warming flash of a message. It is twelve o'clock before I get a reply.

**'Hiya. Sorry overslept this morning. We can meet at the usual place later? At seven?'**

I had snatched the phone up and I feel a chilling disappointment at the coldness of the message. I reply with a brief acknowledgement back but I keep my tone distant as well. I have missed Emma all weekend and I am hurt that she seems so reserved. It is strange because when women are emotional or needy, it switches me straight off. I want to open up to her and tell her how I feel but I know that could have the same effect on her that it normally has on me. It is still early days.

***

The day drags by and I wonder how every week can pass so slowly, and yet I look back and wonder where the time went. I potter into the lab to do some odds and ends because I am close to falling asleep at my desk. Martin has not left his office all afternoon and I imagine that he is frantically working on his CV like the rest of the team. I am bored to the point that I cannot concentrate and that is not a good state for me to be in. I have been stuck reflecting on the past far too much recently and time to think is the last thing I need. It was good of Janice to have warned me but I cannot think of her without picturing that night together. My mind then wanders off down the avenues of what might have been. Normally I would pull myself together and bury myself in work but instead I stare out of the lab window and run scenarios of alternate lives.

I give up at three o'clock. I wander back to the office to find it deserted with only a lonely light on in Martin's office, announcing that the captain is still at the helm even after the crew has deserted. I pick up my things and walk out. I mean, what is the worst they can do? Fire me? If you have never walked out of work without a care in the middle of the afternoon, then I would add it to your bucket list. It felt amazing. All those months of pointless toil to do things that really don't matter, and let's face facts: that pretty much describes most office jobs. I jump in the car and fire up the engine, looking around to see if Martin is chasing me and calling me back, but of course there is no one there. I am home in twenty minutes and then enjoy the greatest luxury that an adult can occasionally indulge in: an undisturbed nap.

***

Needless to say I am at the restaurant early, having been to the gym and feeling completely refreshed. I have had a shower and run through my full regime to ensure that I look and smell amazing. I choose my best shirt and shoes and do not hold back on the cologne. My house is also ready with fresh sheets on the bed and a quick spring clean to give the best experience possible. There is a selection of nice wines chilling in the fridge and some flowers on the kitchen table to give the room a pleasing scent. I am not lying when I say that it has been a long time since I have felt this good and the rush of excitement means I feel happy.

I am at the table a full twenty minutes before I am due to arrive and I order a gin and tonic with lashings of ice. I have my phone out to check that she hasn't cancelled and then sit back calmly to enjoy the evening. I have come here a lot over the years and one of the reasons is the turnover of staff. I am not sure that I would feel comfortable coming to a place where the staff had seen me with dozens of other women. I mean that would look really bad, as if I were a professional or something. It is only the second time I have been here with Emma, so I have no idea why she called it our usual. Something to tease her about later. I have demolished my drink by the time she arrives at quarter past seven, and it has started to go to my head. I lurch to my feet to give her a hug.

"Hey," I say. "I missed you."

She holds me for a second before releasing. I may have gone to town on my appearance but Emma looks distinctly casual. Her hair is pulled back in a ponytail and there is only evidence of a dab of makeup. She is wearing trousers, a pullover and distinctly flat shoes. I am disappointed. She smiles at me but doesn't say anything. We sit down.

"How was the weekend?" I ask.

Emma gives a shrug and pulls a face, and for a moment I am concerned that she is going to play the mime for the whole evening but she begins to speak.

"It was okay, I suppose. I mean it's lovely down there once you suffer the four-hour drive but the roads are crammed with tourists at this time of year. My parents have a small cottage, which I used to love when I was little but it feels really cramped now," she explains.

Her voice is tired and she is not making eye contact. These are not good signs. I wait. It is best not to push the conversation or it will feel like an interrogation. The waiter arrives. We order gin and tonics and water for the table. She seems to begin to relax when the drinks arrive.

"So what did you do?" she asks.

"Apart from miss you?" I say and am rewarded with a smile. "Not a great deal to be honest."

"I am sorry there was no reception down there," she says.

"It is okay. I had an interview to prepare for and some parents to looks after."

"They okay?"

"Yeah, they are. They are worried about me though which feels a bit odd. At this point in life, I should be the one looking after them. It's like they still see me as a small child."

"Ahhh, that's so sweet."

"So we have this strange deal. I go around and do whatever chores my parents need and my mum cooks a massive roast meal."

"What about your dad?"

"He sips sherry and dozes somewhere, the garden in summer and the conservatory in winter."

"I would like to meet them."

"You will."

This is the breakthrough and she rewards me with the sweetest smile. She reaches her hand through the condiments and cutlery to take mine.

"I did think about you a lot but part of that was how I was going to explain it to my family."

I squeeze her hand. There is no point denying this an issue because it is, and I feel that I am in denial about it. It may be fine for now but if the relationship becomes serious then it will be a real issue in ten years.

"We will work it out."

It is all I can come up with but it seems to work. We let go of each other when the waiter returns to take our food order. He is nicely aloof so I am not concerned that he is judging us, although I am certain he is internally.

"So how was work today?"

"Well, very strange. Not that many people in and Martin looks like he's been given a death sentence. I just can't describe how worried he is. He gave us this big speech about how we should keep striving hard until the end, and I was like, why bother?"

"Crazy guy, thought he would have got the message!" she laughs. "What about your friend Denise?"

We shared a lot on our last night together but I am struggling to recall how much I actually told her.

"No sign and not responding to messages. I am not sure what to do about that."

The truth is that I have no idea where she lives. We have always been work friends primarily, even if we have met up outside of work occasionally. I have never been to her house (or any of my current colleague's for that matter). It is a world away from Hamiltons where we used to visit each other all of the time. I don't want to seem like a bad friend to Emma so I rack my brains for another way I could reach out to get. My panicked mind does not disappoint.

"I think I will try messaging her mum on social media," I add quickly.

"It must be so difficult for her," muses Emma. "When is your interview?"

"Tomorrow at ten," I reply. "It will be fine."

"Hmm, does that mean that someone needs a night of undisturbed sleep?" she asks.

She has kicked off her shoes and I feel her foot stroke up my thigh. Her smile is pure evil and I find myself responding.

"I think that I can manage just fine, thank you for asking."

"Oh good," she replies.

She takes my hand again. Her foot has worked its way to my groin and my breathing picks up. I am oblivious to anything else which is what makes the next few minutes so difficult.

"What's this?" demands a voice.

For an instant, I imagine that one of the staff has worked out what Emma is doing under the tablecloth and has taken offence to it. However, Emma rips her hand away from me and her foot vanishes. Her cheeks are flushed crimson in shame and she hunches up in a ball.

"What is what?" I reply turning my attention on the voice.

I am taken back by the sheer level of fury I encounter. A pudgy youth is stood by the table, rocking on his heels with his arms folded. It looks like he is about to physically attack us but despite his anger, he also looks soft. He has the physique of someone grown plump on computer games and streamed films.

"Who are you? And what are you doing with my girlfriend?" he demands.

"Your what?" I reply.

My voice may be steady but the shock is disorientating. I rise slowly to my feet and turn to face the accuser. I am taller than him and despite my age, have a much better physique under my tight-fitting shirt. I can see him take this all in and calculating the odds if it all kicks off.

"Emma is my girlfriend," he snaps. "We have just got back from a lovely weekend together and then I find out she is seeing you on the side!"

"Is this true?" I turn to Emma. "You weren't with your parents?"

Emma gives a shake of her head. She is practically balled up against the wall with her head down.

"So there was no problem with network coverage, you were just with someone else," I state.

"The coverage down there is just perfect," snaps the boyfriend, looking from one of us to the other.

"I did not see that coming," I say. "After that lecture you gave me about playing games, I must admit to being a little surprised."

Emma is saying nothing. There may not be many people in the restaurant on a Monday night but they are all enjoying the show. They make no secret of staring at us, their faces plastered with pleasant surprise. The anger seems to be fading from the boyfriend and now everything is just awkward and embarrassing.

"You coming or what?" he snaps to Emma.

She uncoils from her chair, picks up her bag and walks out without looking at either of us. The boyfriend follows without a backward glance. Everyone goes back to their food and two minutes later the waiter shows up. His demeanour has changed and he is quietly sympathetic.

"Hey, sorry man. I should have warned you. This guy walked by outside seconds after she arrived and clocked you two together. He was straight on his phone and I should have known it was trouble from his expression."

"I had no idea she was seeing someone else," I reply. My hands have started to shake slightly.

"Women, what can I say, man?" he offers with a shrug as though this was some occupational hazard of the catering industry. "What you want to do?"

"I will pay for the drinks and the food we ordered and then leave, if you don't mind," I say.

"Sure, man, I will just get you the bill," he says.

I think he is going to give me a shoulder squeeze for a second and I am grateful when he does not. There is only so much empathy I can deal with from someone twenty years my junior. I pay quietly and give him a large tip, and then I leave calmly but my cheeks are flushed and I fix my eyes ahead trying to ignore that everyone is watching me.

***

I stop at the local take away on the way home because I need to eat. It is annoying to have paid for two meals in the restaurant but eaten nothing. I want to text her. I know that I must not. I cycle between anger and upset. When I get home, I pour my food onto a cold plate, wedge a bottle of wine under my arm, and grab a glass before heading upstairs. My laptop sits in its usual place on my desk and I head towards it. I have chosen fried rice so that I can eat it with just a fork, but I take a few moments to organise my things and pour myself a generous glass of wine. I know that I will go on to finish the bottle. I boot the laptop and shovel the food down as it slowly whirrs its way to working. I click on my favourites and select my first choice dating site.

The rice is washed down with large swills of wine. I log in and click on "new arrivals" to check out the fresh meat. The selection is unimpressive but there is only way to distract from what I am feeling. I need validation. I need to connect with someone and right now I am not too concerned who that person is. This is why I end up on dates with people with whom I have no interest. I know all of this but it makes no difference. I click on the first profile, scan her description, and then look at her photos. She is a fresh arrival who has been on the site around two hours. Excellent.

'HoneyBunny22' is in her mid-thirties and a single mother. The usual comment about her child being her life. Yuck. She looks a bit overweight and her face isn't much. Never mind. The odds of getting a response are low so I may as well send a message. I read her profile a couple of times so glean some hook to get the conversation started, something that will make me stand out from the barrage of "how u doing?" comments that will fill her inbox. She likes holidays. Good, but who doesn't? There is a photo of her at some exotic beach. That will have to do. I type up a flirty response introducing myself, flattering her photos (nothing crude) and asking her where the beach photo was taken since it looks so amazing.

The next one has the moniker 'FemmeFrancaise' and is a French speaking lady born in the Caribbean. I am immediately drawn to her amazing photos. I know I am shallow but she has a long, slender body and amazing hair. Her profile is interesting. Family is important to her and she is religious. I am unsure about the latter but check out her legs again, and that swings the deal. Just because she believes in the Lord does not mean that she won't be fun, and her profile states how she loves dancing and travelling. I take my time in crafting a response, apologising for approaching her directly and mentioning the name of the local parish church. This last point is a gamble but I just need to get her attention.

I pour out a second glass of wine and work my way down the list. There are four new people and I message them all before turning my attention to a wider search. I scroll through the screens and run through the profiles for the local area. The majority are old and stale, people I have unsuccessfully messaged, and there are even a few I have dated. I look for any that are online now in the hope that they are clearly looking as well and therefore more responsive to a message. I send out six further messages but receive no instant replies.

I sit back for a moment and contemplate what I am doing. I have eaten every last grain of my dinner and I pour myself the third and final glass of wine to empty the bottle. I have an interview tomorrow and I know that I should consider an early night but I know that I will not sleep at all. The wine will only make the insomnia worse but then again, I have no idea what would really help. The wine is nice. It would have been lovely to share. I savour the taste and look out of my bedroom window. It is night time and the streetlights are on. It all looks so peaceful. Suddenly a message pings into the chat window.

**'Hi, how are you?'**

A boring response to my thoughtfully crafted message from HoneyBunny22. She had not been a first choice or even a second but at least she responded. I know that she is sat at home bored and only really seeking some brief attention, but that is fine. I crack my knuckles, take a deep draught of wine and get to work.

This is what I am good at. I just need that first bite.

# Chapter 17 – Sophie

I get out of bed at six am having finally given up on sleep. I did doze for some brief periods but that came with strange dreams, a little bit like the ghosts of girlfriends past. My temperature had oscillated up and down during the night, one moment wrapping myself up tight in the duvet for warmth and then later kicking it off as I flushed with sweat. I do not feel good and those lovely fresh sheets do not feel fresh anymore. I know that my only hope of making it through the day is coffee, specifically lots and lots of coffee. I pull on my dressing gown and head to the kitchen to put the coffee maker on, taking the time to gather the dirty dishes from yesterday. I do have a dishwasher but sometimes it is better just to handwash the dishes. I create so little washing up that I would need to wait days to be able to fill the dishwasher up, and by then the sauces will be caked dry on the plates and it will smell. I wash up and dry as I wait for the coffee pot to fill. The warm water feels really refreshing against my skin, and the taste of coffee then revives me.

I am unable to resist padding back upstairs to find my phone. I sit up in bed, sip the coffee and then scroll through my messages. There is depressingly little. A couple of delayed responses from the website (including a lovely one from FemmeFrancaise so my approach on the church was correct) but most importantly nothing from Emma. I browse the news and social media but there is nothing exciting on either. I debate going into work but the tiredness has made me too lethargic and I want to save my energy for the interview. I go downstairs for a refill and wonder to myself why I don't just move the coffee maker upstairs and make my life easier. I run a bath as I drink the second cup, and then take a third into the bath with me.

I slip into the warm, bubbly water and realise that this is what I should have done last night. I am tired and my eyes sting, but at last I can relax. I fold a towel and put it behind my head and lean back to soak. There are few greater pleasures than a hot bath, but a quick shower is what I normally choose in the morning. I close my eyes and there is the danger that I will finally fall into the slumber I so needed during the night, but I don't let myself. When the water finally starts to cool, I begin the same regime I did last night for Emma to make sure that I look amazing. The chances are that the interviewing panel will make their judgement based on the first glance, so long as I don't mess up the following questions too much.

I get out the ironing board and refresh my shirt to remove any cupboard creases and it takes me three goes to get my tie knot looking just perfect. I wear my best suit and freshly polish my shoes, and to be fair when I admire myself in my full-length mirror, I do look good. I skip breakfast and rely on the caffeine to keep me going. I leave the house by nine to ensure that I am there in plenty of time, taking the same leather folder that my father gave me for my first interviews. It looks a bit worn in places but somehow that adds to the image. I have my business cards and several copies of my CV inside. I feel ready.

Socratech is a German owned technology company that has bought up a number of smaller UK firms and consolidated them onto one campus. It was the second company that I had a telephone interview for but the first to offer me a face-to-face. It looks impressive as I pull into the visitor car park (having clocked the large, multi-storey one for employees) and admire the new buildings of steel and glass. There are gardens dotted around the place and an impressive fountain in the middle, with tables arranged in the grass. I notice the number of employees drinking coffee and pretending to work. I could see myself doing that as well. The lady in reception is both stunningly pretty and friendly. She searches for me on the system, asks to see my identification, and then asks me to take a seat. There are a number of comfortable chairs to sit in but I notice a lone woman, who also looks dressed for an interview, and I head over to sit by her. She looks up, notices my visitor badge and gives me a smile. She looks chatty.

"Morning," I say. "Are you here for an interview as well?"

"How did you guess?" she smiles back.

"Impressive looking building," I reply, stuck for something to say. "They must be doing really well."

She pulls a face and looks at me directly.

"Impressive building. Big fountain. Probably haemorrhaging money and slowly going bust."

I look at her closely to see if she is joking but her face is serious.

"Oh OK," I reply slightly. "So do you normally look for employment with companies that are going bust?"

This provokes an explosion of laughter and she looks at me again. She has noticed me. I can't help but want to push it further. I like the way her eyes sparkle when she laughs.

"Good point," she concedes. "I am here for a contract role so six months maximum."

"I used to do the contracting thing but I am looking for a little more security."

"I would too at your age," she says.

She realises how this sounds immediately she says it. She looks at me and then explodes again as I try to look offended, but I cannot hold it for more than a couple of seconds and then laugh too.

"Sorry," she gasps between bursts.

"Well, you two look like you're having fun."

I look up to see a woman looking down at us. I freeze for a moment as she looks like Sophie, Karen's younger sister. Well, that isn't true but she has the same body type even if the face and hair and completely different.

"Are you Johnny?" she asks.

"Yes," I reply and stand to shake her hand.

"I am Calvina. I am the HR business partner who will be supporting the assessment today."

She really is short and I tower above her. She has a sharp looking face, with lots of dark freckles and a severe haircut, which is cropped close to her head. Her tight suit shows off her curves and she is wearing heels which look uncomfortably high.

"Pleased to meet you, Calvina," I reply with my most charming smile. It falls flat. She is immune.

"Kindly follow me," she asks, and turns to walk off without checking whether I am following.

"Well, nice to meet you," I say to my new friend.

"It was good to see you Johnny. I am Anita by the way. Hope to see you around," she says, still giggling.

We shake hands and then I hurry after the HR robot called Calvina, who is waiting by the security booths.

"Please scan your pass and then enter the booth. I shall then scan you in and the booth will open at the other side," she commands.

The booths are rather intimidating and look like they have been pinched from a science fiction film. I scan my pass and step inside. The door closes behind me and for a moment I am trapped in a large plastic cylinder. The second door swings open and I scuttle through, waiting for Calvina on the other side. She seems rather pleased that I can follow basic instructions.

"We are on the first floor," she says and heads off to the staircase.

I follow obediently and watch her skirt ride up her muscled thighs as she strides up the stairs. She turns to say something and catches me looking. I am mortified but she cracks a smile and turns back. Maybe not a robot after all. I suddenly have an image of her wearing some really exotic lingerie underneath but I keep this vision to myself. We arrive at a meeting room with glass walls and a screen outside which says who has reserved the room. There are two men sat inside. One looks close to retirement and whose face could define the word anxious. He has a younger colleague who has crooked teeth and curly hair that is losing the fight to baldness. They both stand up to greet me as I enter and we shake hands.

"I am Philip," says the older man. He sounds like he may be wrong about this and is worried that I may correct him. I don't.

"I am Robert," says the younger guy.

"Good morning, guys. I am Johnny. Really pleased to meet you," I reply and notice that I appear to be speaking in bullet points.

"Would you like coffee?" asks Calvina.

"Ooh, yes please," I reply as though this is some unusual treat. "That would be lovely."

The two men act like she has not spoken and Calvina gives a gentle sigh before disappearing out of the room, and an uncomfortable silence descends. They just stare at me and it is really awkward.

"It is a great facility you have here," I say in my friendliest tone to try and break the ice.

"Is it?" asks Philip.

He makes a point of turning around and looking out at the window at the fountain and the shiny buildings. He is acting as if this was the first time he had seen them.

"Yes, I suppose it is a nice facility," he says in a surprised tone.

I look at Robert but he is sat with his arms folded, looking off into the distance. He looks furious about something, and part of me is curious but a larger part of me is more worried about what his temper is doing to my chances. My eyes rest on him but Robert shows no sign of acknowledging that I am there. I am glad when Calvina returns with two drinks. She didn't ask me how I like my coffee and has made an executive decision on white. She leans in close as she places it in front of me and she reminds me again suddenly of Sophie. This does not help the sudden and hugely inappropriate surge of attraction I feel.

"Thank you, that is really thoughtful," I gush at her, and am rewarded with a smile.

Calvina sits herself down, opens her day book, and prepares to make notes. Robert suddenly breaks out of his reverie and turns on her peevishly.

"Which interview is this?" he snaps.

"Test House Manager," replies Calvina, her tone showing that she is only repressing her irritation because she is more professional than he is. The pair obviously has history.

"We used to be sent packs before an interview. We have been sent nothing! What happened with that?" pushes Robert.

I have seen long time married couples do this as they are working up to a furious row in front of other people. It is as though the presence of friends and family are enough to slow the argument, but not to prevent it. I do not want them arguing. It means if one of them likes me, then the other one won't just to be contrary, and I need a full house if I am going to nail this stupid job. This is supposed to be about me. People can be so selfish.

"I have brought some spare CVs," I say.

I unzip my folder —and my mind jumps back to my first interview with Dr Phillips all those years ago — and hand out three CVs, one to each of the panel. Calvina rewards me with another smile but Robert makes a noise that is somewhere between a snort and a grumble. Philip may as well be in another room.

The interview begins.

***

It was not my intention to daydream my way through the questions but somehow it happens. It is Calvina's fault: her mannerisms, her tone of voice and the way she tilted her head to think before she spoke. They may have a general similarity of body shape but there was no way that one could confuse them physically. Sophie had a cute face with large brown eyes and a pinched nose, but with long, tight black curls. They both had something of Daphne from Scooby-Do about them, but my mind could not lose the image of my ex-wife's sister. It was a strange experience, my face pulling the appropriate expressions, my voice recanting supporting anecdotes to their questions, and my hands making the right amount of body language to appear sincere. It does not take a lot of narrative retelling to make the most mundane CV sound like a glittering career. In the meantime, my brain wandered off down memory lane.

Sophie was the black sheep of the family. The mention of her seemed to cause Karen's father physical pain at the loss of what could have been had she not succumbed to the allure of the left wing, filled her head with nonsense, and taken a career in a questionable "so-called" academic establishment rather than marrying and raising a family. Her romantic entanglements were even worse, including several inter-racial relationships and — shock, horror — even a member of the communist party who could quote Das Kapital and who had an awful, scatty beard and John Lennon glasses. I mean, one could not make this stuff up. Sophie was never happy in love. She seemed to collect strays that needed looking after, and her type seemed to be ungrateful and emotionally demanding men who took advantage of her good nature and then dumped her. I watched the cycle a few times and had to listen to Karen's dad recount bitterly her latest romantic debacle over lunch. I was incredibly curious about her by the time I finally met her.

Karen was endeavouring to establish a rapprochement in her family. We had set the date of the wedding and Karen was determined that she wanted no drama on her big day (notice "her" and not "our"). She invited Sophie around for dinner and drinks and I was disappointed that the legendary trouble maker showed up punctually, looked rather smaller and more charming than the stories suggested, and had even brought a nice bottle of red wine. Dinner was a disaster. Karen had assumed that her vegetarian sister would be happy to pick the chicken lumps out of her coq au vin, and it was a difficult moment when Sophie explained that she did not wish to eat the vegetables which had been cooked in meat juice. Karen had made nothing else and her response of "can you stop that vegetable nonsense for one evening?" was not well received. Sophie, like a lot of people I have met with strong political beliefs, was incapable of laughing it off and had to explain in great detail the evils of meat production, while we ate a lovely casserole and she had a plate of boiled rice.

We drank a lot. I laughed at her explanations. She started to get annoyed and then saw the funny side of it too, and relaxed. I have known a lot of bigots from both sides of the political spectrum and the only difference I have found other than the specific flavour of their deep beliefs, is that those on the right wing tend to have more of a sense of humour. Every time that Sophie tried to reiterate some heartfelt political point, I deflected her with a joke. It annoyed the hell out of her but she couldn't help enjoying it as well. She socialised entirely with those of the same thoughts as her own, where laughing about important political matters would be treated as heresy. The wine lifted me up, and I was fast and witty with a slight edge that she found attractive. When Karen disappeared to the kitchen to warm the supermarket pudding, Sophie regarded me sternly for a while.

"Well, you were not what I was expecting," she said bluntly.

I laughed and almost regurgitated my wine.

"What were you expecting then?"

"I don't know. Some younger clone of dad, I guess."

"You two are not that close?"

"You already know that answer to that, you've been making enough underhand comments about it all evening."

"Me?" I replied, placing my hand on my chest and putting on a wide-eyed, innocent face. "I have no idea what you mean!"

"Well, we don't see eye-to-eye on much to be honest, and I was worried that you'd be another Daily Mail reading Tory."

"How do you know that I don't vote Conservative?" I demanded with fake outrage.

"I suppose I don't," she replied, narrowing her eyes.

"I am actually forming a local group to dismantle the NHS and ensure the profits go to rich people everywhere," I said, adopting a fake posh voice.

Despite her intense beliefs, she could not help but smile and she leant over the table and gently smacked my elbow. I knew then that she liked me. I liked her too, even though we were poles apart. Sophie had a good heart and genuinely wanted to help people but her views used to tie her in knots. Her conviction in, say, gay rights and gender equality, got her called a racist once for not respecting the views of more conservative societies. She was devastated: I don't think any other insult could have stung her more. She was giving too in bed, and I still remember the feel of her riding me, leaning forward so that I could suckle her ample breasts as she smiled down at me.

"So how did you persuade my sister to go to the US? Hiking in the Grand Canyon is not her thing. She is more of a reading a romantic novel by the side of the pool kind of a girl."

"We'll find time to go swimming as well," I replied, deliberately misunderstanding the point she was making.

"I think you're good for her," said Sophie. "I have rarely seen her this content."

I noticed even then the use of content rather than happy, but I passed it off at the time. I suppose that Sophie knew that I was unlikely to be perfect if I was flirting with my future's wife sister when she was out of the room. I had a sudden urge to get her phone number.

"The good news is that we've already started to choose the bridesmaid dress. We saw this lovely peach dress at the weekend."

"What, are you joking? I can't tell. Please not peach, that is an awful colour."

"I am sure that it won't make you look like a funny coloured sausage," I continued with a smirk. "Still, you don't want to upstage the bride."

"Oh no. This is not just one bad clothes day, I will be made to look at those photos every year for the rest of my life," she said.

I dug in my wallet and found my business card with my new mobile number on it. I handed it over.

"Here. Text me next week and I'll let you know how the search continues."

"OK," she replied.

She took the card and hid it in her bag. I got a text on Monday morning. It was the beginning of a close friendship.

***

The interview is wrapping up. My story about my career at Chimera being a valiant attempt to protect local jobs in the face of short term greed from a foreign multi-national has hit a chord with Robert, who is spitting with anger on my behalf. I learned long ago how to manipulate the permanently angry men. Philip has laid out what I guess are his current woes and I have given concise answers to how I would approach them. It was quite charming to see him making frantic notes and I have no doubt that this afternoon he will be trying them out. As to Calvina, I make a point of respectfully listening to her questions and giving serious answers, while trying not to picture her riding me naked wearing only those uncomfortable heels.

Calvina brings the interview to a conclusion by asking me if I have any questions. I have a few based on scouring their website, but once these are done, I shake hands with the men and she leads me back to reception. As she is taking my pass off me, she suddenly feels the need to mention the tension between her and Robert.

"I apologise if things seemed a little off there with Robert," she said, looking at the ground from embarrassment. "He does not value the HR function."

"Aaah, that is probably because he has never worked in a company without a strong HR function," I reply. "He would then realise what he was missing."

Of course, if every date is like an interview, then I am already a master at this. Calvina gives a happy smile and a small blush.

"Thank you, Johnny," she says quietly. "I am sure we will see each other again soon."

We shake hands and I walk calmly back to the car. Robert will definitely recommend me and now so will Calvina, seeing me as an important future ally. Philip will be unable to make his mind up about anything and therefore will go along with the other two. I hop in the car with a sense of satisfaction and for a moment consider going back into work before heading home. What are they going to do, fire me?

***

I am home early again. It is the strangest feeling that my life is slipping by and yet when I do have spare time, I seem to lack the drive to do anything. I am worried about going out in case I am seen when I should be at work, and so instead it is back to the laptop and the comfort of my dating sites. I browse through them efficiently but there are not many people active at the moment as it is still within office hours, and I have a prejudice against chatting to unemployed single mothers unless I am really desperate. I know, I know, it's a terrible prejudice blah, blah, blah but what can I say? I have tried it many times and I have never found one that I could just chat to easily. On the fourth site, I do notice that Rebecca is active. There is a small icon with a compressed version of her main picture. It is so small that one can only see a tiny, round head and a mass of hair. I linger for a moment and consider messaging her — I mean she did have the most amazing, toned body — but I know deep down that I don't actually like her and I need to start choosing my dates more wisely if I am not to be doing this as a pensioner. However, Rebecca has also seen me and takes the initiative. A small dialogue box pops up.

**'Hey! We seem to have fallen out of contact. How are you?'**

I am genuinely torn. I know I should shut this down quickly and politely. She may not be for me, but there is someone for everyone and I should not distract her from finding him.

**'Hi Rebecca. I am okay. Had a difficult week at work which has demanded my full attention.'**

There. Perfect. A credible excuse to cover hurt feelings and the perfect start to a let-down. I just need to hold the course.

**'Yes, I hadn't seen you online for a while so I wondered what had happened. All ok now?'**

I met someone I really liked was what happened, and she really hurt me. Karma I guess. It's not like I haven't done the same to dozens of women before so I suppose I deserve a taste in return. I would not say that Emma managed to break my heart but I feel her absence every moment. I had hoped that with all the disappointment and let down in my life that my heart would be bulletproof.

**'I think so. Just one of those job things that crops up now and again. I need to win the lottery or something.'**

Or have a really wealthy ex-spouse like Rebecca does who can pay a small fortune for me to potter along in a nice insulated bubble, indulging my interests and never having to worry where the next mortgage payment is coming from.

**'Ha ha! Yes, wouldn't that be amazing? Listen I was meaning to ask you something.'**

My internal alarm goes off. She is about to ask me out. I can tell. I need to think quickly how I can refuse. On the other hand, it is so flattering when a woman makes the first move. It means that she must be keen. If you spend your life chasing strangers for dates then there is something so sweet about being chased back.

**'Yes?'**

A nice abrupt answer. The best way to start switching her off.

**'We never did get to try that restaurant.'**

Oh no. A vegan restaurant. I can think of few things worse. One would be able to smell the smug, privileged self-satisfaction a mile away. The thought of having to listen them drone on about climate change or how evil vaccinations are based on ten minutes internet research sickens me. This is my moment. I shall let her down easily.

**'Sounds lovely. When were you thinking?'**

My brain looks on in horror as some dark part of my subconscious takes over. However awful dinner will be, it will be better than sitting home alone searching the internet for something I will never find.

**'Wednesday?'**

Tomorrow. So soon. At least I have nothing else planned. Better than pining for someone who hurt me.

**'Perfect!'**

I should feel some self-disgust but I am just numb. She is good looking after all.

**'I still have your phone number. I will text you the name and the address. Got to go. Time for the school run.'**

She disappears and the dialogue box greys out. Perhaps I am wrong. Perhaps there is more to her and I just need to give her chance. It's not like what I am currently doing is working, so perhaps Rebecca is my chance out of it.

## Chapter 18 – Consultation

"Welcome to the first of your consultations as we go through the process," says Martin.

He is sweating really badly and straining to read out the printed notes in front of him. The printer has nearly exhausted its cartridge but as one of the many penny pinching (sorry, cost saving) measures, we won't change it until it is completely empty, even though we can read nothing we print off. I feel sorry for him, I really do. He has his own stuff to worry about and he has this piled on top. Chimera could have at least paid for some consultants to handle it but no doubt it was cheaper this way, and Martin is on the way out anyway, so why would they care?

"You alright, mate?" I ask with genuine concern.

His hands tighten on the paper, crumbling the edges which are already damp with perspiration, and he looks forlorn and bewildered.

"Yeah, I am okay. Just getting through this," he says with a shallow, transient smile.

He knows that I can clearly see that he is lying. It must be the first time he has been cut loose by a company. It feels like getting dumped and he always did swallow the whole "we care about our people" corporate rubbish. It is harsh but in a couple of years he will be glad of this, once he has a better job and can take the family to the Greek Islands for their holidays.

"Am I the first?" I ask.

"Yes," he says and looks worried.

"Well, the good news is that this isn't my first time, so I will go easy on you," I reply with a wink.

The humour elicits a genuine smile and he relaxes.

"I suppose corporate has already done yours?" I ask.

"Yesterday," he says.

I can see that any distraction will work to keep him away from this dreaded task. He knew that I would be the easiest, but he has to face down the sales team later, and some of them were discussing getting lawyers in order to improve their settlements. Idiots. There is no chance of getting better than statutory. I mean, this isn't exactly the Civil Service.

"They did it over the phone?"

"Yeah."

"Wow, that's harsh."

I am upset on his behalf.

"Was it Janice?"

"What?"

"Did Janice run the consultation?"

"No, it was someone I've never heard of."

I am disappointed. I am also disappointed in Janice. She was the nearest thing we had to a manager over there and at least she would have done it competently and with compassion.

"How was it?"

"Quick. After all, there's not much to say, is there?"

"There never is," I say. "Look, I know the form. The office is closing and my role is at risk of redundancy.

However, that risk is 100% because there will be no roles left in Europe. We will have a total of three meetings, although I have no idea what we'll be able to talk about in the latter two, and I shall leave the company in around three months with the minimum amount that the company can legally get away with paying."

"Yeah, that's pretty much it," says Martin.

He put the faded, damp, and crumbled piece of paper down in front of him. He first looks relieved and then upset.

"Look, it'll be okay, you know," I reassure. "There are lots of other jobs out there and this company was always a bit crap."

"Why did you stay?" he asks unexpectedly.

"Because I was too lazy to make the change and this has given me the kick up the bum I needed to get moving and find something better," I said. "You should do the same. This will look like good experience on your CV."

"I know. I need to start looking," he replies, looking forlorn. "You know, I had a bad time before I got this job. It took a fair while for someone to take me on. I was asked to leave my last place, you know how it is, they have a quiet word so that you can resign without going through the formal process."

Oh dear, that is really bad. It also explains why he wound up in a dying company that couldn't attract anyone better. He is a nice guy and he has inherited a team which runs itself to all intents and purposes. It also explains why he cannot manage the more difficult sales team.

"Well, it's different this time. The whole office is being closed. But I would not hang about if I were you."

We seemed to have switched roles and I have no desire to become my manager's confidante. He stares at the floor and I am worried that he may break down on me. Don't get me wrong: I love a bit of drama but I don't want to be part of it. Remember what I said about being part of the audience and not the cast?

"Look, shall I just read the paper and then sign it so that we can pretend we had the full consultation?" I offer.

"Yes please."

***

"How did it go?" asks Ben.

He has his appointment after lunch and seems quite excited by it all. He has been on a few websites which offer advice and is convinced that he can negotiate himself a better deal than is being offered. I can't seem to get through to him that without a voluntary redundancy round, then there is no chance to push for anything.

"Yeah, it was fine. What can I say? It's not the first time I have been through this."

"Will you look over my CV later?" he asks.

"Yeah, sure. No issue. You need to get it up on the job boards quickly."

"I will. You have told me that twenty times."

"I know, sorry. It is just easier to find a job when you have a job."

"You think I'll have a problem?"

"No, I had a quick look. There seems to be a lot of things out there. Good chance to get a decent pay rise as well."

"Cool," he replies.

He squints as his monitor and I can make out the format of a CV on the screen. He really should have this ready to go but I just bite my tongue. I potter over to the kitchen area and make us both a cup of coffee. I have not turned my PC on all week and I just can't face it. I could just go home. Martin will be caught up in consultations and I could just say that I had another interview. I take the coffees back and Ben gives a grunt of thanks before something else occurs to him.

"Hey, you heard from Denise yet?"

"No, still nothing," I reply.

I am lying since I have not messaged her. It is on my list and in my defence, she has not messaged me either. My recent activity on the dating sites has stirred up a number of messages to respond to but I feel too apathetic.

"You seeing anyone at the moment then?" he asks.

I consider asking him how his marriage is but that would be considered rude, and anyway chatting about myself is both pleasant and avoids me needing to do anything.

"I am having dinner tonight as it happens. Second date. A rather attractive divorcee who does a lot of yoga and it shows."

"Oooh!" replies Ben and sits up with interest.

His CV is just not going to get done quickly.

"So, she sounds attractive. Why don't you sound more keen?"

"She's vegan."

Ben explodes with laughter. It causes the sales team to stop plotting mutiny and look across at us angrily. This is clearly no time for levity. I sip my coffee and wait for the forced gales of laughter to finish.

"Oh dear, that is terrible," he gasps between laughs.

"It's a dieting fad, she's not a serial killer," I snap.

I hear how defensive my voice sounds, and I am caught in the strange position of admitting to myself that it is a bit terrible.

"Oh no, I mean your response to it. She could be perfect but that one thing is enough to turn you off and get you pulling that face. The poor woman is history."

"I haven't made my mind up yet."

"Your face says otherwise. I am guessing you are only stringing her along because there is nothing better on the horizon."

"I am not like that!"

"You are exactly like that. You want me to start listing the names of the other victims of the 'Johnny string along' process?"

"You have a name for it?"

"Well, Denise came up with it to be fair, but yes of course we have a name for it."

"Ok fine. You may be right, and yes I may have done this before. I just don't know what to do because she looks really nice."

"And that's what counts is the looks," replies Ben with his theatrical eye roll.

"Well, it certainly matters!" I snap back.

I hate it when he does this, catching me off guard and then going in for the kill on some thoughtless statement.

"So if that's what you want, why does it matter that she's vegan?"

My rationale brain warns me to be quiet but my emotional side wants to vent. It is never a surprise that it wins.

"Because it's one of those stupid beliefs that attention seekers do, who want to feel good about themselves. Trying to make themselves seem less boring and somehow more worthy than normal people. I am sorry that she has some pathetic craving for attention, but it is really inconvenient and I just want to go to a normal restaurant and eat normal food without a whole performance about where we're eating and what is in it."

"So you mostly don't like the fact that a vegan girlfriend may be occasionally inconvenient?"

"And the general air of smugness from people who drive massive cars, run up thousands of air miles and have their food flown in from exotic parts of the world at heaven knows what carbon cost, and then want to act all sanctimonious."

"So you resent wealthy people too?"

"Yeah, a bit to be honest."

We fall silent. I feel a lot better from having got this off my chest. I really do need to make more male friends who I can say these things to. I have not got to the point of posting my feelings on social media and then enduring the collective shaming from a thousand trolls who see themselves as the guardians of the latest political correctness mandate.

"So where are you taking her?"

"A vegan restaurant."

The laughter comes with a power and volume of hysteria. Ben is doubled up and his laughs come out as incoherent bellows. The sales team stand up to watch him, unsure whether he is having some sort of episode. The noise is replaced by coughing and choking as he runs out of air. When he finally looks up, his face is red and streaked with tears.

"Thank you," he gasps. "Thank you so much."

***

Sophie and I used to text each other daily. There was no flirting or anything inappropriate, just the banter of friends, stupid observations that we wanted to share with someone who would be amused, jokes and exaggerated anecdotes. She was genuinely upset about the chasm with her father and I pushed Karen to get her invited to Sunday lunch, and then pushed Sophie to eat fish if her mum would cook it. I felt rather good that everyone agreed to the arrangement and that the tedium of the monthly Sunday dinner with the future in-laws became a lot more fun. I was not sure that Sophie felt the same, since her father would lecture her relentlessly on politics and her life choices, all the while looking to me for support. At first, I tried to mediate but then I used humour to tease them both and it seemed to work and keep the tension at a manageable level.

Sophie was also very indulgent about the constant wedding talk, since Karen and her mother seemed incapable of speaking about anything else. I found it strange how two daughters from the same household could look and think so differently. The months raced by and it dawned on me what was happening. I was going to marry this woman. I was going to take joint responsibility for raising her son. I was going to waste one precious Sunday a month having dinner with her dreadful parents. I was going to grow old with her. She would be the only person I would make love to. I would share every holiday with her, and most activities. It was sinking in then how little we had in common and how I was finding her company increasingly boring. I did not want to spend most evenings sat on the sofa watching tedious television, maybe occasionally going out to some restaurant and having nothing to say to another that did not concern our impending nuptials.

Their father assumed that my singular lack of interest in the wedding was just because I was a proper man, after all, he had suffered the wedding day as well and had no interest in the planning of that either. Sophie was more perceptive than that and began to work it out after the first couple of months. It did not help that when I tried talking about the honeymoon and all the things we could see in the US, Karen responded as if this was some penance she was doing as a labour of love for me, rather than something she might enjoy. I knew it was a mistake. Occasionally I thought about calling it off, but how could I do that when our lives were already intertwined? We had a house together and a joint bank account. Her son had started to call me Dad, and I was really fond of the lad. Deposits were placed with venues, caterers and chauffeurs. We had booked the honeymoon and it looked fantastic — I certainly did not want to give that up. So I threw myself into work and ignored the problem.

It came up fast, although to be honest I was looking the other way. I had dusted down enough of my university friends to ensure that I had a respectable stag night and that there were enough ushers at the wedding. We stayed at a small hotel within walking distance of the church and met in the bar for dinner and a nightcap. Sophie did not stay at her parents' house — citing not enough room in the cars to the church — and stayed with us. She looked good. She had lost a weight and started wearing these knee high boots which made her legs looks longer, and even worse for a committed feminist, was wearing makeup. She sat next to me. We all drank and laughed at the bar. Our knees touched under the table. Neither of us moved away. It felt close and intimate. It was midnight and I rose.

"Chaps, this has been great but I need to get some sleep for tomorrow," I said.

My friends gave the required drunken roar as if I was making some innuendo. It was that kind of evening.

"I need to turn in as well," said Sophie.

We walked to the stairs. It was a funny old hotel that felt more like a couple of mismatched houses knocked together with random sized rooms and wonky staircases. We walked up the stairs together and our hands brushed. It made me tingle.

"I have some whiskey in my room if you would like a final nightcap."

The question hung in the air for a long moment. She knew exactly what I was asking.

"Yes."

She replied and I knew exactly what she was agreeing to. I felt a surge of excitement that I hadn't felt since the first night with Anna. The wedding in the morning was forgotten. This was everything that matters. I led her to my room in silence. The door had an old-fashioned metal key with a large dongle on the back with the room number handwritten on it. I fussed for a moment before I could get it unlocked. It swung open with a creak revealing a compact room with the faintest whiff of damp. It could not be more quintessentially low budget British. There was a trouser press next to the door, under a faded plan of the escape route in case of a fire. There was a chipped desk under the window with tea and coffee making facilities, complete with small packets of biscuits long past their sell-by date. The bed was soft and on an incline that suggested a pronounced sag. It had seemed good value until I saw what I was getting for my money.

Sophie walked into the room as I closed and locked the door. She was facing me as I placed the key down on a shelf.

"You don't want to marry my sister in the morning, do you?"

Perhaps she came back to my room for a heart to heart. I wanted her so much that I could think of nothing else. She saw my expression and mirrored it back.

"Let me show you what I want," I replied.

I walked over and took her head in my hands and kissed her hard. She relaxed into it initially and then was kissing back harder. I could smell her skin and it was delicious. It made me so aroused that I was in pain. I pulled off her pullover, which lifted her breasts up and I watched them bounce back down as it cleared over her head. I unfastened the bra and she rolled her shoulders left and right so that I could pull it off quickly. I was kissing her neck, down her chest and then sucking her nipples.

"Oh God. Oh God. Oh God. Please," she gasped.

She sat down on the bed and the fight began to remove her boots. It took both of us and some comic antics to get them off. I was onto her leggings, which were a doddle by comparison, which left her lacy pants. Lace pants. I think by now you know what that means. I slid them off and then I noticed how moist she was. Her pants were soaking and as I worked my fingers between her legs, she spread herself and was gasping for breath. I put my mouth to work. After my mouth, I used my fingers. She came to orgasm quickly and she was loud. Her voice must have carried through the thin walls of the hotel.

I stepped back as she recovered herself, and stripped off my clothes. I knew that I wouldn't last long, I was far too over-stimulated for that but I needed to be inside her, no matter how quickly. She looked up at me naked and shook her head when I tried to mount her. Sophie leant over the side of the bed, located her handbag and found a condom.

"Get on your back," she instructed. "I am going to fuck you."

"I won't last long," I replied.

"Maybe not the first time," she smirked and pushed me back onto the bed.

She ripped open the packet and rather expertly put it on me without once breaking eye contact. The stimulation of her hands was nearly enough to set me off. She straddled me gently, before using her hand to position me and then she slid down on top of me. We both groaned. She smiled and lowered her breasts down in front of my face.

"Suck," she commanded.

She rode me rhythmically as I nuzzled her gently, rolling her hips forward and backwards slowly. She was so wet that I felt myself slip around as she moved and it felt amazing. She watched me with an indulgent smile as she gradually increased the tempo.

"This is how a feminist fucks," she giggled.

I was incapable of an answer apart from groans and gasps to a God I didn't believe in. She moved faster and faster, culminating in a few hard slams to make me finish and I gave into her. The noise of my climax was even greater than hers.

"Good boy," she said when I had finished.

She leant forward and kissed the top of my forehead with a happy giggle, before resting her head on my shoulder as we felt me go limp inside her. It was sweet and intimate, but there was a hint of revenge to the family to which she has always been an outcast. After we cleaned up and disposed of the condom, we pressed into each other and drifted in and out of sleep, occasionally stirring to kiss and make love again. We did it three times in total and I knew then that I would be too drained to do much on my wedding night. Maybe it was deliberate on Sophie's part, but I was so happy I didn't care. We woke at six in the morning and she looked cute with her hair in disarray. She wriggled out from my embrace and started to get dressed.

"I should at least pretend to have slept in my room," she said.

I saw the guilt now the passion had worn off and I regarded her as she got dressed. Her body was soft and although I liked her curves then, I knew in a few years that she would turn to fat. Her mum had done the same and I feared that Karen would also go that way.

"You could stay a little longer," I ventured. "No one will be up for another hour at least."

She flattened her hair down, shook her head sadly and then pulled on her boots. I could not help but find this erotic and felt myself responding. Sophie hesitated for a moment and then turned to face me.

"We could just make a run for it. I mean, they would never speak to us again but I can live with that," she said.

I tried to work out whether she was joking or not and that second of hesitation was enough. She turned and was gone from my room before I could open my mouth.

***

My mind returns to the present as I prepare for my next date with Rebecca. I arrive at the restaurant early and feeling very anxious. I decided to take a taxi, which means I intend to drink and that is not a good mix with anxiety. The restaurant is called Lemongrass and despite my misgivings, it looks like a small family place and only a close inspection of the menu outside would tell you that it was anything other than normal. I loiter for a few minutes before I feel really uncomfortable and head inside. The maitre d' gives a welcoming smile as he looks up from the seating plan and I try not to sound nervous.

"Sorry I am a little early," I say. "I have an appointment at half seven."

"No problem, sir," he replies calmly. "Why don't we get you settled at the bar with a drink and I shall make sure that your table is ready?"

I admit that I am starting to like this place and I follow him over to a traditional looking bar with high stools and vast array of drinks, very few of which I am familiar with.

"Is this the first time at our restaurant?" he asks.

"It is, and the first time at any vegan restaurant," I blurt.

"Well, we are glad that you have given us a try," he says warmly. "What can we get you?"

"A glass of dry white wine would be nice," I say.

"Coming right up."

He sorts me out a generous size glass of wine before disappearing back to his post at the door and I take the time to survey the other diners. I am disappointed to see that they are all quite normal looking. I hate it when my prejudices are challenged. Not one of them is announcing that they are vegan in a loud braying voice.

I tune out in a contented haze, sipping the wine and feeling comfortable. I fail to recognise Rebecca completely when she walks in, only noticing a lovely pair of legs. It is not entirely my fault as she is wearing massive aviator sunglasses, which hide her face, and she has combed her hair flat and straight. It is only when the maitre d' nods in my direction and she heads straight for me that my distracted brain stutters into life. She looks amazing in a tight-fitting dress and strange shoes that look like something a gladiator would have worn, with the straps worked around her shins and up to her knees. As she approaches, she removes the sunglasses and looks at me in concern. I put my drink down and stand up to greet her.

"Rebecca. Hi," I blurt. "You look amazing."

The faux posh accent I put on at our last date has evaporated completely but I realise that my transformation must seem a little confusing, and in the fake world of dating perhaps even alarming. She folds her sunglasses and puts them away in her designer handbag, while allowing me to kiss her cheek.

"Thank you," she replies eventually as she stares at me. "You seem a little different to last time."

"Well, you look a lot different too," I try to deflect but it is too late to put the accent back on.

"I didn't mean in looks," she replies. "But I suppose we all put on a different face for the profiles."

She seems tired but wise, and I wonder whether the empty headed routine was all an act last time. She sits down gracefully and I watch in anticipation as her dress creeps up to the middle of her thigh. My inner schoolboy gives a roar of glee in my head. I make no attempt to hide the fact that I am studying her closely and at this proximity, the signs of aging are there. The skin around her eyes is wrinkled, her neck is no longer smooth, and her hair has started to thin from the regular dying. I know her diet and fitness are what give her a flat stomach but a few extra pounds would look good on her, and allow her to look less gaunt even with the well applied makeup.

"What do you think?" she says with a wave of her hand to indicate the restaurant.

"It is really nice," I reply.

"Nice," she repeats with a shake of the head.

This is not the conversation I thought I would be having. I decide to engage my intellect before I lose her completely. I give a confident laugh.

"OK, nice is not the most descriptive adjective," I reply. "I have never been to a vegan place before and I was worried that I would really hate it, and when I say hate it I mean not just the food but the attitude of the people."

"I know what you mean," she answers, giving the newly arrived bartender a complicated series of gestures to say she will be having whatever I am drinking. "We do have a bit of a reputation for being up ourselves but it is important to me, even if people assume it is some fashion. I will probably give up though."

"Why?"

"Because it is hard. I miss eating meat, I really do. And I love eating out and it just makes it more difficult. Sure most places cater for it now, but there will be only a few things on the menu and they will taste vile and I will have to pretend that overcooked vegetable mush is amazing."

I laugh and this makes her look up and smile.

"You are very different this time," I state.

"I know but I am also tired of putting on a face, you know, pretending that everything is great and that I am some super contented mummy who is loving her life."

She stops and takes a huge swig of wine that nearly empties the glass. I signal the bartender for two more.

"Come on, your life is not that bad," I state.

"I know, it isn't. I just wish that sometimes it felt more significant. I know what you see and I know what you think," she says and looks hard at me for my reaction. "The handbag that you have already clocked is the genuine article but it is five years old, and I shall carefully look after it until it falls apart. The Range Rover, which is the de rigueur article for the yummy mummy on the move, is third hand and I shall lovingly keep it until it rusts and the wheels fall off. Yes, what I have is nice but I don't have many things and I look after them."

"Wow," I reply. It is all I can think of.

"Yes, wow," she dismisses. "I bored you last time, didn't I?"

"Yeah."

"I know. I am boring though and I know that. And I am lonely and when I meet new people, I just open up and all this trite rubbish comes out and I hate it."

She finishes her first glass with a flourish and picks up the second.

"What are you really upset about?" I ask.

"Isn't that enough?" she snaps in exasperation. "You kissed me to shut me up, didn't you?"

"I did. Sorry."

"That's fine. It was a good kiss and it made my toes tingle. It is the only reason I contacted you again. So, you kissed me and then didn't call, so who you been with then?"

"I was seeing someone else. It didn't work and I got hurt and was left feeling foolish."

"Younger woman?"

"She was."

"She won't bring your youth back."

"Harsh but fair, but it wasn't that. I really liked her."

"You liked her because you felt like you did when you were young, when we had opportunities and our bad choices were still ahead of us."

"I still have time to make some more bad choices," I counter with a smile. It is all getting too serious.

Rebecca laughs with a deep and genuine roar, one hand holding her wine glass and the other covering her perfect white teeth. She looks up at me from under her long hair. She likes me but not enough. I need to be open with her.

"So now that I have told you my stuff, what about you?" she demands.

"I feel awkward in a restaurant where I don't know what to order and don't want to look unsophisticated and coarse," I reply.

"It was a test, I suppose, asking you to come here. I wanted to see if there was more to you than met the eye. To see if I was worth coming out of your safe, familiar world for," she says.

She reaches onto the bar and holds my hand.

"Tell me what you like and dislike and we can work it out together."

***

Eighteen years ago, I sat on the front pew of a ghastly, modern church sweating in a rented morning suit. I had hardly slept and I had drunk too much, and my body seemed to know that this is all a big mistake. My best man was sat next to me with his eyes closed and I suspected that they had had a few more drinks while Sophie was making me regret my choice of sister. I could hear the church filling up behind me, even recognising some of the voices of friends and family. It suddenly hit me how I had let this get so far, that all that planning and fussing was not just a distraction to a tired relationship but had an outcome. There were going to be two hundred people here to watch me give myself to this woman. I was too late to run. I felt as if I had stumbled into a trap and was just waiting for it to all be over.

The vicar arrived at the lectern and gave me this massive, supportive smile. He must have thought that it was nerves why I looked so pale and close to fainting. I was scared. Too scared to run. Too scared to stand up and call it off. Too scared to look around in case I saw Sophie staring at me with unforgiving eyes. I was trapped hoping for it all to be over like an unpleasant dream from which I was unable to wake.

***

"Are you kidding me? Anti-vaxxers are insane! I mean, it is like risking your child for your own stupidity. I hate big pharma as much as the next person but there is like a ton of scientific evidence one side and a few cranks on the other."

"Vegan cranks," I reply.

We are sat back at the bar having a few for the road having put down a few bottles of wine over dinner. We are happy drunk and it feels really good. When I tease her, she leans over and slaps me on the bicep (no doubt both to flirt and test out my muscles). I respond by placing my hand on her thigh. She looks at me with a raised eyebrow. She doesn't mind but that is as far as things are going this evening.

"I told you before that the two are unrelated."

"Maybe."

"You are soooo annoying."

That is a good sign. It means she is interested. She puts her hand down on top of mine, pressing me against her thigh. I could not be happier.

"Well, I know what you yummy mummies are like, five minutes of internet research on some conspiracy websites and you know better than the consensus of scientific research," I tease.

"I will tell you a story, Mr Know-It-All. My best friend persuades me to go for some treatment. I forget what it was called, water of life or something? It was expensive but hey, I am worth it right?" she says with a smile that gets my blood pumping somewhere it should not be.

"Stop fishing for compliments," I say and squeeze her thigh.

She gives a shrug and carries on.

"So we go to some health clinic which felt like a research lab with lots of plants from the Amazon."

"The store Amazon?"

"No, the actual Amazon basin," she says with mock annoyance. "Now, listen. The people, well they called them technicians, were all dressed up like scientists and it was all therapeutic music and scented candles. And they take us into the room and we take our shoes off and put them in these bathes of saltwater. Then they attach a battery to some nails and drop them in the water."

She stops for a glug of drink and then continues.

"And they tell us that the process will extract all the toxins from our bodies, especially all the plastics we consume because we all full of plastic."

"Bad news for all that plastic surgery you ladies had."

She stops holding my hand to slap my arm again. She is speaking fast from the alcohol and the need to get to the punch line.

"And I watch and the water turns brown and there is this smell of chlorine, and I am like: oh wow, this is working! All that bad shit is coming out of my body. And I feel so good. And I go home and tell my kids, and my thirteen year old daughter points out that it is basic electrolysis and it would have been the same whether my feet were in the water or not . I mean, salt is sodium chloride right? So I paid two hundred pounds for a nail to rust and some chlorine to be released!"

We are both leant forward laughing on our stools. We slip our arms around each other for stability. Our faces are so close, then I move slightly and our lips touch. I kiss her gently. She smiles. I adjust and kiss her forehead and sniff the scent of her hair. We like each other.

# Chapter 19 – Karen

"So," says Ben in his inquiring voice. "Did you do the deed?"

We are having coffee and chatting before the workday has really begun. The day really should have begun since it is close to ten o'clock but we are not even pretending to be motivated. Martin has not even made it in yet and I hope for his sake that he is at an interview. Ben has kicked his shoes off and is sat back with his feet on the desk, and has the air of someone who is looking forward to the show. I should be annoyed that I am the show and resent the intrusion, but I like the attention and I need to talk to someone about it. I have a flash of worry about what will happen when I leave this company and how I will find an outlet for this personal stuff.

"No, of course not," I reply in the best injured tone I can manage. "I am not like that."

"You are absolutely like that," he laughs back.

He is right, of course. I am exactly like that.

"Well, we kissed lightly at the restaurant and had a cuddle outside as we waited for the taxis to arrive but that was it."

"You going to see her again?" he pushes.

"Yes. No. I don't know."

"Oh dear. Here we go again."

"Come on, don't be like that."

"Well, you are clearly into her physically."

"I am, yes," I reply.

There is no denying that. She is a beautiful woman and however I may sneer at her diet and regimen, she has a body that women half her age would envy. She had looked amazing last night and who does not want that?

"And she seems nice and able to laugh at herself. In fact, very different from the shallow stereotype you described after the first date."

"Yeah, that is true. Once she dropped that whole persona, I did like her a lot more."

"So sounds like a third date is not a bad idea?"

I give a heavy sigh and shrug my shoulders. Everything he says is true but I can also see the road ahead and experience has taught me the outcome. A third date is commitment.

"Look, this isn't like when you and Sally were dating. You don't just get a person, you inherit the sum of all their baggage. Yes, she is nice. Yes, she is attractive. Yes, there may be something there. However, she comes with three children and all the compromises that entails, plus the hassle of having them in your life as well. The arguments and tantrums, the lack of much real time together and when you do, she's always tired from looking after the kids so you wind up as another thing to be crammed into a busy schedule. The children may resent you. There are the awkward custody exchanges with the former spouse. You will never be her main focus. Maybe all of that is worthwhile if she is perfect, but Rebecca is far from perfect."

"Wow," replies Ben dramatically. "Okay, let's work with that. Apart from the diet and wellbeing fads, what is imperfect?"

"She's just not clever enough," I reply. "I don't want a life watching reality television with a wife obsessed with fashion and cosmetics."

"Even if she does look really hot."

"And yet you will see her again."

"You don't know that."

"I think I do. Denise and I have seen you like this dozens of times. She calls it 'Johnny disorder' where you know it's not right but you are physically attracted to them and will sleep will them until the buzz wears off and then move onto the next one."

"That is not true!"

It is though. It is exactly what has happened dozens of time and I can see it happening this time. Probably. Almost definitely. I am concerned how many of my behaviours they have names for. The mention of Denise causes me to look at her empty desk. We used to have little signs on our desk that said our names and position when I first joined. Denise once replaced the paper in mine with a little sign that said, 'A woman is for life and not just for Xmas.' I laughed along with the rest of the office but I didn't find it at all funny.

"Still nothing from Denise?"

I sense a flash of annoyance from Ben. He has not finished wringing every detail out of me from last night and he loves to perform some post-analysis. He looks over at her desk as well and frowns.

"Still nothing. I must have sent her five messages with no reply, plus it goes to voicemail when I ring."

I have not even sent her a message yet and I resolve to rise above my current issues. She is one of my closest friends and I know that I have been selfish, but I can't seem to help myself.

"I will try today. I hope she is alright."

"She probably just needs some time alone to adjust."

"I suppose."

Ben sits up and drops his feet back to the floor, so that he can lean close to his monitor. I can see across the desks that he is reading an email.

"Yes! I have an interview," he shouts and gives a funny little fist pump.

"That is good news, well done," I respond with a smile.

Ben is wrapped up in the details and starts making frantic notes on a Post-it note. I turn back to my work but suddenly Ben stops what he doing and looks at me.

"Hey, isn't it the big five-oh soon?"

I freeze. No matter how much I try and put it from my mind, I am staring at the milestone and it is coming up fast. No matter how much I have shared with Ben over the years, the dread I feel of this is too much. I decide to shut it down fast.

"I have a little time yet."

"Any plans?"

"I'll sort something closer to the time."

This is a lie. I will hide away from it and pretend that it is not happening.

***

It would make sense to write the most about my marriage, seeing as it was by far the longest of my relationships, and yet looking back, it is like a dead time to me. Karen and I made so few memories together that those seven long years feel like a blank or even a gap in my recollections. The passion had fizzled before we tied the knot and we both went into a strange state where we never did anything. We had no interests in common and this resulted in two separate existences under a shared roof. Sophie and I cut contact through a mixture of shared guilt and what I suppose was her anger that I had gone through with a sham wedding. I still miss her friendship and think of her occasionally, but the truth was that it would have worked no better with her either, and a few years later she immigrated to the US to take up a teaching post in a college over there. Our contact had reduced to polite platitudes at family gatherings.

I actually missed Karen's son Martin more than I missed her. He had started off an awkward and introverted child of thirteen and over the years, I saw him mature into an adult. He was obsessed with console gaming but I managed to encourage him outdoors, and we did a lot of hiking and sight-seeing together. I could never encourage him into sports but at least he did a lot more exercise, and when he brought his first girlfriend home aged eighteen, I must confess a certain pride in him. I don't know what happened that pushed me to divorce but there must have been some trigger and perhaps it was when Martin left for college. I started exercising a lot as I had become very out of shape through a diet of ready meals and no proper exercise. I started cooking for myself, which turned out to be a good thing as I just felt better not eating food that was loaded with salt and sugars, and then I went on holiday alone so that I could do the things that I wanted rather than be stuck by the pool for a week.

I don't know if Karen was aware that the relationship was unravelling, or even if she cared that much. When I decided to move out, there were tears but no passion to fight for us. I moved into a one bedroom flat and I cannot describe the feeling of relief that I experienced. I used to compare it with having completed a prison sentence, which was not fair but was the only metaphor I could think of for the sense of elevation I felt after I left. I went to see her father to tell him the news. He reacted with cold fury, scolding me for being a disappointment and for hurting his family. He had a loveless marriage and could not understand why I expected anything different. A house and a cooked dinner every night should be enough to make a man happy, so what was I talking about? He refused to shake my hand at the end and I left feeling glad that he was out of my life as well. It is so liberating to shed all those people who have dragged you down, but the exception was Martin. He took the news as if I was divorcing him as well and cut me off. I sent him birthday cards and wrote him letters for years after and never received a response. One year, I missed his birthday and then it was like a switch was thrown within me and I stopped making further effort. I told myself that it was his choice not to stay in contact, but I wish I had been a bigger person and made more effort. He was a quiet child, with few friends, who had been deserted by his father, and I should have considered how devastating it was to lose his surrogate father as well. Occasionally, I think that I should try again but I have no address for him and I can't bring myself to ask Karen.

The divorce went through with little fuss. I gave her the house and that seemed to be all that she was concerned about. We promised to stay in touch as friends but there never seemed to be any reason to contact one another. After all, we were barely friends when we were together. I have rarely heard from her or seen her since, our lives were truly divorced from one another. I had hoped that Sophie would write to me when she heard the news, but she didn't. I realised that rather than having an outcast from the family in Sophie, they now had a common enemy in me, and that was fine. My life was easier without them. That may be the reason why I have struggled to commit since. Actually, I know that this is a lie but it is a comforting one that I tell myself.

***

My mobile phone rings just before eleven o'clock. I don't recognise the number so I head quickly towards an empty meeting room before I answer it. I have had a barrage of calls from recruiters over the last few days which has been wonderful for my ego and made the whole search for a new job rather exciting. I answer it as soon as the door is closed.

"Hello?" I ask excitedly.

"Good morning, am I speaking with Johnny?" says a female voice.

"Speaking," I reply. "How may I help?"

"It is Calvina from Socratech," she replies. "You came in for an interview."

"Yes, of course!" I blurt out with far too much eagerness. "How are you?"

"I am very well, thank you," she replies, her voicing changing and softening. "Have I caught you at an okay time?"

"Yes, yes. I just ducked into one of our meeting rooms so we can talk."

"Well, okay then. So I just wanted to provide some feedback on your recent interview," she begins.

My heart is beating like mad and adrenalin is coursing through me. A quick response like this either means I have been discounted easily or that I made a really good impression. I cannot call which way it went.

"Oh great. Thanks," I ramble.

Calvina pauses and I can sense her shifting position in the background before she speaks again.

"We normally move to a second interview if a candidate achieves the minimum threshold for a position, however we were discussing your application with our general manager during one of our recruitment meetings and she directed us to proceed straight to offer and to accelerate the on-boarding process," continues Calvina.

"Oh wow, that is good news."

"So we shall of course be following up with a formal offer in writing because our general manager was most insistent that we move quickly on this, as we know you will have other irons in the fire so to speak."

She proceeds to lay out an offer including car and bonus which is based on a salary that is a third more than I already earn. It is more than I was expecting and I am too surprised to be able to act cool on the phone.

"So how does than align with your expectations? Is it in the right ball park?"

"Wow. That is a really good offer. I am lost for words."

"Yes, we pushed to the upper end of the range to catch your attention."

"You have certainly done that."

"So, do you think that you would be interested in joining the team?"

"Well, yes. Based on that I shall be happy to sign the paperwork when it arrives."

I don't know what to say really. The offer is good and is certainly the lifeline I need at the moment, but more than that I am seduced by the idea of actually being wanted. I have not felt like that professionally for a long time, and it excites me more than the money.

"That is excellent news, Johnny," replies Calvina and I can practically hear her smiling at the other end of the line. "Please let me give you my number in case you have any questions when the paperwork arrives."

I write down her number and process her voice which had become borderline flirtatious. I have an image of her on the stairs looking back at me smiling as I checked her legs out. The flush of embarrassment is overwhelmed by the elation of being offered the job. We both go into a loop of thanking the other person which makes ending the call protracted, but I am smiling with joy at the end. I know better than to rush back into the office, since I need to play this cool to get my redundancy pay out. So I sit down and stare at the window, tapping my phone on my lips. Beneath the happiness, a different emotion starts to rise: shame. Now that I have sorted out my own immediate concerns, there is something that is long overdue. I open up my phone, select Denise from the contacts, and begin to type.

**'Hey you. Just to say that we're all thinking about you at work and have fingers crossed for a quick recovery. We know that you have a lot going on but please let us know you are okay when you have a moment. The office is like a morgue at the moment with the sales team deserting en masse and Ben and I bored to death without you. Talk soon x'**

It takes less than thirty seconds to type out and hit send. I really should have done this earlier but there is a strange paralysis in my life sometimes, like my mind just blanks things out if they are difficult. I consider messaging Rebecca but then hesitate. We had joked the previous evening about who texts first after a date and whether it makes you sound desperate or not. She had maintained that the man should always reach out first, but I called her a coward and replied that in an age of equality, men should not be assumed to have to do all the chasing. I am caught between being unsure whether she is right for me and the need for some attention. It is the same conundrum that gets me into all sorts of problems, with me essentially leading women on because I need the reassurance from someone, and it doesn't always matter who. I wait five minutes for an answer from Denise before putting my phone away and heading back to the office.

***

Those first few months of being single were the most exciting time since I moved away to college. I bought my current house and loved having my own place and being able to organise it without consideration for anyone else. I rented an enormous TV set and bought the best computer that I could. I recovered my old record player from the attic — where it had resided as it did not "fit in" with Karen's interior decoration — and dusted off my old vinyl so I could listen to them in the bath. I enjoyed having a double bed to myself and bookshelves full of books I liked to read. It was a like a second childhood where I could choose whatever I wanted. I moved back to Reading to make sure I was close to a lot of hiring companies and then went back to contracting, also escaping from a dead end job that somehow had made Karen feel more secure.

The other thing I had in abundance was time and I used it how I wanted to. I exercised regularly and with a passion that only someone who had grown soft and has come to despise the shapeless rolls of his or her body can understand. I shed weight quickly and my muscles returned, and I don't mind admitting that I grew to enjoy looking at myself in the mirror again. However, the other thing I discovered was the internet. I became obsessed with dating sites and signed up to them with abandon. It didn't matter to me whether they were free or I had to pay, as I assumed that the latter would offer better options. I trawled them all, endlessly fascinated with an extensive catalogue of women of every flavour. Ben made a joke years later about me being like a child in a sweetshop, which is a tired old metaphor but was surprisingly accurate. I gave these websites more attention than I gave my career, spending hours to refine every aspect of my profiles. I also used to study the profiles of other men to know what I was up against.

I know how bad that sounds when I explain it now, but there was a huge empty area in my life and this was the way to fill it. There are worse addictions after all. My life became tightly timetabled between work, the gym and the internet. I scanned through the profiles of women, making notes from their photos and their bios to ensure that my messages would attract their attention. I came to stereotype them as well into groups, and tried to refine different types of approach. Horrible as that sounds, it did wonders for my hit rate. This all led to a tonne of dates and ultimately continual disappointments. It is not like that there were not periods of stable relationships over the years but things were never quite perfect, and why would anyone ever compromise when there are dozens of other options in the catalogue? The invention of the smartphone only added to the efficiency as I moved from texting to running the relevant applications and staying connected to the sites throughout the working day.

I cannot honestly say how many hundreds of women I dated over that period. I can only remember a handful of the names of the best (and the worst!) of them. I met them all: the crazy cat women; the bitter divorcees; the bored spouses looking for something on the side; younger women looking for a sugar daddy; older women looking for a toy boy; the depressed; the paranoid; the self-obsessed; the independent ones who would never make time for you; the needy ones who you could never satisfy with enough; the tall women on a hunt for a man who they could date and wear heels; the short ferocious women; the intelligent ones who worried that they would have to settle for a thickie; the successful ones who worried they would intimidate men; the obese who still thought they deserved a man with a six pack; the picky eaters who were a pain to dine with; the passionate whose touch I still miss in the lonely hours; the rude ones where the date could not be over fast enough; the mind-numbingly dull ones; the funny ones who made every date amazing; the damaged ones who should have been spared the horrors of online dating; the obsessive gym bunnies who were amazing to look at but dead between the ears; the ones with beautiful photos who turned out not to be; the pretty ones who perfected their appearance but lacked a personality; the ones who sparkled and made the world a better place; the ones who cared and made you feel like you mattered; the crystal healers who refused to countenance scientific method; the overly religious with their narrow beliefs; the mildly religious who just seemed too nice to have fun with (despite the temptation to try and corrupt them); and the ugly ones who still thought they looked amazing. And yet among all of these, I never found one that kept me interested for long and I did not notice the years were rolling by and I was not getting any younger.

Those websites are fine to find someone and settle down — assuming that you find someone you want to settle with — but I stayed on too long. Some of my potential dates started asking some reaching questions about how long I had been looking. Their conclusions were brutal, ranging from calling me a player that was in love with seeking love, to a toxic bachelor who was too damaged to be with anyone. I suppose now that I finally stop and look back that they may have had a point. I should have come up for air and seen this before with so many broken relationships behind me and so many teary break ups. I worry how many people I have hurt and how little they have meant to me. I am not afraid of time running out of me, which perhaps I should be, but rather that I should feel more: more discouragement, more isolation, more loneliness and more compromise. Instead all that remains is a peculiar nostalgia for the past.

I had been living in Reading for somewhere between six months and a year when I took an afternoon off to go back to Hamiltons. I don't know what I expected to find but I know that I hoped for a glimpse of Anna again. The company must have been on its way down then, but I sat in my car at the end of the road and watched as people went home in the evening. I stared into every passing car looking for a glimpse of her, in my mind the same girl as the one I had abandoned a decade before. I did not see her but two of the production operatives noticed me as they were walking home and pointed. I started the engine and drove off, never to go back. I knew that she was long gone and probably married with a family of her own, and I realised that what I really wanted was a second chance. Every six months I still scour the internet for any sign of her. The advent of social media did not help either and I found myself trawling through profiles for the girls I had liked from school and university but there was no happiness to be found there either. I traced through the jubilant profiles of the happily married with picture perfect families, and in a strange way I felt so left behind. And that meant there were only the dating sites remaining, and once more that's where I returned. There were no other avenues open to me.

Something has to change. I pull out my phone again and message Rebecca.

**'Hey you. Thanks for yesterday. I really enjoyed the evening and it was great to get to know you a little better x'**

I know. It's lame. But one of the many things I have learned is that it doesn't matter. I had made the effort and that is what counts.

# Chapter 20 – Claire

We met at a normal restaurant that is supposed to offer adequate vegetarian food. Rebecca has relaxed her stance slightly, although more for practical rather than ideological reasons. We have managed only one other date in the last three weeks, as we have both had a lot going on. I have been busy since taking my pay-out early and leaving Chimera and I suspect that her distractions are an aspect of her lifestyle. I know this means that it's not going to work. I need a lot more attention than that, but I have also forced myself to stop going on the dating sites. I am excited. I start work at Socratech on Monday and despite having made a number of career changes over the years, this is a big thing for me. I feel that I am re-entering the main stream after years of hiding away. I suddenly want a career and a job that somehow feels significant and worth showing up for in the morning.

I arrive early and have taken up position at the bar. It seems to be a habit from our previous dates and I quite like it. Part of me wants to go on a pubcrawl. I have a taste for a lot of alcohol but Rebecca politely declined via text as she can't get back too late because of the babysitter and she also needs to be up early to look after the children. The spectre of my fiftieth birthday is less than two months away, but the recent activity has made me feel that I am finally sorting my life out, and as I sit sipping a gin and tonic, I reflect that life is not bad after all. I see Rebecca enter and she gives me a little wave before heading over. I rise and we kiss cheeks before settling ourselves at the bar.

"I think I'll have one of those," she says with a nod towards my drink.

The waitress overhears and gives a smile. The place is pretty dead for a Saturday night but I suppose it's only six o'clock. I imagine it will liven up in an hour.

"You okay?" I ask. "You look a little stressed."

"I am alright," she replies in a voice that suggest she isn't at all. "It just takes so much preparation to get ready. I mean, there are three meals to be cooked and routines sorted before the babysitter can take over at the same time that I am trying to get myself ready."

"Well, the effort paid off: you look amazing," I say.

I am being genuine. She looks stunning. I suppose that is one of the reasons why I haven't walked away yet, the combination of the fact that she looks good and seems to like me. That counts a lot to me. Rebecca smiles and squeezes my hand.

"Thank you. It is nice that you noticed."

The use of the word 'nice' had a hint of sarcasm about it. Her drink arrives and she takes a larger gulp than one should with spirits at the start of the evening.

"Well, here is to our fourth date," she says, raising a toast after her swig.

"To number four!" I reply.

"So, will there be a number five?" she asks directly.

I am unsurprised by this. It is what happens after a few dates. I mean normally we'll be sleeping with each other before we have the 'what are we?' conversation, but she doesn't want to be wasting her time if I am not serious. It is fair enough, she still suspects I may be a player, apart from the fact that I am in no hurry to take her to bed. I do not rush to answer the question but take a sip and consider carefully what I am going to say, as the honest answer is that I have no idea. I am coming to resent how much of my life I have wasted on people I care nothing for. I don't even know why I did it. It was not for the sex, since that would have been better with a professional; it was trying to recreate what I had lost. I feel a flush of shame for chasing people that were not worth it and I had no real interest in.

"Well, we both like each other, otherwise we would not have given it a fourth chance," I begin. "But I suppose it is fundamentally difficult."

"Because I have children?"

"Yes, and that will always be your focus. It is not like it has proven easy for us to find time together and that won't get any easier."

"So we should call it a day?"

"I didn't say that."

"I would rather you told me sooner rather than later."

"Come on, I am trying to be honest here. I mean, what is it you want?" I reply with a hint of wounded anger in my voice. It seems to pay off.

"Good question. I suppose I find life demanding and boring, and I want some excitement."

"So you are just after a fling as a distraction?"

That makes her think. We sit in silence, both pondering our drinks.

"I would not have said so, but the way you put it is making me think. I don't want another husband and certainly I am not after another father for the children, but I do miss some male companionship. What about you?"

"I am after more than occasional companionship," I reply.

"Like what?"

"Like the full deal."

"You sure? I don't want to be rude," she begins and I brace myself, for she is about to be rude. "But based on what you told me, you have not exactly been the settling down type."

Ouch. Harsh.

"I have not found the person I want to settle down with but that does not mean that I don't want to settle down."

Rebecca drains her drink and signals for two more.

"So you are telling me that in all those dates you had with all the women you have met, there was not one that was worth keeping?"

My mind fast forwards from when I divorced until the present. I don't like the answer.

"It is more complicated than that. I mean, there were loads of women I liked and some I even had long relationships with."

"How long?" she demands,

"Well, one was at least a year."

Rebecca gives a loud snort and looks at me incredulously. It takes her a second to realise that I am serious.

"Okay, well tell me about that one."

"Well, what is there to say? Chloe was nice, attractive and we got on well. We had fun when we were together."

"Did she have children?"

"No, she wasn't able to. It was why her husband left her because he wanted to be a father."

"So she sounds perfect and had no baggage. What was the problem with that?"

My mind flicks back to her. She was lovely and she was keen as mustard. If I hinted I liked something, then she would make it happen. She wanted me to be happy. She didn't nag me about the state of my house or the relationship. She was pretty. She was funny. You could take her anywhere.

"On paper nothing, she ticked every box. I just never fell in love with her, and although I enjoyed her company, it just became clear that she wasn't someone I felt strongly enough to be with. She did nothing wrong, in fact, quite the opposite, but I never missed her when she wasn't there."

"I see."

"It's like when you are somewhere and you see something amazing or taste something exquisite, and then you immediately want to share it with someone? I never felt that with her."

"So you basically broke her heart and moved on?"

"Basically? Yes."

"Wow," she says, her eyebrows raised. "That's it?"

"Well, there was Natalie I suppose."

"Natalie?"

"Yes," I reply, oblivious to the warning signs.

"Tell me about her."

"It was weird because we were not suited at all. She was this tattooed goth girl with a penchant for leather, fishnets and heavy, dark makeup."

"So it was about the sex then?" she says, her eyes fixed forward.

"We had this amazing physical connection and, for a while, it seemed to overcome everything else. We kept breaking up but couldn't stay away from each other. In the end, she moved to Australia, which was very odd because she didn't really like sunshine or hot weather."

"Right," snaps Rebecca.

I see this as a warning signal. I've long come to recognise this as a sign of extreme shock at an unbelievable level of stupidity or thoughtlessness. I don't know what to say without making it worse. Before I was married, there were at least a couple of women who I could have been with, but how can one compress decades of disappointment into a few succinct sentences? It worries me that for hundreds of dates, so few of them resulted in anything.

"Come on, everyone has a history. Relationships are difficult and they don't always work out. What happened to you and your husband?"

This is the correct approach. I observe how her expression changes immediately.

"I suppose we should never have married. He wanted a pretty wife and I wanted security. Although, that is an oversimplification. I suppose it felt more like a mutually convenient transaction, rather than a happily-ever-after. It is not surprising that we grew apart if I am honest."

"OK."

"Actually, do you want to know what really annoys me?" she demands and does not wait for an answer. "Is that I obviously bored him. The looks were not enough to keep his attention and I suppose that is why he went off with someone he worked with. At least, they had lots to talk about. And I know I said that I wanted security, but I chose not to have a career and I think that I deeply resent that. I don't feel, well I don't know the word, but something like significant. Suppose I were to suddenly disappear from this world, the children would lose a maid and a taxi but who would actually notice?"

"I would notice," I say and nudge her knee with my knee.

She laughs and gives me a smile that restores my confidence in the evening. There is nothing like sharing to produce intimacy.

"So, what we going to do then? A quick dinner and then back to yours for a quick romp around the bedroom?" she pushes.

"You are so posh," I laugh back. "Jilly Cooper was the last person to describe it as a romp. And no, no sex tonight."

"Why not? I didn't get all dressed up like this for nothing, and you should see what I have on underneath."

"Oh dear, please don't tell me things like that or I shall lose all powers of concentration for the evening. But I think that being physical too soon with people is a mistake. I have come to the conclusion that you only should when you really like them, otherwise it just seems to kill the interest."

"So what does that mean for us?"

"Well, it is clear that we both have our issues and baggage, and maybe we should just try and find our ways through this."

"That doesn't sound very romantic."

"Maybe not, but at least it is practical."

"Not even one quick shag?"

"No," I dismiss. It is the hardest 'no' I have ever had to say.

"You can tie me up?"

"Still no."

"Spoilsport," she says. If she keeps this up, then I am going to give in.

"Look, there is something I would like to ask you."

She looks at me directly and raises an eyebrow.

"It is my fiftieth in a few weeks and I was wondering if you wanted to go away for a couple of days. Maybe one of those Country House Hotel Spas or something."

"You serious?" she asks. I have her full attention and I nod deeply.

"I was not expecting that, but actually it does sound very sweet. I would like to spend some time with you," she replies but then leans forward so her lips brush my ear. "But only if you take me home and make me scream."

"OK, then," I give in.

"Lovely," she replies. "Let's order some food then. I am famished!"

"Yes, my lady," I reply sarcastically.

I secretly like the fact that she is posh. I have also closed my dating profiles. We go back to mine afterwards.

***

I arrive at Socratech half an hour early on a cold and wet day. The car park is rammed full and I circle for ten minutes until someone leaves, finally creating a space. I did not bring an umbrella and run through the rain to reception, arriving both soaked and out of breath. The receptionist gives me a huge smile and talks me through the on-boarding process. I join a queue of a dozen people who are led into a conference room where the tedious series of lectures begin. We are each given a checklist to return to our future line manager, which each presenter has signed that we have been briefed on security, health and safety, parking etc. I should not mind as I am being paid the same regardless but it is so tedious once you have been through a few of these. It is eleven o'clock by the time we are done and we return back to reception to await collection.

I am quietly fretting and distract myself by thinking about the upcoming weekend. Denise, Ben and I have plans to meet for brunch, the first time that we have been together since Chimera. They have both found other jobs and it feels like I have some real friends outside of work. My happy daydream is disturbed when Calvina shows up. We have the obligatory handshake and make false platitudes about how glad we are to see each other through forced smiles. She then leads me off in search of a coffee machine, chatting away relentlessly.

"We have twenty minutes before the introduction to the General Manager. She has blocked out an hour this morning to meet with you."

"Is that usual for the general manager to do that?"

"Not really, no. I mean, obviously for her direct reports but it is rare for the wider team. When she saw your CV, she became very animated. It is one of the reasons that we got through the process so quickly. What number do you want?"

We have arrived in a break out area with an oversized dispensing machine. It has a huge number of options, all of which no doubt taste grim. I scan the numbers and quickly give up.

"Oh, white coffee would be lovely."

"Number fifteen, okay."

She punches in the number, waits and then hands me the scolding hot cup. She repeats the process but I notice that she orders tea. We sit down in a pair of lurid, lime green chairs and sip our drinks. I scan around the office, which is bright and fresh. This area is no doubt supposed to be a creative area for innovative thinking, but is really the perfect place for a good gossip.

"Thanks, that's lovely," I say.

I am lying. It is cheap powdered coffee with hot water. I know that it is best to drink it hot so that my taste buds don't register how bad it really is.

"So you have completed your induction?" she asks.

"Well, everything apart from HR and the line manager bit," I reply.

"We have some time after lunch for me to brief you," she replies with a coquettish smile. "I will then introduce you to the team."

"How is the team?" I ask in my most serious voice.

"We have our challenges to be honest, some performance and some behavioural, but I suppose that is what you are here to help with," she replies. "I know you have some experience of transforming under-performing teams."

"So you would rate the team as under-performing?"

"Well, we have struggled to get to grips with it to be honest. It does not help that the local management is massively defensive of their teams, but we are changing as an organisation and some of those old-fashioned behaviours are severe growth inhibitors."

I hear the jargon in her words and know that she is repeating verbatim what has been said in the senior management meeting. It seems like Socratech is a house divided. This does not seem right to me for a new company.

"Old-fashioned? Isn't this a recent expansion into the UK?"

"It is but it was done through acquisition of a UK company."

"Oh. Got it. And you have a rump of the old guard who still want it to be 1983?"

"Yes," says Calvina with a sideways glance. "Only we are now a multi-national and not just some shed. To be honest, it was your previous experience in that area that attracted us."

I have little idea what I said at the interview that gave her that impression. I am stuck for an answer but Calvina checks her watch and suddenly her body language becomes agitated. She stands up quickly, pours her half-finished tea down the sink and begins to flatten down her skirt. It seems that a visit to the general manager is to be taken seriously. I drain my coffee and drop the plastic cup into the recycling bin.

"We better get going. Her office is on the top floor," says Calvina.

She is off quickly without checking to see if I am following. I am a lot taller and it was a brisk walk for me, so she is practically jogging to the lifts. She fidgets as she waits for the lift to arrive, and when it does, we ascend in silence with her eyes fixed in a thousand-yard stare. We race through the fifth floor, which is buzzing with activity, and she leads me towards the large corner office.

I can see the general manager from a distance, she is stood with her back to us, one hand holding her glasses. She looks an idealised version of a senior executive in some film, with her long, straight black hair, and tight-fitting suit that shows off her waist and hips. I can't help wondering if she knows we are coming and this is all for our benefit.

Calvina knocks nervously on the glass door. The General Manger spins around with a flick of hair and a swish of her skirt, she is practically beaming as she waves us in.

"Claire, this is Johnny," says Calvina nervously. "You have an eleven o'clock with him."

"Thank you, Calvina," replies Claire in a tone that is both friendly and letting her know that she is dismissed. "It is good to see you again, Johnny. Please do come in again."

I step forward and shake hands, while my brain races to recognise this woman. If you have dated as many people as I have done, then running into a vengeful, former lover is always a risk, and I have dated a lot of Clares and Claires in my time. The initial panic wears off as I slowly recognise it was Claire from Schema, who I worked for all those years ago.

"Oh wow, Claire! You've… well, you've…," I began and then stall.

"Changed?" she says with a smirk. "Haven't we all? I see you have a 'Silver Fox' thing going on, which suits you if I may say so. Anyway, sit down, sit down. There is fresh coffee coming up. Calvina didn't give you that muck from the machine?"

"She did."

"Yuck! And I am sure you were too polite to pour is straight down the sink."

"It wasn't that bad," I laugh in embarrassment.

"Still too polite to make a fuss, I see," she replies.

We sit down and she makes no secret of that fact that she is studying me, taking in every detail of my appearance.

"Well, where have you been? Are you that last professional on Earth not to have an online presence? I have lost count of the number of times that I have sent my useless recruiters to find you but if you are not on a professional network then the idiots have no clue."

"I was happy where I was," I lie.

I don't want to look ridiculous in front of her, nor do I want to point out that I have a broad, online presence but her recruiters were looking in the wrong places. Claire dismisses my comment with a snort.

"Nonsense! I know your company would have done anything to keep you where you were. Your line manager was no doubt desperate to have someone they trusted and who had their back."

I don't think Martin would have thought that at all. I give a humble shrug, which convinces her that she is right. She sits back and crosses her legs, which I find worryingly erotic. I imagine her wearing stockings, before a quick flush of shame kicks in.

"Well, I have changed. The kids have now left home and I am able to concentrate on my career. You cannot imagine how hard it was for me over the years, balancing a family and a job with no support. And yes, I said job not career. I had to watch lesser people be promoted over me again and again. So I decided to change and I have worked hard."

She looks better now than she did twenty years ago. She is no longer flat-chested and there is no hint of grey in her hair. She has put on some weight, but only in the right places. There are crow's feet around her eyes, which sparkle with mischief. Her clothes appear to come from a boutique and her makeup looks like it was done by a professional. She watches me appraise her and it amuses her.

"Don't judge me too harshly, this job is all politics and appearance. I wish that I could go back and tell my younger self that, it would have saved a lot of hard slog."

"I wasn't judging."

"I can see what you're thinking. You know, we always had a spark for one another. I did wonder whether if I had been in a different place, something might have happened."

I am a little shocked by this. I wonder how she remembers our brief time together professionally. We always got on well and were a highly effective team, but there was definitely no spark. Well, not on my side at least.

"So, what is your situation personally? Wife, children?"

"No, I am still unattached."

"Excellent. There will be a lot of travel and late nights for us to get this company in order, not the thing for someone with family commitments."

The brief moment of sentiment has gone and she is the woman I remember: focussed and determined. The comment about children cuts me emotionally but I freeze my expression. She opens up her day book. I reach down and open up my leather folder, now battered and tired from so many years service, and find a pad to start writing.

"Okay," she says, now completely absorbed in her job. "We have just under an hour for me to give you the headline brief. I noticed that you were recruited merely as a testhouse manager and that's fine, it will give you a chance to get under the skin of the company and work out what's what. You will be my eyes and ears down there, and as soon as we have our plans together, then I will promote you to one my direct reports."

I hear the office door open behind and coffee being brought it. My mind is still racing to process everything but for the first time in as long as I can remember, I feel happy. It feels like I have a purpose.

If you have enjoyed this book, please can you leave feedback at Amazon (for e-books) or send to alexander.moran2020@hotmail.com for print versions!

Printed in Great Britain
by Amazon

61058787R00218